GUY DE MAUPASSANT

UNE VIE

Translated by

KATHARINE VIVIAN

Introduction by

MERVYN HORDER

Lithographs by

LASZLO ACS

London

THE FOLIO SOCIETY

1981

SET IN TEN POINT OLD STYLE NO. 2 TYPE
LEADED TWO POINTS WITH KLANG
FOR DISPLAY
AND PRINTED BY
WESTERN PRINTING SERVICES LTD, BRISTOL
ON SPECIAL SMOOTH BOOK WOVE PAPER
ILLUSTRATIONS PRINTED LITHOGRAPHICALLY
BY WESTERHAM PRESS LTD, KENT
BOUND BY THE PITMAN PRESS, BATH
USING SCHOLCO BRILLIANTA CLOTH
AND PRINTED PAPER SIDES

Printed in Great Britain

List of Illustrations

Introduction

HENRI-RENÉ-ALBERT GUY DE MAUPASSANT (1850–1893) was Normandy born and bred, and forever proud of it. Not merely are his writings full of the sights, sounds and smells of the place; he celebrated too the traditional sturdy farmer's and sailor's virtues that it engendered, coupled with the added local specialities of boastfulness and what he somewhere calls the 'sly malice' of the Norman; coupled also with a proper mistrust of the English, who had so often ravaged his homeland.

His parents separated when he was ten, and lacking a father's guidance he grew up a rebellious child: the stories of midnight teenage cognac feasts on the school roof are such as might adorn other authors' biographies; but Guy was always the ringleader and this earned him at one point the supreme honour of expulsion. The rebelliousness was harnessed to the military service of the state by the Franco-Prussian War of 1870, in which he was present when the Germans occupied Rouen, and from which he brought away many of the experiences on which his early stories were based, notably the famous *Boule de Suif* (1880). After demobilization he lived for eight years in Paris as a minor civil servant, first in the Ministry of Marine, then of Education; in these years his literary fortunes were slowly forwarded by contact with such influential figures as Turgenev, Zola, Taine, Daudet and Edmond de Goncourt, though he remained throughout a reader's rather than a critic's writer.

In these years, too, in 1877 to be precise, he gathered himself for the spring and began work on his first full-length novel *Une Vie*, which was finally published in 1883, after it had first appeared serially in *Gil Blas*. I do not mean to discuss the content of this book any further, since above all other novels it requires to be read without any dilution of surprise, without the slightest foreknowledge of what is coming next. It is enough to say here that it is the life story from adolescence onwards, with all its ups and downs, of Jeanne, an upper-class Normandy woman; that it is to some extent, but by no means exactly, based on the experiences of his mother and father; and that it shows a consummate understanding of his contemporary Frenchwomen and 'what made them tick'.

It was indeed his mother who had early made up her mind that Guy should be a writer, and had called on her old family friend Gustave Flaubert – another Norman, as was Corneille – to help her bring this about. Flaubert, a longer-limbed, more painstaking novelist than his pupil had it in him to be, remained down to his death in 1880 Maupassant's literary godfather, not always approving, but doing a good deal to help place his early writings. (The all-important moralising final sentence of *Une Vie* actually reproduces a sentence in one of Flaubert's letters to his pupil, though Flaubert writes of 'things in general' (*les choses*) rather than 'life' (*la vie*); can there be any other famous novel in which the last sentence has actually been composed by someone else?)

Une Vie was thus in gestation for some six years during the author's late twenties, subjected to endless redrafts, cuts, corrections, afterthoughts and attempts to refine his personal *style de vision*.* Several characters were jettisoned altogether in this process, Jeanne's brother Henry among them, and the mousey Aunt Lison replaces a whole chorus of more talkative female relations. The book was strong meat for its time, was banned on railway bookstalls and brought its author instant fame and money. He was able to finish building a substantial villa at Etretat which he looked on as home for the rest of his short, wandering life. At first he thought of calling it Maison Tellier, after one of his early stories; but since the Maison Tellier of the story is a brothel, his friends soon laughed him out of that and he chose instead La Guillette, a diminutive

* I take this phrase from André Vial: *La Genèse d'*Une Vie (Paris, 1954) a monograph essential for all who want to pursue in full and fascinating detail, through all the extant drafts, Maupassant's attempts to streamline his own work.

version of his own name. At the end of the same year he was lucky enough to sign on as his valet and cook an intelligent Belgian, François Tassart, who stayed with him for life and later wrote a charmingly respectful memoir of his master, who remained always a hero to him.*

The ten years that remained to Maupassant were a steady decline from these days of glory. With his long moustaches and sergeant-majorly good looks he was physically robust, a keen sailor, oarsman and swimmer. Compulsively addicted to the girls (he was fond, too, of other animal pets), given to practical jokes and not unappreciative of his status as a literary lion, he was all the time being slowly rotted from within by the syphilis in his blood, probably a hereditary taint; nor could any amount of restless journeying, to Algiers, to the Riviera, to French spas of every kind, and once to England, halt the downward progress. As the years went on, he became a prey to hallucinations – not being able to see himself in his shaving mirror was one of them – to eye troubles, headaches and insomnia. (*Lui?* and *Le Horla* are two of the stories in which he made copy out of his own sufferings.) Taine, who found him at Aix-les-Bains in 1888 described him as 'the unhappy bull' (*le taureau triste*). In 1891, a year or two after his younger brother Hervé had died of general paralysis of the insane, he tried to cut his own throat, and was later confined in a private asylum at Passy in the heart of Paris for eighteen months before he died there in July 1893, aged only forty-two. His mother, whom he adored to the end, outlived him by ten years. He was unmarried, not indeed the marrying sort. After *Une Vie* he wrote only two more major full-length novels: *Bel-Ami* (1885) and *Mont-Oriol* (1887). The first presents for our admiration, for perhaps the first time in fiction, one of those successful scoundrel-heroes now so commonplace; and is one of the few novels ever to deal interestingly with the newspaper world. *Mont-Oriol* shows some relaxation of what contemporaries called Maupassant's natural

* Published in English by John Lane in 1912 as *Recollections of Guy de Maupassant by his valet François.*

pessimism – it was hardly more than a relentless candour about truth however paradoxical – and includes two of his happiest descriptions of the first awakening of love in young girls, a subject in which it is a surprise to find that this rather rakish author always excels; for these reasons his publisher hoped for a bigger public success than before, but was cheated of this by rumours of another war with Germany about the time of publication. There was no falling off in the collection of Maupassant's short stories, sometimes three a year, but more and more of these stories as time went on had to be rewrites of earlier work. By the time of his death some 200 stories had been published.

Tolstoy, who was introduced by his friend Turgenev to Maupassant's writings, went on record as finding *Une Vie* not merely the best Maupassant novel but 'perhaps the best of all French novels after Victor Hugo's *Les Misérables*'. He found united in it all the three qualifications he looked for in a true work of art: a correct moral relationship between the author and his subject, beauty of expression, and sincerity, that is a true feeling of love or hate for the people he writes about. It was in the first of these that Tolstoy found the rest of Maupassant's work deficient; 'Lacking a knowledge of the difference between good and evil, he loved and described that which he should not have loved and described.' Only in *Une Vie* were the author's sympathies all and wholly on the side of good. 'I saw behind it no longer a chatterer and joker, such as Maupassant had appeared to me from his first book to be, but a serious man, investigating life deeply and already beginning to see his way in it.' Tolstoy's standards may seem to us a bit stately and old-fashioned, after the upheavals of two World Wars have caused us to feel that life itself leaves you with an occluded moral viewpoint, not knowing whether to laugh or cry, to applaud or hiss; and that the closer an author gets to life itself in all its perversity, the better author he is.

Laconic and off-hand in manner, a master of the short paragraph – apt to be shorter than ever at points where the story takes an important step forward – Maupassant is now type-cast as one of the world's masters of the short story. Most of his stories are built round an identifiable central *clou*, often clinical or physiological in content, like the erratic action of chloroform which gives *Yvette* its point; and for such stories a single such *clou* suffices, whether remembered from his own observation or told him by his friends from their own experiences. (One such *clou* in *Une Vie* is the bizarre incident of the shepherd's hut rolling down off the cliff top, an incident of deep significance to psychologists; I feel sure that Maupassant had actually seen one somewhere, probably a disused Etretat bathing-machine towed by a thrifty farmer onto an upland meadow to end its days as a shepherd's shelter.) It is, however, when Maupassant was prepared to do what he always found difficult, the business of stitching many such incidents together – if necessary in some kind of imposed biographical framework as in *Une Vie* and *Bel-Ami* – that he reaches greater heights. There are six such full-length novels in all, and these are the books that made the biggest impact in France during his lifetime. When in 1891 he wished to bring a piracy action against an American publisher, he collected the figures to help his lawyer state the case: 180,000 of these six novels had been printed, only 169,000 of the thirteen volumes of short stories.

Une Vie was almost immediately translated into English, by John Eggers, who paid £300 for the rights; and it was published as *A Woman's Life* in 1885 by the publisher who was later associated with, and prosecuted for, Zola's English appearances. Of the nine or ten other English translations that have appeared since, here and in America – about one per decade since 1883 – four have used Eggers' title, others have settled for *A Life, A Woman's Soul,* and one for just *Life.* Katharine Vivian has perhaps been wise in letting the French title stand; those two highly charged three-letter French words seem to carry enigmatic overtones that can never be precisely conveyed in English.

Unlike that of his illustrious contemporary Zola – unlike

Tolstoy's for that matter – Maupassant's genius was descriptive rather than inventive, his stories a kind of triple-distilled journalism, extrapolated from life itself. 'According to me,' he once told his valet, 'a writer must only describe what he has felt; to express a thing well it must have been seen and understood. I think also one must not only understand it, one must either love or hate it, in fact be imbued with every detail of one's subject, see them distinctly and have studied them thoroughly.' Tassart adds elsewhere that he only once saw his master make a note of anything – he always wrote from memory and hardly ever hesitated. And as Joseph Conrad emphasises: 'Maupassant thinks very little; it is by the energy of his perception that he achieves great results.' Though an admirable irony and a certain amount of rhetoric give force to his writing, it is all as hard as diamonds; there is nothing meretricious or sniggering to be found there.

Truth is, however, many-sided, and it is not to be supposed that Maupassant's visions and versions of it at once carried conviction to the public. His was a unique new voice and his readers were quick to discern puzzling and clashing tones in it. The Paris critics vied with each other in assembling epithets for the opposing polarities they found: 'audacious and discreet', 'irritating and exquisite' – these were two of the combinations, while a third, less fulsome, was prepared to concede that the stories were 'banal but readable'. A hundred years on, now that Maupassant has settled comfortably into his niche, without followers, without rivals (though I should want to locate W. Somerset Maugham somewhere in the same side-aisle of the cathedral of literature) we need not be so tentative. His work remains to remind us of the bursting, woman-centred vitality of the man himself; and of that work there is no more vital example than *Une Vie*. It is the finest wine, decanted here *à point* in this sympathetic new translation. Let us enjoy it without further delay.

MERVYN HORDER

UNE VIE

1

AS SOON AS JEANNE HAD FINISHED PACKING SHE went to the window and looked out. The rain was still coming down.

It had rained all night, a heavy downpour that beat against the window panes and drummed on the rooftops. It seemed that the sky had burst at last under the weight of water and discharged its burden onto the earth, dissolving the soil like sugar into a liquid mush. The wind was fitful and sultry. Water gurgled in the gutters and overflowed into the deserted streets, where the houses soaked up moisture like sponges until their walls were sweating from cellar to garret.

Jeanne had left her convent the day before and was free at last, free for ever, eager to grasp at all those delights in life of which she had dreamed for so long, and now she feared that her father would be unwilling to set out on a journey if the weather did not clear; for the hundredth time that morning she peered out, scanning the horizon.

Then it occurred to her that in packing her travelling bag she had forgotten to put in her calendar. She took it down from the wall, a small card marked out in months, with the date of the present year – 1819 – in gold encircled with a design. She drew a line through the first four columns, crossing out the name of every saint up to May 2nd, the day she had left the convent.

A voice outside the door called: 'Jeannette!'

She called out in answer: 'Come in, Papa,' and her father entered the room.

Baron Simon-Jacques Le Perthuis des Vauds was a gentleman of the old school, eccentric and kind-hearted. An earnest disciple of Jean-Jacques Rousseau, he had a lover's passion for nature, for fields, woods and animals.

As a nobleman born, he naturally detested the events of '93; but, since he was philosophical by temperament and liberal by education, his hatred of tyranny took a harmless, declamatory form.

Both his greatest strength and his greatest weakness lay in his kindness of heart, a benevolence that never had arms or hands enough to caress, bestow, embrace: the benevolence of a creator, unrestrained and undiscriminating – almost a vice, a leakage of energy, as if some nerve in his will were paralysed.

He was a great believer in theories and had thought out in detail a scheme for his daughter's education, designed to make her happy and good, upright and affectionate.

She had lived at home until she was twelve, and at that age – although her mother wept bitterly – she had been sent to the Convent of the Sacred Heart.

There she was cloistered in strict seclusion, a stranger to the world of human affairs and knowing nothing of them. He wished her to be returned to him pure and chaste at the age of seventeen so that he himself could immerse her, as it were, in a sort of pool of intelligent poetry; and out in the fields, with the fruitful earth all round them, he would awaken her soul, dispelling the mist of her ignorance with the sight of the simple, artless loves of the animal world, the serenity of nature's laws.

Now that she had left the convent she was radiant, bursting with life, hungry and eager for all the joys and unforetold pleasures that she had already tasted in imagination during long nights and idle days, in the solitude where hopes are born.

In looks she was like a portrait by Veronese, in which shining fair hair sheds its lustre on the skin – an aristocratic skin with only the faintest tint of rose and a bloom of down like pale velvet, visible for a moment when the sunlight falls on it. Her eyes were blue, the opaque blue of a little delftware figure.

There was a tiny mole on her left nostril and another on the side of her chin, with a few curling hairs so like the skin in colour that they were hardly visible. She was tall and full-breasted, with a supple waist. Her clear voice sounded occasionally too sharp a note; but her laughter, free and unconstrained, radiated happiness all round her. She had a way of putting both hands to her forehead in a natural gesture, as if to smooth her hair.

She ran to her father's side, kissed and hugged him and asked: 'Well, are we going?'

With a smile he tossed back his hair, already white and somewhat long, and pointed to the window:

'How can you think of travelling in weather like this?'

She pleaded with him, coaxing and affectionate: 'Oh, Papa, do let us go. It's sure to be fine this afternoon.'

'Your mother will never agree.'

'Yes, she will, I promise; leave it to me.'

'Very well, if you can persuade your mother I'm perfectly willing to start.'

She hastened off to the baroness's room. She had looked forward to this day of their departure with mounting impatience.

She had seldom been away from Rouen since the day when she first entered the convent, for her father would allow her no distractions until she reached the age appointed by him. On two occasions, indeed, she had been taken to Paris for a fortnight, but that was just another city, and it was of the country that she dreamed.

Now she was going to spend the summer at their estate of Les Peuples, the family's old country seat perched on a cliff-top near Yport; and she looked forward eagerly to the freedom of life beside the sea. It was understood, besides, that the house would be hers when she married, and that she would continue to live there.

The rain, which fell without respite from dawn until dark, was the first great disappointment she had known.

After three minutes, however, she came running out of her mother's room and shouted through the whole house: 'Papa, Papa! Mama agrees! Order the carriage.'

The storm was by no means subsiding; indeed, it seemed to have increased in fury by the time the carriage drew up at the door.

Jeanne was about to step in and take her seat when the baroness came downstairs, supported on one side by her husband and on the other by a big, strapping maidservant with the strength of a lad. This girl was from Caux in Normandy, and looked at least twenty years old although she was no more than eighteen. Her place in the family was almost that of a younger daughter, for she had been Jeanne's foster-sister. Her name was Rosalie.

Her principal duty was to assist her mistress in moving about, for the baroness had become exceedingly obese a few years before after an enlargement of the heart, about which she complained unceasingly.

With much puffing and panting the baroness reached the top of the flight of steps at the entrance of the old mansion, looked down at the deluge streaming into the courtyard and said in a faint voice: 'Really, this is not wise.'

Her husband was still smiling as he answered: 'It's your choice, Madame Adélaïde.' (Because she bore the rather affected name Adélaïde, he always preceded it with 'Madame' in a mockingly deferential tone.)

She set herself in motion again and climbed painfully into the carriage, making all the springs sag. The baron took his seat beside her, while Jeanne and Rosalie settled on the opposite seat.

The cook, Ludivine, brought out a pile of cloaks to spread over their knees, and two baskets which were stowed away under the seats; then she climbed up onto the box beside old Simon and wrapped herself in a large rug that covered her from head to foot. The lodge keeper and his wife came out to shut the door of the carriage and wish them goodbye; they were given final instructions about the luggage which was to follow in a cart; and the journey began.

Old Simon the coachman lowered his head and hunched his back against the storm, huddled down in his carrick coat with its triple cape. The wind moaned as it beat on the windows, and the paving was flooded with the rain.

The pair of horses took the berlin down onto the quay at a

brisk trot, past the line of tall ships with their spars and rigging standing out bleakly against the streaming sky, like trees stripped of their leaves; then the carriage turned into the long Boulevard du Mont Riboudet.

Soon they were driving through the grasslands; now and then the outline of a drowned willow-tree, its branches dangling inert like the limbs of a corpse, could be discerned through the haze of water. The horses' hooves splashed through the mud, and the four wheels of the carriage churned it up into haloes of spray.

They were all silent; their spirits seemed to be as damped as the sodden earth. Dear Mama leaned back and closed her eyes. The baron looked gloomily out at the dull, drenched landscape. Rosalie sat in a dream, holding a parcel in her lap, in the bovine rumination of working people. But Jeanne felt her spirits rise in the warmth and the rain like a plant brought out into the fresh air; happiness enclosed and sheltered her heart, like a screen of foliage, from the gloom around her. She said nothing, but longed to burst into song, to hold out her hand until it filled with rainwater and drink; and she revelled in the motion of the horses as they carried her along at a brisk trot, in feeling safe and dry in the midst of the floods as she looked out at the desolate fields.

Steam as from boiling water rose from the horses' haunches gleaming in the heavy rain.

The baroness gradually fell asleep. Her face, framed by six neat dangling ringlets, sank little by little on the soft support of the three great billows of her neck, which flowed like waves into the open sea of her bosom. Her head was lifted at each intake of breath, then fell again; her cheeks filled out, and a sonorous snore came from her parted lips. Her husband leaned over and gently placed a small leather purse in the hands crossed over her ample stomach.

She awoke at the touch; she stared at the object in her hands with a drowned look, in the bemused state of someone suddenly roused from sleep. The purse slipped off her lap to the floor and fell open. Gold coins and banknotes were scattered all over the carriage. At that she came fully awake; and her daughter's high spirits broke out in a peal of laughter.

The baron gathered up the money and placed it in her lap: 'This, my dear, is all that is left from my farm at Eletot. I sold it to pay for repairs at Les Peuples, since we shall be spending much of our time there now.'

She counted up six thousand four hundred francs and calmly put them in her pocket.

It was the ninth farm sold in this way out of the thirty-one inherited from their parents. An income of twenty thousand livres still remained to them, however, from property which would easily have yielded an annual return of thirty thousand if it had been well administered.

That income would have been sufficient for their plain way of living if there had not been a bottomless hole in the household, namely their open-handedness. This drank up the money in their hands as the sun dries up the water in a marsh. It trickled away, leaked out, evaporated. How? No one knew. Somebody was always saying: 'I don't know how it's happened. I haven't bought anything in particular, but I've spent a hundred francs today.'

It was, besides, one of their greatest pleasures in life to be free in giving; and they were all splendidly, touchingly in agreement on that point.

Jeanne asked: 'Does it look beautiful now, my château?'

The baron replied gaily: 'You'll soon see, little girl.'

The downpour gradually decreased in violence, and soon it was no more than a sort of mist, the finest powdering of shimmering drops. The cloud vault seemed to lift and whiten; and suddenly through an invisible gap in the clouds a long, slanting ray of sunlight shone down on the meadows.

Now as the clouds dispersed the blue depths of the sky came into view; then the rent grew wider, as though a veil were torn; and a glorious clear sky of deep azure spread out over the world.

There was a cool, soft breath of wind as though the earth

gave a contented sigh; and in gardens or woodland paths could be heard the occasional bright notes of a bird drying its plumage.

Darkness fell. All the occupants of the carriage were sleeping now, except Jeanne. They stopped twice at an inn to give the horses a rest, and a little hay and water.

The sun had set; bells were ringing in the distance. In a small village lamps were lit; and the sky too was alight with a scatter of stars. Lighted houses could be seen here and there, piercing the darkness with a fiery shaft; and from behind a hill, between the branches of fir trees, the moon rose huge and red, languid as if with sleep.

It was so warm that they lowered the windows of the carriage. Jeanne lay back in her seat, tired out with day-dreaming, content with her visions of happiness to come. As she remained motionless in the same position, from time to time a twinge of cramp would make her open her eyes; then she would look out of the window to see the trees of a farm go past in the moonlit night, or cows lying down in a field raising their heads as the carriage passed. Then she changed her position, trying to recapture the outline of a dream; but her ears were filled with the continuous sound of the vehicle's motion, which was fatiguing to her mind, and she closed her eyes again with a sense of being constricted in spirit as she was in body.

At last, however, the carriage came to a halt. Men and women were standing at the doors with lanterns in their hands. They had arrived. Jeanne woke with a start, and quickly sprang to the ground. Papa and Rosalie, lighted by a farmer's lantern, half carried the baroness who was utterly exhausted, moaning with distress and murmuring incessantly on a faint, expiring note: 'Oh dear, oh dear! Poor things, poor things!' She refused to eat or drink, but retired to bed and immediately fell asleep.

Jeanne and the baron had supper together alone.

They smiled at each other and clasped hands across the table; then, after they had eaten, a childish excitement came over them and they set out to explore the redecorated manor-house.

It was one of those big, high Normandy mansions, part farm, part manor-house, built of white stone grey with age, spacious enough to house an entire clan.

A vast hall extending the full length of the house divided it in half with two main doors opposite each other, one on either side. This entrance hall was surmounted by a double stairway, the two flights of stairs meeting in a landing on the first storey, with an open space underneath.

The drawing-room, an immensely large apartment, was to the right of the entrance on the ground floor; it was hung with tapestries in a design of birds. All the furniture was covered in *petit point*, with illustrations of La Fontaine's fables; and Jeanne thrilled with pleasure when she saw a chair she had been fond of as a child, with a picture from the tale of the Fox and the Stork.

Adjoining the drawing-room was the library, its walls lined with old books, and two more rooms which were not in use; the dining-room on the left was newly panelled, and next to it were the linen closet, the servants' hall, the kitchen and a little room with a bath.

A corridor ran the whole length of the first storey. A row of doors along it led into ten rooms. They went into Jeanne's apartment which was on the right, at the far end. The baron had just had it redecorated, making use of some antique tapestries and pieces of furniture that he had found lying neglected in the attics. The bedchamber was peopled with the curious characters of the old Flemish tapestries, but it was the sight of the bedstead that drew cries of delight from the young girl. Four great oaken birds, black and shining with polish, supported the bed standing one at each corner, as though they were guarding it. The sides were carved with broad festoons of flowers and fruit; and the bedposts were finely fluted columns crowned with Corinthian capitals, sustaining a cornice of interlaced roses and amoretti.

It stood there like a monument; yet although the darkness

of the wood blackened with time lent it an air of austerity, it was not without grace.

The counterpane and tester hangings glittered like the heavens at night. They were of old silk, deep blue and starred with large fleurs-de-lys worked in gold.

Jeanne first admired it in every detail, then raised her candle high to examine the tapestries closely, trying to make out the stories in the pictures.

A young lady and gentleman quaintly dressed in green, red and yellow were conversing beneath a blue tree with ripening fruit on its boughs. A large rabbit of the same colour nibbled at some greyish plants. Five small round houses with pointed roofs could be discerned, just above the heads of the two figures, against a conventional background; and high up, almost in the sky, was a windmill all in red.

A pattern of flowers was interwoven through the whole picture.

The two remaining panels much resembled the first, except that they depicted four manikins in Flemish dress coming out of the houses, raising their arms to Heaven in a gesture of extreme surprise and anger.

The last tapestry portrayed a drama. Here the young man was stretched out on the ground, seemingly dead, while the rabbit was still browsing on the grass beside him. The lady looked down at him as she pierced her breast with a sword; and the fruit on the tree had turned black.

Jeanne had given up trying to understand it all, when she noticed a small creature in a corner, so tiny that the rabbit could have swallowed it up like a blade of grass. This animal, however, was a lion.

At that point she recognized the sad story of Pyramus and Thisbe; and although the simplicity of style of the pictures amused her, she felt happy at having round her the adventures of those two lovers who would whisper to her their cherished hopes and whose ancient, fabled love would hover each night above her slumbers.

The remainder of the furniture was a collection from many

different periods. It was made up of all those pieces that are passed down in a family through successive generations, turning old houses into the kind of museum in which everything is jumbled together. A fine Louis XIV chest of drawers bound with brightly polished copper stood between two Louis XV armchairs in their antique covering of brocaded silk. A rosewood writing-desk opposite the mantelpiece displayed an Empire clock in a glass globe.

This clock was made in the shape of a bronze beehive, suspended between four marble columns above a garden of gilt flowers. A small bee with enamelled wings was kept hovering over the flowerbed in perpetual motion by a slender pendulum emerging from a narrow slit in the hive. The dial of painted faience was set in the side of the hive.

The clock began to strike eleven. The baron kissed his daughter and retired to his own apartment, and Jeanne went reluctantly to bed.

She took a last look round the room before putting out her candle. Only the head of the bed rested against the wall, and to the left of it was a window with moonlight streaming through and casting a patch of light on the floor.

This brightness was reflected on the walls of the room, and shed a faint pallor like a caress on the motionless loves of Pyramus and Thisbe.

There was another window opposite the foot of the bed, and through it Jeanne could see a tall tree bathed in soft light. She turned over on her side and closed her eyes, but opened them again after a few moments.

She still had the sensation of being jolted along in the carriage, a movement that seemed to continue inside her head. For a time she lay without moving in an attitude of repose, hoping in that way to induce sleep; but her restless state of mind soon spread through her whole body.

Excitement rose within her, with a nervous twitching of her limbs as the feeling grew. At last she left her bed, barefoot and bare-armed, and, like a ghost in her long nightgown, stepped through the pool of light on the floor and flung open the window to look out.

The scene was as clear under the brilliant moon as in the full light of day; and Jeanne was able to recognize every part of the countryside that she had known and loved since her early childhood.

Immediately below her was a wide lawn, creamy in the nocturnal light. Two great trees rose high in front of the château, a plane-tree to the north, a linden to the south.

Beyond the expanse of turf the domain was bounded by a small copse, protected from the ocean gales by five rows of ancient elms, twisted, bare and scarred, shaped to the slope of a roof by the never-ceasing fury of the wind off the sea.

This part of the grounds, the park, was enclosed on each side by a long avenue of towering poplars* separating the manor-house from the two adjoining farms, one of which belonged to the Couillard family, the other to the Martins.

These poplars had given the château its name of 'Les Peuples'. A broad expanse of waste land outside the park stretched away to the edge of the sea, and day and night the wind whistled over it as it beat its way through the scattered gorse. This level ground fell sharply away to the top of a sheer white cliff a hundred metres high with the sea waves licking at its foot.

Jeanne gazed out at the distant expanse of the waves, with their surface like watered silk, asleep under the stars.

All the odours of the earth breathed out in a long sigh of release from the heat of the sun. The persistent, penetrating scent of a jasmine climbing over the windows below mingled with the faint fragrance of young foliage. A fitful breeze drifted past the window bringing a tang of strong, salty air in its languid passage and the sticky, sweaty smell of seaweed.

The girl abandoned herself for a time to the sheer pleasure of breathing; the scene was as restful and soothing to her as a cool bath.

* Poplars (*peupliers*) were known in Normandy as 'populars', literally 'peoples' (*peuples*).

The semi-darkness was astir with the almost noiseless activity of all the creatures that awake at nightfall, whose obscure lives find refuge in the tranquil dark. Large birds cleft the air without a sound, showing only as a smear, darkening the air like a shadow; the humming of invisible insects was the lightest touch upon the ear; there was a silent scurrying through the dew-soaked grass, over the sand of deserted paths.

The only sound came from a few melancholy toads crying out to the moon in harsh, monotonous croaks.

Jeanne felt her heart full to bursting, filled with murmurous life like the clear night itself, suddenly invaded by a host of errant desires like the creatures of the night whose heartbeats surrounded her. She was at one with that living poetry; and in the bright, warm night she felt unearthly tremors coursing through her, the pulsing of indefinable hopes, the breath of an unguessed happiness.

She began to dream of love.

Love! For two years she had thought of its approach with growing expectation. Now she was free to love; she had only to meet Himself!

What would he be like? She did not precisely know, nor did she so much as wonder about it. *He* would be *he*, that was all.

She knew only that she would worship him with all her heart and he would love and care for her with all his might. They would go out together on evenings like this, beneath the ashen light of the stars. They would walk hand in hand, pressed close, feeling each other's heartbeats and the warmth of each other's shoulders, their love transfused with the smooth, limpid air of a summer night, so much at one that they entered freely into each other's inmost thoughts through the sheer power of their love. They would go on for ever in this way, their love serene and indestructible.

Suddenly she seemed to feel him there, close beside her; and a faint tremor of sensual pleasure ran through her whole body. She pressed her arms to her breast in an unconscious movement, as though to clasp her dream; and when her lips, expectant of the stranger, were brushed by a light passing touch she almost swooned, as at a lover's kiss borne on the breath of spring.

At that moment she heard the sound of footsteps in the night, out on the highway behind the château. In a wild flight of imagination, a transport of belief in the impossible, in acts of Providence, divine presentiments, the romantic machinations of Fate, she wondered: 'Can it be He?' She listened eagerly to the walker's measured footsteps, sure that he would stop at the gate to ask hospitality.

When he had gone past she felt almost disappointed, even though she realized that her hopes had been fantasies, and smiled at her own folly.

Her mood had quietened, and the thoughts that drifted through her mind were now more realistic as she sought to see into the future, to plan her life.

She would live here with him in this peaceful manor-house by the sea. Doubtless she would have two children, a son for him, a daughter for herself. She pictured them playing on the lawn between the plane-tree and the linden, while their parents gazed at them fondly and exchanged passionate looks above their heads.

She stood there a long time lost in dreams, while the moon reached the end of her journey across the sky and disappeared into the sea. The air grew colder. The horizon lightened in the east. A cock sang out in the farm on one side, and was answered from the other. Their raucous calls seemed to come from a long way off beyond the chicken runs; and, as the immense vault of the sky turned slowly, imperceptibly paler, the stars faded from sight.

A bird woke with a chirrup somewhere near. Twitterings began among the foliage, tentative at first, then growing bolder until a joyous trilling echoed from bough to bough, from tree to tree.

Jeanne realized with a start that she was bathed in light; when she raised her head from her hands to look up, the sunlight was so dazzling that she closed her eyes.

A mountain of purple cloud half-hidden behind the great

avenue of poplars cast gleams of light like bloodstains on the awakened earth.

Slowly, splitting the blazing clouds asunder, engulfing trees and plains, the ocean and the whole fiery horizon, the immense globe of flame came into view.

Jeanne was wild with delight. In the presence of all that splendour she was moved to an ecstasy of joy, suffused with infinite tenderness. The sun was hers! this was her dawn! the beginning of her life! the sunrise of her hopes! She stretched out her arms to the radiant sky in a yearning to embrace the sun; she wanted to speak, to utter god-like words at that divine dawning of a day; but for all her ardour she was stricken dumb, powerless to express it. She dropped her head in her hands, felt tears come into her eyes; and she wept for joy.

When she looked up again the superb panorama had disappeared. She felt appeased, a little tired, chilled. Leaving the window open she went to lie on her bed, dreamed for a few minutes longer, then fell into such a deep sleep that she did not hear her father call her at eight o'clock and only wakened when he came into her room.

He was anxious to show her the improvements he had made to the château, her château.

A large, enclosed apple orchard lay between the façade overlooking the grounds, and the lane. This lane was a by-road which passed between the boundaries of the two farms and half a league further on joined the main highway from Le Havre to Fécamp.

The drive ran straight from the wooden gate to the main entrance. There was a row of small outbuildings, built of shingle and roofed with thatch, on each side of the apple orchard along the dykes that bounded the farms.

The roofing and walls of the château and all the woodwork had been repaired, the rooms re-carpeted and the whole of the interior painted. The gleaming fresh paint on the shutters, the patches of new plaster on the tall grey frontage stood out like white stains on the shabby old mansion.

On the other side of the house, one of Jeanne's windows commanded a view over the copse and the row of wind-racked elms to the distant sea.

Arm in arm, Jeanne and the baron wandered about looking at everything, inspecting every corner; then they strolled along the great avenues of poplars that enclosed what was known as the park. The grass had grown and spread a carpet of green under the trees. The copse at the far end of the lawn was charming, with small paths winding between leafy hedges. Suddenly a hare started up, startling the young girl, then leaped the bank and made for the rushes at the top of the cliff.

Madame Adélaïde was still exhausted, and when she announced after luncheon that she would take a rest the baron proposed that they should go down to Yport.

They started by walking through the hamlet of Etouvent, to which Les Peuples belonged. Three rustics greeted them as old acquaintances.

Next, their way was down a wooded hillside through a winding valley that led to the sea.

Presently the village of Yport came into view. Women sitting outside their houses, mending clothes, watched them as they passed. A stream ran down the middle of the steeply sloping street, with piles of rubbish beside it, and there was a strong smell of brine. The brown nets, in which a few shining scales still hung like small pieces of silver, were drying on the doors of the hovels, and through the doorways came the odour of large families crowded together in a single room.

Pigeons strutted beside the stream and pecked a living from the debris.

Jeanne stared about her, finding it all as strange and unaccustomed as a scene on the stage.

Then as they rounded the corner of a wall she caught sight of the sea, a smooth opaque blue, flowing out to the horizon.

They stopped at the beach, to look at the view. Sails like the wings of white birds went floating past far out at sea. On either side of them rose towering cliffs. The view in one direction was bounded by what appeared to be a headland, and on the other side the line of cliffs stretched away as far as the eye could see.

In a break in the cliffs nearby a quay and a few houses could be seen; little waves edged the water with a fringe of surf as they broke lightly on the shingle.

The local boats hauled up on the shelving pebble beach lay on their sides as though they were offering up to the sun their round cheeks shiny with tar. Some of the fishermen were making them ready for the evening tide.

A seaman came up to offer them some fish, and Jeanne bought a brill from him to take back herself to Les Peuples.

He then offered his services to take them out in a boat, repeating his name over and over again so that it should be firmly impressed on their minds: 'Lastique, Joséphin Lastique.'

The baron promised not to forget it.

They started on their way back to the château.

Jeanne soon found it tiring to carry the big fish, and she passed her father's walking-stick through the gills so that each of them could take one end; they walked gaily home along the cliffs, chattering like two children, their eyes shining as they headed into the wind, while the brill gradually weighed down their arms until its thick tail swept the grass.

2

JEANNE'S EXISTENCE NOW WAS DELIGHTFULLY unconstrained. She read, daydreamed, wandered alone through all her surroundings. She took leisurely walks in the lanes, her footsteps slow as her thoughts drifted off into dreams; sometimes she would go running and skipping down into the little winding valleys, where the brow of the hill on each side was crowned with a golden mop of gorse in flower. Its strong, sweet scent went to her head like wine; and the distant sound of waves breaking on the beach lulled her spirit like the rocking of a cradle.

There were times when a feeling of languor would make her drop down and lie full length on the thick, springy turf on a hillside; and at moments when a turn in the path gave a sudden glimpse, through a funnel-shaped gap in the grass, of a triangle of blue sea sparkling in the sun and a sail on the horizon, she would feel a wild, unreasoning joy as though some mysterious happiness were hovering close above her.

She came to love solitude in the cool tranquillity of that countryside, the peace of its rounded horizon; and she would stay out long on the hills until little wild rabbits went bounding past her feet.

Often, exhilarated by the light breezes from the sea, she would break into a run along the cliffs, all a-quiver with the exquisite pleasure of motion and tireless as a fish in water or a swallow in the air.

She sowed seeds of memories everywhere like scattered corn, the kind of memories that take root and endure until death. It seemed to her that she let fall a piece of her heart in every fold of the valley.

She became an enthusiastic bather. She would swim until she was out of sight from the shore, for she was strong and venturesome without any thought of danger. She loved the sensation of the cold, clear blue water bearing her up, rocking her to and fro. When she was far out from the land she would turn on her back and lie with arms crossed on her breast, gazing up into the deep blue of the sky at the swift flight of a swallow, the white silhouette of a seabird. There was nothing then to be heard but the distant murmur of waves on the shingle and a vague sound from the shore that came to her over the water, indistinct, scarcely perceptible. Then Jeanne would raise herself up with shrill cries of pleasure and splash the water with both hands.

Sometimes when she went out too far a boat would come out to bring her back.

She would return to the château pale with hunger but treading on air, lively and bright-eyed with contentment.

The baron in the meantime had grand agricultural schemes in mind; he wished to make experiments, introduce progressive ideas, give new implements a trial, bring in and acclimatize foreign breeds; and he passed some of his time conversing with peasants who shook their heads in incredulity when they heard what he proposed.

Often, besides, he went out with the Yport boatmen. After he had visited the caves, springs and headlands in the vicinity, he wanted to go out fishing like an ordinary seaman.

On days when a breeze was blowing, filling the sails and sending the plump cockle-shells of boats flying over the waves, and when the long line trailed on each side of the boat sank almost to the sea-bed with shoals of mackerel in pursuit, his hand trembled nervously as he held the thin line that would quiver when a fish was hooked and wriggling on the end of it.

He went out by moonlight to pull up the nets put out the day before. He liked hearing the creaking of the mast, and drawing in cool breaths of the whistling night breeze; and after the boat had tacked to and fro for a long time to find the buoys – steering by the tip of a rock, a church steeple or the Fécamp light-house – he enjoyed the sudden stillness, as the first rays of the rising sun struck a gleam of light from the slimy backs of the big ray spread out like fans on the deck, and the thick bellies of turbot.

He talked about these expeditions with enthusiasm at every meal; and dear Mama for her part told him how many times she had walked from one end to the other of the great avenue of poplars beside the Couillard farm, since there was not enough sun on the other side.

As she had been advised to 'take exercise', she had taken up walking. As soon as the chill of night had gone from the air she came downstairs on Rosalie's arm wrapped in a cloak and two shawls, her head muffled in a black hood with another – of red wool – on top of that.

Then, dragging her left foot which was less active than the

other – it had already drawn two powdery furrows through the grass the whole length of the path, one on her outward way and one on the return – she started off on the journey from the corner of the house to the nearest of the bushes in the copse. She had had a seat placed at each end of this path; and every five minutes she would stop and say to the poor, patient maidservant who supported her: 'Let us sit down here, girl, I am a little tired.'

Each time they stopped she would leave a garment on one of the seats, it might be the woollen hood or one of her shawls, next the second shawl, the remaining hood, and lastly her mantle; all this made a big pile of clothes at each end of the avenue for Rosalie to carry back under her free arm when they went indoors to luncheon.

In the afternoon the baroness would set out again, walking more slowly and with longer pauses for rest, occasionally even dropping into a doze in the chaise-longue which had been wheeled out for her.

She called this taking 'her exercise', just as she talked of 'her hypertrophy'.

A doctor she had consulted ten years earlier when she was suffering from shortness of breath had talked about hypertrophy. Although she hardly knew the meaning of the word, it had been fixed in her mind ever afterwards. She persisted in making the baron, Jeanne and Rosalie feel her heart, which in fact it was no longer possible to do, as it was now buried so deep under the swollen flesh of her breast; however, she firmly refused to allow a new doctor to examine her, for fear that she might be found to have other ailments; and she mentioned 'her hypertrophy' on every possible occasion, so frequently that it might have been supposed to be a condition peculiar to herself, something of her own, like a unique object to which no one else could have a claim.

The baron spoke of 'my wife's hypertrophy' and Jeanne of 'Mama's hypertrophy' just as they would have said 'her gown, her hat, her umbrella'.

She had been very pretty as a girl, and as slender as a reed.

After waltzing in the arms of every uniform in the Empire she had read *Corinne,* which made her weep; and it seemed she bore the mark of that novel for ever afterwards.

As her waist grew thicker, her spirit soared to higher flights of poetry; and when obesity nailed her to a chair she roamed in thought through amorous adventures in which she saw herself as the heroine. She had favourites among these exploits which she always made repeat themselves in her dreams, as a musical box endlessly repeats the same tune when the handle is turned. All the languishing romances about captive maidens and swallows invariably brought tears to her eyes; and she even liked some of Béranger's bawdy songs because they struck a nostalgic note.

She would often sit for hours lost in dreams; and it gave her tremendous pleasure to live at Les Peuples where the house provided a setting for the stories passing through her head, since the nearby woodlands, the barren heath and the sea not far away called to her mind the books of Sir Walter Scott which she had been reading for the past few months.

On rainy days she stayed in her room going through what she called her 'relics'. These were all her old letters, from her father and mother, from the baron at the time of their engagement and others besides.

She kept them in a mahogany writing-desk ornamented with copper sphinxes; and her voice took on a particular tone when she said to her maid: 'Rosalie, child, bring me the souvenir drawer.'

The maid would open the desk, pull out the drawer and put it on a chair beside her mistress, who would begin to read the letters slowly, one after another, occasionally letting fall a tear on one.

On the days when Jeanne took Rosalie's place and accompanied dear Mama on her outings, her mother talked of her childhood memories. The young girl, seeing herself in those stories of bygone days, was surprised at the similarity of their thoughts, the kinship of their desires; for every one of us imagines that ours is the first heart to tremble at a host of sensations, even though these are the very same that quickened the pulse of the earliest created beings, the same that will flutter the hearts of the last man and woman on earth.

Their progress was slow, matched to the pace of the story which a few moments' breathlessness interrupted from time to time; and then Jeanne's thoughts raced ahead of the events being related, to project themselves into a future crowded with pleasures and to revel in anticipation.

One afternoon when they had paused to rest on the seat at the far end of the avenue they saw a portly priest advancing towards them.

He bowed while he was yet some distance away, assumed an air of benevolence, bowed again when he had come within three paces of them and called out: 'Well, Baroness, and how are we today?' He was the parish priest of the district.

Dear Mama, who had been born in the Age of Enlightenment and brought up at the time of the Revolution by a rather sceptical father, seldom went to Mass, although from a sort of feminine religious instinct she had a liking for priests.

She had quite forgotten about her parish priest, Father Picot, and blushed when she saw him. She apologized for being unprepared to receive him. But the good man did not appear in the least put out; he glanced at Jeanne, complimented her on her looks and sat down, placing his tricorn on his lap and wiping his forehead. He was very stout, very red in the face and streaming with perspiration. Every few minutes he pulled a huge, sweat-soaked check handkerchief from his pocket and passed it over his face and neck; but the square of linen had scarcely been tucked away in the black recesses of his gown before drops of moisture had broken out afresh on his skin and fallen on the cassock over his rotund stomach, making a paste of the dust from the high roads and covering him with small round spots.

He was a merry fellow, a typical country priest, talkative, tolerant, a thoroughly worthy individual. He told them anecdotes, talked about the people in the neighbourhood and appeared not to have remarked that his two parishioners had not yet come to the church, the baroness attributing this omission to the vagueness of her beliefs, while Jeanne was thankful to be released from the convent where she had been surfeited with pious ritual.

They were joined by the baron. His religion was pantheistic and he was not interested in dogma. He was affable to the priest, with whom he was distantly acquainted, and invited him to stay to dinner.

The priest knew how to make himself agreeable, thanks to that unconscious subtlety with which the manipulation of souls endows the most mediocre of men when they are called upon by chance to exercise power over their fellows.

The baroness made much of him, drawn to him perhaps by the kind of affinity that exists between like natures, for it consoled her as she panted and wheezed in her obesity to see her stout guest's sanguine complexion and shortness of breath.

By the time dessert was on the table he was displaying the animation of a priest off duty, with the verve and freedom of manner of a convivial guest.

He gave a sudden exclamation as though a happy thought had just entered his head: 'But I have a new parishioner whom I must introduce to you, Viscount de Lamare!'

The baroness had all the nobility in the province at her fingertips, and promptly inquired: 'Is that one of the Lamares of Eure?'

The priest inclined his head: 'Yes, Madame, he is the son of Viscount Jean de Lamare who died last year.' Then Madame Adélaïde, who loved the aristocracy above everything, put a number of questions to him; she learned that after paying his father's debts the young man had sold the family seat and set up a modest establishment in one of the three farms belonging to him in the township of Etouvent. This property yielded an income of five to six thousand livres in all; but the viscount was of a close, careful disposition and intended to live simply for two or three years in this unpretentious lodging, in order to save enough to cut a figure in society and make an advantageous marriage without contracting debts or mortgaging his farms.

The priest added: 'He's a charming young fellow; sensible, you know, and steady. But there's very little to amuse him in these parts.'

The baron replied: 'Bring him to visit us, Reverend Father; that may provide a little distraction for him now and again.'

They went on to talk of other things.

When they retired to the drawing-room after coffee had been served the priest asked if he might go out into the garden, as he was in the habit of taking a short turn after meals. The baron went with him. They strolled slowly to the end of the white frontage of the château, and then retraced their steps. Their shadows fell behind or in front of them as they walked towards the moon or turned their backs on it, one thin shadow and one round one topped with a mushroom. The priest was chewing a sort of cigarette that he had taken from his pocket. He was outspoken, as country people are, in giving his reason for this: 'My digestion is rather sluggish and it helps me to bring up wind.'

Suddenly he looked up at the brilliant moon and exclaimed: 'That's a sight one is never tired of seeing.'

Then he went indoors to take leave of the ladies.

3

ON THE FOLLOWING SUNDAY THE BARONESS AND Jeanne went to Mass, prompted by a sense of delicacy and consideration for their parish priest.

They waited to see him after the service, to invite him to luncheon on Thursday. He left the vestry with a tall, distinguished-looking young man at his side who gave his arm to the priest with an air of familiarity. As soon as Father Picot saw the two women he exclaimed, with a gesture of surprise and pleasure: 'This is a happy chance! Baroness,

Mademoiselle Jeanne, allow me to present your neighbour, Viscount de Lamare.'

The viscount bowed, declared that it had long been his desire to make these ladies' acquaintance and began talking easily and without constraint, in the manner of a well-bred man with some knowledge of the world. His looks were of the kind that women dream of and men all find displeasing. His dark hair curled over a smooth brown forehead; the heavy eyebrows were so evenly shaped that they might have been false, and lent a profound and tender expression to his dark eyes with the whites faintly tinged with blue.

There was a passionate eloquence in his gaze from beneath long, thick lashes, of the sort which makes the haughty belle of the drawing-rooms lose her poise, the girl in a bonnet with a basket on her arm turn her head as she goes down the street.

The languorous charm of those eyes made people think his ideas profound, his lightest words full of weighty meaning.

The glossy, well-trimmed beard, fine in texture, hid a jaw somewhat too strong.

They parted with a profuse exchange of compliments.

Monsieur de Lamare paid his first call two days later.

He came when they were looking at a rustic seat which had been placed that morning under the big plane-tree outside the drawing-room window. The baron wished to put another seat under the linden, to balance it; dear Mama did not care for symmetry and was against the idea. The viscount, on being consulted, pronounced himself in agreement with the baroness.

Then he discoursed to them about the surrounding country, where in the course of his solitary rambles he had discovered many charming 'beauty spots', and declared it to be very 'picturesque'. From time to time his eyes met Jeanne's as though by chance; and the sudden glance, abruptly withdrawn, gave her a strange sensation like a caress of admiration, the hint of a dawning attachment.

It soon emerged that Monsieur de Lamare the elder, who had died the year before, had known an intimate friend of dear Mama's father, Monsieur des Cultaux; and the discovery of this acquaintance gave rise to an interminable conversation about marriages, dates and family relationships. The baroness performed prodigious feats of memory, recapitulating the lineage and descendants of other families and moving unerringly through the labyrinth of complicated genealogy.

'Tell me, Viscount, have you heard about the Saunoys de Varfleur? – the elder son Gontran married a de Coursil, a Coursil-Courville, and the younger married a cousin of mine, Mademoiselle de la Roche-Aubert, who was related to the Crisanges. Of course, Monsieur de Crisange was a close friend of my father and must have known yours as well.'

'Yes, indeed, Madame. Wasn't that the Monsieur de Crisange who emigrated, whose son was ruined?'

'The same. He proposed to my aunt after her husband's death, Count d'Eretry; but she would not have him, because he took snuff. By the way, do you know what has become of the Viloises? They suffered a reverse in their fortunes and left Touraine in about 1813; after that they settled in Auvergne, and I have heard nothing more of them.'

'I believe, Madame, that the old marquis died after a fall from his horse, leaving one daughter married to an Englishman and the other to a tradesman who had seduced her, a person by the name of Bassolle, well-to-do, so they say.'

Names familiar to them were mentioned, names they had heard as children and in the conversation of their elders. Marriages in those families of equal rank took on in their minds the importance of great public events. They talked of people they had never seen as of familiar acquaintances; and those same people in other parts of the country spoke of them in the same way; thus they felt themselves at ease with such people, on friendly terms almost even at a distance, by the sole fact of belonging to the same class and caste, being of one blood.

The baron, who was of a retiring disposition and had not been brought up in the beliefs and prejudices current in his world, knew scarcely any of the families in the neighbourhood and questioned the viscount about them.

'Oh! There are not many of the aristocracy round here,' Monsieur de Lamare informed him, in the same tone in which he might have observed that there were few rabbits on the hillsides; and he entered into details. There were only three families of more or less the same background: the Marquis de Coutelier, head as it were of the Norman aristocracy; the Viscount and Viscountess de Briseville, people of very good family who for the most part kept to themselves; and lastly the Count de Fourville, an ogrish figure who was said to have broken his wife's heart; he was a keen sportsman, and lived in the château of La Vrillette built over a mere.

A few self-made persons had bought property here and there, and were on friendly terms with each other. The viscount had no acquaintance among them.

He took his leave; his last look was for Jeanne, a farewell glance with a suggestion of special warmth and tenderness.

The baroness thought him charming and, above everything, of good family. Dear Papa replied: 'Yes, he's certainly a very well-bred young fellow.'

He was invited to dinner the following week. After that he became a regular visitor at the château.

He arrived usually at about four in the afternoon, when he joined dear Mama in 'her avenue' and gave her his arm to take 'her exercise'. When Jeanne had not left the grounds she supported the baroness on the other side, and all three walked slowly to and fro straight from one end of the long path to the other. He seldom spoke to the young girl. But the glance of his eyes often met Jeanne's, like black velvet encountering blue agate.

On several occasions the two of them went with the baron to Yport.

One evening when they were on the beach old Lastique came up to them, and remarked as he continued to smoke his pipe, the absence of which might have occasioned even more surprise than that of his nose: 'With this wind, now, M'sieu l'Baron, we'd have no trouble making as far as Etretat to-morrow, and back again.'

Jeanne clasped her hands, pleading: 'Oh, Papa, couldn't we?' The baron turned to Monsieur de Lamare:

'Will you be one of the party, Viscount? We would go over there to lunch.'

Thus the expedition was agreed on between them.

Jeanne was up at dawn. She waited for her father, who was slower in dressing, and they set out to walk through the dew, over the heath and then through the woods, which were alive with bird song. When they arrived at the quay the viscount was seated on a capstan beside old Lastique.

Two seamen helped them to put to sea. The men put their shoulders to the bulwarks and shoved with all their strength. The boat would scarcely move over the flat stretch of shingle. Then Lastique slid greased wooden rollers under the keel, returned to his post and chanted in a continuous drawl: 'O-ay hup!' to keep everyone in time.

When they came to the edge where the beach shelved steeply to the sea the boat went down in a rush, sliding over the round pebbles with a noise like tearing cloth. It stopped short at the line of surf along the edge of the waves, and they all stepped in and took their seats; then the two seamen, who had remained on shore, pushed it out on the water.

A light, steady breeze ruffled the surface. The sail was hoisted, it filled and rounded a little, and the boat rode smoothly over the waves with a gentle rolling motion.

They sailed at first straight out to sea. The sky above the horizon stooped until it met and mingled with the ocean. To landward the tall, sheer cliff cast a long shadow at its foot, and grass-grown crevices in it caught the sunlight. Far away behind them brown sails were moving away from the white jetty at Fécamp, and in the distance ahead an oddly shaped round rock with a hole right through it looked very much like a huge elephant dipping its trunk in the water. That was the small port of Etretat.

Jeanne gazed into the distance, one hand on the side of the

boat, lulled into a trance by the rocking of the waves; it seemed to her that there were only three really beautiful things in the whole of creation: light, space and water.

No one spoke. Old Lastique, holding the tiller and the sheet, took a drink from time to time out of a bottle under his seat; and he puffed continually at his stump of a pipe, which appeared to be inextinguishable. A thin thread of blue smoke rose from it unbroken, and an identical one issued from the corner of his mouth. No one ever saw the old boatman re-light the clay pipe, its bowl blacker than ebony, or fill it with tobacco. Sometimes he would take it out of his mouth, and from the same corner from which the smoke had spiralled eject a long jet of brown spittle into the sea.

The baron sat in the prow of the boat and watched the sail, taking the place of a deckhand. Jeanne and the viscount found it faintly disturbing to be seated beside each other. Their eyes met, moved by some unknown power, both looking up simultaneously as though at the touch of an unseen hand; for there was already in the air between them the subtle, tenuous attraction that forms so quickly between two young people when the boy is not ill-favoured and the girl is comely. They were happy, their thoughts perhaps straying towards each other as they sat there together.

The sun rose high, to survey with a wider glance the great expanse of waters beneath; but the sea like a coquette hid from his rays in a veil of light mist. It was a transparent golden haze, very low-lying, not thick enough to conceal the view but only to blur it softly. Rays of fire shot out and dissolved the shining cloud; when the sun rose to the full the mist vanished altogether; and the sunlight's reflection shimmered in the smooth mirror of the sea.

Jeanne murmured, deeply affected by the scene: 'How beautiful it is!' The viscount replied: 'Yes, indeed, it is beautiful.' The serene splendour of that morning aroused, as it were, an echo in both their hearts.

Soon the great arches of Etretat came into view, standing in the sea like a cliff on two legs, high enough for ships to pass through; while a white rock, pointed like a needle, rose up in front of the first pillar.

When they came in to land, the baron went ashore first and pulled on the rope to hold the boat steady on the beach while the viscount lifted Jeanne and put her down on shore without wetting her feet; they were both a little agitated by the brief embrace, and then as they climbed the steep shelf of shingle together they heard old Lastique say to the baron: 'Seems to me they'd make a fine pair.'

Luncheon was a delightful meal at a small inn beside the beach. The sea had stilled their voices and numbed their minds, reducing them to silence; at table they became talkative again, and chattered like schoolchildren on holiday.

They laughed irrepressibly at the smallest things. When old Lastique sat down to table he tucked his still-smoking pipe carefully into his beret; they laughed at that. A fly, no doubt attracted by his red nose, kept settling on it, and when he flapped at it but was too slow to catch it, it flew away to a muslin curtain already stained by many of its fellows, from which vantage point it apparently kept a sharp watch on the old seaman's nose, for it soon darted back to perch there again.

Each of the insect's sallies was greeted with a peal of merriment; and when the old man muttered, annoyed by the tickling of the fly: 'It's danged obstinate,' Jeanne and the viscount laughed until they cried, convulsed and choking, pressing napkins to their lips to stifle their mirth.

After coffee, Jeanne said: 'Shall we go for a walk?' The viscount rose; but the baron preferred to bask in the sun on the beach. 'Off you go, children, you'll find me here for the next hour.'

They started out by the few local cottages; and after passing a small manor which looked like a big farm they came to a grassy vale opening out before them.

The motion of the sea had affected their normal mood, making them drowsy, then the keen salt air had sharpened their appetites and the meal had induced a torpor, and finally they had become weak with laughing. Now their spirits rose, and they would have liked to rush wildly about the fields. There was a humming in Jeanne's ears, and swift, unfamiliar sensations stirred within her.

The sun blazed down on them. The ripe crops on both sides of the road were bowed beneath its glare. Grasshoppers numerous as blades of grass gave out their thin, shrill cry everywhere, in the corn and barley, in the clumps of gorse on the cliffs.

No other voice was raised to the torrid sky, which shimmered with faded blue as though it were on the point of turning red, like overheated metal.

They saw a small wood on their right a little way ahead, and turned aside into it.

There was a sunken path running straight between two banks, through tall trees with foliage that shut out the sun. As they entered it a sudden chill descended on them, moist and penetrating, bringing the skin out in gooseflesh. The grass had disappeared, starved of light and fresh air; but the ground was covered with moss.

They walked on: 'Look, we can sit down over there for a while,' Jeanne said. Two dead trees had made a hollow in the greenery into which a shaft of light shone down, warming the earth, awakening the seeds of grass, dandelions and creepers and raising a fine mist of small white flowers, and foxgloves like rockets. Butterflies and bees, heavy-bodied hornets, huge gnats like skeletons of flies, a swarm of flying insects, ladybirds pink and spotted, devil's coachmen, iridescent or black and horned, all peopled that warm lustrous bowl hollowed out in the cool shade of the dense foliage.

They sat with their heads in the shade and their feet in the sunlight. They stared at the host of tiny organisms that spring into view in a ray of light; and Jeanne kept repeating with emotion: 'How lovely it is here! How lovely the country is! Sometimes I wish I were a fly or a butterfly so that I could hide among the flowers.'

They talked about themselves, their habits and tastes, in

the quiet tone of intimacy, the tone in which confidences are made. He said that he was already disenchanted with Society, weary of that useless way of living; it was always the same; there was nothing true, nothing sincere to be found in it.

Society! She would have liked to know what sort of life it was; but she was already certain that it could not be as good as life in the country.

The closer they felt to each other in their hearts, smiling as they gazed more profoundly into each other's eyes, the more formal they became in their speech, addressing each other as 'Monsieur' and 'Mademoiselle'; and they felt that something new and good had entered into them, that their hearts had opened out and they were receptive to a thousand impressions they had never before perceived.

They retraced their steps; but the baron had started out to walk to the Chambre-aux-Demoiselles, a grotto high in the top of a cliff; and they waited for him at the inn.

He did not reappear until five o'clock, having taken a long walk along the coast.

They re-embarked. The boat ran sluggishly before a following wind without a break in its motion, so that they had no sensation of moving forward. The sail filled at each warm gust of the fitful breeze, then dropped again limp against the mast. The water was opaque and dead-looking; and the sun, exhausted by its own ardour, drew slowly nearer to the sea as it followed its circular course.

Once again everyone fell silent, lulled to stupor by the sea.

It was Jeanne who broke the silence: 'How I should love to travel abroad!'

The viscount said in reply: 'Indeed, yes, only it is dull work travelling alone, there should be two people at the least to exchange impressions.'

She considered that: 'That is true . . . and yet, I like walking by myself . . . It's so pleasant to dream, when one is alone.'

He said, with a lingering look: 'Two people can dream, as well as one.'

She lowered her eyes. Was that a hint? Perhaps. She stared

at the horizon as though trying to see beyond it; then she said slowly: 'I should like to go to Italy . . . ; and Greece . . . yes, Greece . . . and Corsica! It must be so wild there, and so beautiful!'

He preferred Switzerland, with its lakes and chalets.

'No,' she said, 'I should like to see quite new countries, like Corsica, or very old ones like Greece, full of the past. It must be so interesting to discover traces of peoples whose history we learned when we were children, and see places that were the scene of great events.'

The viscount, less carried away by enthusiasm, declared: 'England has a great attraction for me; there is much to be learnt there.'

Then their conversation ranged all over the world as they discussed the attractions of every country from the poles to the Equator, rhapsodizing over imaginary landscapes and the improbable customs of other races such as the Chinese or the Lalpanders; but they concluded in the end that the most beautiful country in the world was France, with her temperate climate, cool in summer and mild in winter, her fertile plains and verdant forests, broad calm rivers, and that veneration for the fine arts which had been found nowhere else since the age of Athens' greatness.

A long silence followed.

The sun was lower now and seemed to be shedding blood; and there was a broad, shining trail like a dazzling path across the sea from the horizon to the wake of their boat.

The breeze expired in a few final puffs and dropped altogether; the ripples on the water vanished, leaving the surface smooth; and the motionless sail glowed red. It seemed that a boundless calm had stilled the air, creating a space of quiet about that meeting of the elements; the curve of the sea beneath the sky was like the lustrous liquid belly of some giant bride waiting for her fiery lover to descend on her. He came down in a swift rush, purple as though with ardour to embrace her. Sea and sun became one; and gradually she engulfed him.

Now a chill rose from the horizon; a ripple ran over the heaving bosom of the waters, wrinkling the surface, as though the star they had absorbed sighed out its contentment over the world.

Twilight was brief; darkness soon spread, with a scattering of stars. Old Lastique took up the oars; and they could see flashes of phosphorescence in the water. Side by side, Jeanne and the viscount watched the darting gleams in the wake of the boat. They sat with hardly a thought in their minds, in a state of vague contemplation, happiness and well-being as they breathed the night about them; Jeanne's hand was resting on the seat and her companion's finger touched it, as though by chance; she was motionless in surprise and pleasure, disturbed by the slight contact.

At home in her room that evening she felt strangely restless, in such a state of agitation that the least thing moved her to tears. She looked at her clock, reflecting that the tick-tock of the little bee was like a beating heart, the heart of a friend; it would be a witness of all her life, its sharp, regular tick-tock an accompaniment to all her joys and sorrows; and she stopped the golden insect to drop a kiss on its wings. She would have kissed anything just then. She remembered putting away an old doll, that she had had as a child, at the bottom of a drawer; she took it out and looked at it with the pleasure that comes from seeing a dear friend again; and, pressing it to her breast, she covered the toy's painted cheeks and flaxen curls with burning kisses.

As she held it in her arms she fell into a reverie.

Could her companion that day be He, the bridegroom promised by a thousand secret voices, sent by the sovereign bounty of Providence to cross her path? Was he indeed the being created for her, to whom she was to devote her life? Was it predestined for them both that their tender feelings should flower into embraces, indissoluble union, and give rise to Love?

She had felt as yet none of those violent transports of the whole being, those wild raptures and turbulent impulses that she imagined the tender passion to inspire; nonetheless, she believed that she was beginning to love him; for at times she felt faint when she thought of him; and she thought of him constantly. Her heart beat faster when she was with him; she blushed and turned pale when her eyes met his, and trembled at the sound of his voice.

She slept very little that night.

From that time, the desire for love grew stronger in her day by day. She consulted her feelings, consulted also daisies, clouds, the toss of a coin.

One evening her father said to her: 'You must look your best tomorrow.' 'What for, Papa?' But he only told her: 'That's a secret.'

When she came down in the morning dressed in fresh pastel colours it was to find boxes of sweets on the drawing-room table and a huge bouquet of flowers lying on a chair.

A cart drew up in the courtyard. There was an inscription on it reading 'Lerat, Pastrycook, Fécamp. Wedding breakfasts'; Ludivine came out and with the aid of a cook's boy lifted down from the back a number of large, flat baskets giving off an appetizing smell.

Viscount de Lamare made his appearance. His close-fitting trousers were fastened under neat patent-leather boots which set off the smallness of his feet. A lace jabot frilled out from a long, tight-waisted frock-coat; his handsome dark head was pushed up high by several turns of a narrow cravat, giving him an air of sober distinction. His features seemed altered, having assumed that particular expression which formal attire can unexpectedly imprint on even the most familiar countenance. Jeanne stared at him in amazement as though she had never seen him before; she thought him splendidly aristocratic, a grandee from head to foot.

He bowed to her, smiling: 'Well, my fellow sponsor – are you ready?'

She said hesitantly: 'Why? What is happening?'

'You'll soon see,' said the baron.

The carriage drew up at the steps. Madame Adélaïde in full

feather came downstairs on the arm of Rosalie, who appeared so much overcome by the elegance of Monsieur de Lamare that dear Papa murmured: 'Really, Viscount, I believe our maid has taken a fancy to you.' He blushed up to the ears, affected not to have heard, and picked up the big bouquet which he offered to Jeanne. She took it from him, even more bewildered. Then the four of them entered the carriage; and Ludivine the cook, bringing out cold soup for the baroness, exclaimed: 'It's just like a wedding, Madame, it is really.'

On their arrival at Yport they descended from the carriage and went on foot through the village, where the seamen in new clothes still creased from folding came out of their houses, bowed and shook hands with the baron and followed them as if in procession.

The viscount had given Jeanne his arm and they walked together in front.

They stopped at the church; and the great silver cross came in sight carried upright by a choirboy, who was followed by a second youngster in red and white bearing the vessel of holy water with an aspergillum.

Then there came three aged choristers, one of whom was lame, next the serpent* player and lastly the priest, his golden stole crossed over the eminence of his paunch. He greeted them with a smile and a nod; then with half-closed eyes and lips moving in prayer, his biretta pulled down over his nose, he walked behind his surpliced troops down to the sea.

There was a crowd of people on the beach standing round a new boat, which was hung with garlands, with ribbons fluttering from her mast, sail and rigging, and the name JEANNE in gold lettering on the stern.

The owner of the boat, which had been built with the baron's money, was old Lastique, who now came forward to meet the procession. All the men doffed their caps; and a row

* Bass wind instrument, in use until the nineteenth century but now obsolete, made of wood covered with leather and curved in the shape of an S.

of pious women, enveloped in voluminous black cloaks, knelt down in a circle as the cross came in sight.

The priest, with a choirboy on each side of him, proceeded to one end of the boat, while the three old choristers, grubby figures in white habits with unshaven chins and solemn expressions, stood at the other, their eyes fixed on their books of plainsong, bawling tunelessly in the fresh morning air.

When they paused for breath the serpent player continued to produce his lowing sound alone; and his small grey eyes disappeared as he drew in a breath and filled his cheeks with air. The skin of his neck and forehead was distended with air until it seemed to come away from the flesh.

The sea was motionless and transparent, seemingly withdrawn into itself as it looked on at the baptism of its small craft, gently raking the shingle with wavelets no more than finger-high. Big white gulls spread their wings and swooped past in huge arcs through the blue sky, out into the distance, to return and circle above the kneeling crowd as though they too wished to see what was going on.

An amen lasting five minutes was bellowed out, after which the chanting stopped; and the priest unctuously pronounced a few words of Latin, of which nothing could be heard but the sonorous endings.

After this he walked round the boat sprinkling it with holy water and then began to murmur some prayers, taking up a position beside the boat opposite the two sponsors, who stood hand in hand without moving.

The young man still looked grave, as befitted his splendid turnout, but the young girl almost swooned in a wave of emotion and began to shiver so that her teeth chattered. Suddenly, in a momentary illusion, the dream that had haunted her for some time past had taken on a semblance of reality. There had been talk of a wedding, a priest was pronouncing a blessing, men in surplices were chanting prayers; was it not she who was being married?

Was there a nervous tremor in her fingers, a message passing through her veins from her heart to her companion's?

Did he know, had he guessed, was he overcome as she was by a sort of frenzy of love? or did he simply know from experience that no woman could resist him? All at once she became aware that he was pressing her hand, lightly at first, then harder, harder still until it must surely break. And he said without a flicker of his features, so that no one remarked it, he did actually say most distinctly: 'Oh, Jeanne, this could be our betrothal if you wanted it.'

She bent her head very slowly in a movement that might have signified 'yes'. The priest, who was still sprinkling holy water, let a few drops fall on their fingers.

It was over. The women rose from their knees. The return of the procession was a stampede. The cross carried by the choirboy had lost its balance; it rushed along swaying from side to side, or leaning forward in peril of falling on its face. The priest, his prayers done, brought up the rear at a gallop; the choristers and the serpent disappeared down a side alley in their haste to disrobe; the seamen hurried along in groups. The same thought had entered all their heads like odours from a kitchen, lengthening their stride, making their mouths water and penetrating to the bottom of their stomachs until they rumbled in anticipation.

A good luncheon awaited them at Les Peuples.

The big table had been set out in the courtyard under the apple trees. Sixty people sat down to it, seamen and peasants. The baroness took her place in the centre with a priest on either side of her, from the parishes of Yport and Les Peuples. The baron sat opposite between the mayor and his wife, a thin peasant woman already aged, who made jerky little bows in all directions. Her face was narrow and pinched under the tall Normandy bonnet, like a chicken's head with a white comb and round eyes perpetually astonished; and she ate with small, rapid movements as though she were pecking at the plate with her beak.

Jeanne, with her fellow sponsor beside her, was floating in bliss. She saw nothing, was aware of nothing as she sat without speaking, her thoughts in a whirl of happiness.

'What is your Christian name?' she asked him.

'Julien,' he said. 'You didn't know?'

She did not answer, but thought: 'How often I shall be saying that name!'

When the meal was finished they left the courtyard to the seamen and went over to the other side of the house. The baroness began to take her daily exercise, leaning on the baron's arm and escorted by her two priests. Jeanne and Julien walked on to the copse and strolled along its small overgrown paths; he took her hands with an abrupt movement: 'Tell me, will you be my wife?'

Again she bent her head; and when he pressed her: 'Give me an answer, I implore you!' she slowly looked up at him; and he read the answer in her eyes.

4

ONE MORNING THE BARON CAME INTO JEANNE'S room before she was up, sat himself down at the foot of her bed and said to her: 'Viscount de Lamare has proposed for you.'

She wished she could hide her face under the sheets.

Her father went on: 'We have not given him our answer yet.' She drew in a quick breath of excitement. The baron paused, and smiled as he said: 'We would not do anything without consulting you. Your mother and I are not opposed to this marriage, but we shall not press you to accept the offer. Your fortune is larger than his, but one ought not to consider money when it is a question of a lifetime's happiness. His parents are no longer living; so that if you were to marry him he would enter our family like a son; whereas if it were somebody else it would be you, our daughter, who would go among strangers. We like the boy. And you – would you like to have him?'

Blushing to the roots of her hair, she faltered: 'Yes, Papa, I would.'

Dear Papa laughed as he looked into her eyes and murmured: 'I rather thought as much, Mademoiselle.'

She went through that day in a state of intoxication, not knowing what she was doing, scarcely able to tell one thing from another, her limbs weak and exhausted as though she had walked a long way.

The viscount came at about six o'clock, when she was sitting under the plane-tree with dear Mama.

Jeanne's heart began beating wildly. The young man came towards them with no sign of emotion. He took the baroness's hand and kissed it, then turned to the young girl and raised her trembling hand to his lips, pressing on it a long kiss of tenderness and gratitude.

There followed the radiant days of their engagement. They had long conversations alone in a corner of the drawing-room, or seated on the grass beyond the copse, looking out over the moorland. Sometimes they would stroll down dear Mama's avenue, he talking of the future while she looked down at the baroness's dusty footprints.

Now that the decision had been taken they were in haste to have the thing done; accordingly it was settled that the ceremony should take place in six weeks' time, on August 15th; and the young couple were to leave immediately afterwards on their wedding trip. When Jeanne was asked where she would like to go she chose Corsica, where there would be fewer people than in a town in Italy.

They were not unduly impatient as they awaited the day of their wedding, wrapped in a cocoon of tender attachment, savouring the exquisite pleasure of light caresses, the touch of fingers, passionate looks so prolonged that their very souls seemed to mingle; only vaguely troubled by the obscure desire for a more intimate embrace.

It was decided that no one should be invited to the wedding but the baroness's sister, Aunt Lison, who lived as a boarder in a convent at Versailles.

After their father died, the baroness had wished her sister to stay with her; but the spinster had a fixed idea that she was an encumbrance to everyone, useless and tiresome, and she retired to one of those religious establishments that give a lodging to people who are unhappy and alone in the world.

From time to time she used to come and stay a month or two with her family.

She was a small woman who spoke little and was always self-effacing; she appeared only at meal-times and immediately afterwards went upstairs to her room, where she passed all her time in seclusion.

Her demeanour was kind and somewhat elderly, although she was no more than forty-two, and her expression mild and sad; she had never been of any account in her family. Since she was neither a pretty child nor a naughty one, it was seldom that anyone hugged or kissed her; and she would stay quietly in corners, a gentle little girl. When she was older, she was always the one to give way. As a young woman, no one paid her any attention.

She was like a shadow, a familiar object, a living piece of furniture that people are so well accustomed to seeing every day that no one ever gives it a thought.

Her sister regarded her as a failure, as her family had always done, a person of no importance. She was treated in a casual, familiar way that concealed a sort of contemptuous kindness. Her name was Lise, a gay, youthful name which seemed to distress her. When it became obvious that she would probably never marry, Lise was changed to Lison. At Jeanne's birth she became 'Aunt Lison', a poor relation, tidy, painfully shy even with her sister and brother-in-law, who were nevertheless attached to her with a vague affection that was part fond indifference, part unconscious pity and part also natural kindness.

Occasionally when the baroness was talking of some childhood event long past she would say, to determine a date: 'It was at the time of Lison's upset.' Nothing more was ever said; and the 'upset' remained, as it were, shrouded in obscurity.

One evening Lise, at the age of twenty had, for no known

reason, thrown herself into the river. Nothing in her life or behaviour could have led anyone to foresee this act of folly. She had been fished out half dead; her parents raised their hands in indignation, and instead of trying to discover what strange impulse had driven her to it they contented themselves with referring to her 'upset' as they would talk of the accident to their horse Coco, who had broken his leg in a rut not long before and had to be put down.

From that time Lise, soon to become Lison, had been regarded as a very poor-spirited creature. The mild contempt that she evoked in her relations gradually affected the attitude of everybody about her. Even little Jeanne, with a child's natural perception, took no notice of her and never went up to kiss her in bed, never visited her room. Rosalie, the maid-servant, who did what was needed to keep her room in order, seemed to be the only one in the household who knew where it was.

When Aunt Lison came down to the dining-room for luncheon the 'little one' would go to her out of habit and put up her face to be kissed; and that was all.

If someone desired to speak to her a servant was sent to fetch her; and when she was absent no one troubled themselves about her or gave her a thought; it would never have occurred to them to be anxious about her or to wonder: 'Why, I haven't seen Lison this morning.'

She had no place in their lives; she was one of those people who remain strangers even to their nearest relations, like a country no one has explored, whose death leaves no empty place in the household, who seem never to succeed in entering into the lives and loves, the everyday affairs of those who go through life beside them.

When Aunt Lison's name was spoken the two words evoked, as it were, no feeling in anyone's mind. It was as though somebody had mentioned the coffee-pot or the sugar-bowl.

She always went about quietly, with small hurried steps; never made a noise or knocked against anything, and seemed to endow even inanimate objects with the property of soundlessness. Her hands might have been made of cotton wool, so light and delicate was her touch on everything she handled.

She arrived about the middle of July, in a great taking about the coming marriage. She brought a number of presents with her, but because it was she who gave them these went almost unremarked. From the day after she arrived her presence in the house was hardly noticed.

Nonetheless a strange emotion was stirring in her, and her eyes never left the engaged couple. She busied herself about the trousseau with remarkable energy in a feverish burst of activity, working like a common dressmaker in her room, where nobody ever came to see her.

She was continually showing the baroness handkerchiefs she had hem-stitched herself or towels she had embroidered with monograms, and asking: 'Is this all right, Adélaïde?' Dear Mama would give these offerings a casual glance and reply: 'You really shouldn't take so much trouble, Lison dear.'

One evening towards the end of the month the moon rose after a day of oppressive heat on one of those clear, warm nights that seem to stir something deep within men's souls, awakening the poetry dormant in them. A gentle breeze from the fields came like a breath into the drawing-room. The baroness and her husband were playing a game of cards in the circle of light from the shaded lamp on the table; Aunt Lison was between them, knitting; and the young people sat by the open window gazing out at the bright moonlit garden.

The linden and the plane-tree cast shadows over the great lawn that stretched away, pale and glistening, to the dark outline of the copse.

Irresistibly attracted by the melting charm of the night, the silvery lustre of the trees and other shapes, Jeanne turned and said to her parents: 'Dear Papa, we're going to walk out on the grass in front of the house.' The baron answered without looking up: 'Very well, children,' and returned to his game.

They went out and started walking slowly across the white shining lawn to the copse at the further end.

The hour grew late, but they had no thought of returning indoors. The baroness was tired and wanted to go to her room: 'It's time to call those lovers in,' she said.

The baron swept a glance over the big moonlit garden, where two shadows were strolling slowly back and forth.

'Leave them alone,' he said, 'it's such a beautiful night. Lison will wait up for them; won't you, Lison?'

The spinster looked up at him anxiously and answered in her timid voice: 'Yes, of course I will wait up for them.'

The baron also was feeling a little tired after the heat of the day, and he said as he helped the baroness to her feet: 'I shall go up myself.' He left the room with his wife.

Then Aunt Lison in her turn rose, put down the work she had begun on the arm of her chair, with the wool and the big knitting-needles, and went over to the window where she leaned out and gazed at the beauty of the night.

The engaged pair were walking to and fro across the lawn from the copse to the drive, from the entrance steps back to the little wood. They went hand in hand, wordless now as though carried away beyond their everyday selves, caught up in the living poetry breathed out by the earth.

All at once Jeanne caught sight of the old maid, a silhouette in the window outlined by the light of the lamp.

'Look,' she said, 'there's Aunt Lison looking out at us.'

The viscount raised his head and said in the indifferent tone of one who is not thinking of what he says:

'Yes, there's Aunt Lison looking out.'

They continued pacing slowly up and down, in their lovers' dream.

But there was dew on the grass, and they shivered at a slight chill in the air.

'Let's go indoors now,' she said.

They returned to the house.

When they entered the drawing-room Aunt Lison had taken up her knitting again; her head was bent over her work; and her thin fingers trembled a little, as though she were very tired.

Jeanne went up to her and said:

'Aunt, it's time to go up now.'

The old maid turned away her face; her eyes were red, as though she had been crying. The loving pair paid no attention; but suddenly the young man observed that Jeanne's thin shoes were wet through. He became immediately solicitous and asked her tenderly: 'Aren't your precious little feet cold?'

At those words her aunt's fingers shook so violently that the knitting slipped from their hold; the ball of wool rolled away across the floor; she quickly covered her face with her hands and burst into convulsive sobs.

The young couple stood motionless, stupefied, staring at her. Then Jeanne in a swift movement knelt down and held out her arms, repeating anxiously over and over again: 'What is it, Aunt Lison, what is wrong?'

The poor woman shrank pitifully into herself and answered in a halting voice choked with tears:

'It's when he asked you . . . weren't your . . . your . . . precious little feet cold . . . no one has ever said anything like that . . . to me . . . never . . . never . . .'

Surprised and moved to pity though she was, Jeanne felt inclined to laugh at the thought of anyone speaking a lover's endearments to Lison; and the viscount was obliged to turn away to hide his merriment.

Aunt Lison rose abruptly and made her escape, leaving the ball of wool on the floor and her knitting on the chair, and groped her way in the dark upstairs to her room.

After she had gone the two young people looked at each other, amused and touched. Jeanne murmured: 'My poor aunt!' and Julien replied: 'Perhaps she's a little mad tonight.'

They were holding hands, unwilling to part, and gently, very gently they exchanged their first kiss in front of Aunt Lison's empty chair.

Next day they hardly gave the old maid's tears another thought.

By the end of those last two weeks before the wedding

Jeanne was calm and serene, as though she were weary of tender emotions.

On the morning of the day itself she had no time for reflection. Her whole body felt curiously empty as though flesh, blood and bones were dissolving beneath the skin; and she observed that her fingers trembled violently whatever they touched.

She did not regain possession of herself until she was in the chancel of the church, at the service.

Married! She was married! All that had been done, all that had taken place since dawn that day seemed to her like a dream, an actual dream. There are moments when everything round us appears altered; even gestures take on a new meaning; even the hours of the day do not seem to be in their usual place.

She felt dazed, and above all astonished. Only yesterday nothing had changed in her existence; nothing but the constant hope of her life coming nearer, so near that she could almost touch it. She had gone to sleep a young girl; now she was a woman.

She had crossed that invisible barrier, then, which conceals the future with all its joys, its dreamed-of pleasures. She felt that a door stood open before her; she was on the threshold of the domain of her expectations.

The ceremony came to an end. They passed into the vestry which was almost empty, since no guests had been invited; and left it again.

When they made their appearance at the church door a tremendous din startled the bride and made the baroness scream; the peasantry had fired a salvo of shots; the sound carried as far as Les Peuples.

A collation was served for the family and the bridegroom, the château priest, the priest from Yport and the witnesses, who had been chosen from among the principal farmers in the neighbourhood.

They walked about the grounds as they waited for the meal. The baron and baroness, Aunt Lison, the Mayor and

Father Picot set off along dear Mama's walk; while the Yport priest strode through the avenue on the other side, reading his breviary.

On the further side of the château the noise of the rustics' merry-making could be heard as they drank their cider under the apple trees. The courtyard was crowded with people from all over the countryside, wearing their Sunday clothes. The young men and girls ran about chasing each other through the trees.

Jeanne and Julien made their way through the copse and up to the top of the bank where they stood without speaking, gazing at the sea. Although it was mid-August, the air was chilly; there was a north wind blowing, and the sun shone fiercely in the cloudless blue sky.

The young people turned to the right across the heath, to seek shelter in the wooded valley winding down to Yport. When they were among the trees there was not a breath of wind, and they left the road to follow a narrow path overgrown with foliage. They could hardly make their way along it; then Jeanne felt an arm glide slowly round her waist.

She could not speak; her heart hammered and her breath came short. Low-growing boughs brushed their hair; they often had to bend low to pass them. She plucked a leaf; two ladybirds, like frail red shells, were curled up on the underside.

Innocent, somewhat reassured, she said: 'Look, here is a married couple.'

Julien's lips brushed her ear: 'Tonight you will be my wife.'

Although she had learnt much from her country walks, she still thought of love only in terms of poetry, and his words surprised her. His wife? Wasn't she that already?

Then he began kissing her lightly, swiftly, on her forehead and neck where the hair first sprang into curls. These man's kisses, to her an entirely new experience, took her by surprise each time and she turned her head away to avoid his caresses, even while she enjoyed them.

All at once they found themselves at the edge of the wood.

She stopped, with a feeling of embarrassment at having come so far. What would people think? 'Let's go back,' she said.

He drew his arm away from her waist and they turned face to face, so close that they could feel each other's breath on their cheeks; and they regarded each other. They exchanged one of those steady, direct, penetrating looks that lead two souls to believe they are meeting, intermingling. They sought each other in their eyes, in what lay deeper, in the impenetrable unknown of another's being; they explored each other in mute, persistent questioning. What would they mean to each other? What would their life together, the life that they were starting now, turn out to be? What joys, pleasures or disillusionment had it in store for them in the long, indissoluble intimacy of marriage? It seemed to them both that they were, as yet, unknown to each other.

Suddenly Julien placed his hands on his wife's shoulders and kissed her full and hard on the lips, as she had never been kissed before. She felt his kiss deep in her veins, penetrating to the very marrow of her bones; and the shock of it was so strange that she pushed at him wildly with both hands, until she almost fell backwards.

'We must go, we must go,' she faltered.

He did not answer, only took her hands and held them in his own.

They went back to the house without speaking again. The rest of the afternoon seemed to them to pass slowly. They sat down to table as darkness fell.

It was a plain meal and somewhat short, contrary to the custom in Normandy. A sort of constraint lay heavy on those at table. The two priests, the mayor and the four farmers who had been invited were alone in showing a little of that bawdy merriment which is supposed to be proper at weddings.

The laughter was beginning to die away, when the mayor said something to revive it. It was nearly nine o'clock; coffee was about to be served. Out of doors, under the apple trees in the courtyard, the rustic ball was starting. All the festivities could be seen through the open window. Candle-ends hanging from branches turned the leaves to a shade of verdigris. Peasants and yokels pranced round in a ring, bawling out a wild dance tune which was feebly accompanied by two violins and a clarinet perched on a big kitchen table for a stage. The musicians were drowned altogether by the rustics' noisy singing; and the faint sound of their instruments was torn to shreds by the uproar of voices and seemed to fall out of the sky in tatters, fragments of a few scattered notes.

Two great casks framed by flaring torches kept the crowd supplied with drink. A couple of servants were continuously employed rinsing glasses and bowls in a tub and holding them out, still streaming with water, under the taps that ran with a crimson thread of wine or a golden thread of cider. Thirsty dancers, placid old people and perspiring girls pressed round and stretched out their hands to get hold of a drinking vessel of some sort, tilted their heads back and poured their chosen liquor in a stream down their throats.

Bread and butter, cheese and sausages were set out on a table. Everyone swallowed a mouthful from time to time, and the sight of that healthy, hearty feast under the ceiling of illuminated leaves gave the wedding guests indoors a longing to be dancing themselves, drinking their fill from the big casks and eating slices of bread and butter and raw onions.

The mayor, who was beating time with his knife, shouted: 'Dang me! This is something like, it's like the marriage of Ganache.'

There was a ripple of stifled laughter. But Father Picot, a natural enemy of civic authority, declared: 'You mean Cana.' The other would not accept the correction. 'No, Your Reverence, I know what I'm saying; when I say Ganache, Ganache it is.'

They rose from the table and went into the drawing-room. Then they went out to join the crowd at their merry-making. Finally the guests departed.

The baron and baroness were having a low-voiced altercation. The baron appeared to be making a request and Madame Adélaïde, more breathless than ever, was refusing it; at last she said, almost aloud: 'No, my dear, I cannot, I should not know how to do it.'

Then dear Papa turned abruptly away from her and joined Jeanne. 'Will you take a turn with me, daughter?' She was moved, and answered warmly: 'If you wish, Papa.' They left the house together.

When they were outside, on the seaward side of the château, they felt a small cold breeze blowing. It was one of those chill summer winds that carry a presage of autumn.

Clouds were racing across the sky, drawing a veil across the stars and then leaving them uncovered.

The baron pressed his daughter's arm to his side and fondly squeezed her hand. They walked on a little way. He seemed to be troubled and irresolute. At last he came to a decision.

'Child, I am going to do something that is really your mother's province, and it will not be easy; she refuses to do it, and therefore I must act in her place. I don't know whether you are entirely ignorant of the facts of life. There are mysteries which are carefully kept from children, especially girls, for girls should remain pure in spirit, pure beyond reproach, until we give them into the arms of a man and their happiness passes into his keeping. It is he who will lift the veil and reveal to them what is life's sweetest secret. Only, if they have guessed nothing of it beforehand, they often recoil from the reality, the crude facts behind their dreams. If they feel wounded in spirit as they are, indeed, in the body, they may refuse their husband what is his by law – both human and natural law – his absolute right. I cannot tell you more than this, my darling; but never forget that you belong to your husband entirely.'

What did she really know? How much did she guess? She had begun to shiver with an oppressive, sad sensation, a kind of foreboding.

They returned to the house. They halted in surprise at the door of the drawing-room. Madame Adélaïde was weeping on Julien's breast. Her tears came in noisy gusts like those from a blacksmith's bellows, and appeared to stream from her nose, mouth and eyes all at the same time; and the young man, awkward and embarrassed, was supporting the stout woman who had flung herself into his arms and begged him to take tender care of her darling, precious, adored little girl.

The baron hastened forward. 'Oh! let us have no scenes, no tears, if you please!' He took his wife's arm and set her down in a chair while she dabbed at her face. Then he turned to Jeanne: 'Now, child, give your mother a kiss and run along upstairs.'

Jeanne, herself on the verge of tears, quickly kissed her parents and fled.

Aunt Lison had already retired to her room. The baron and his wife were left alone with Julien. They were all three so embarrassed that they could think of nothing to say, the two men in evening clothes standing, avoiding each other's eyes, and Madame Adélaïde in her chair, unhappy and shaken by an occasional sob. At last the constraint became intolerable, and the baron began to talk about the journey that the young couple would be starting in a few days' time.

Upstairs in Jeanne's room, Rosalie was in floods of tears as she helped her mistress to undress. Her fingers were all thumbs, she could not find tapes or pins, and indeed she seemed even more agitated than her mistress. But Jeanne was scarcely aware that her maid was weeping; she felt as though she had entered a different world, was walking on strange ground, parted from all that she had known, all that was dear to her. Everything in her life, all her thoughts seemed to have suffered an upheaval; she even found herself wondering, did she love her husband? All at once she saw him as a stranger whom she hardly knew. Three months ago she had not known that he existed, and now she was his wife. How had that come about? Why had she let herself fall into marriage, as one might into an unguarded pit?

Attired for the night she slipped into bed; and the cool sheets brought a shudder to her skin, intensifying the chilled feeling, the sense of loneliness and sadness which had lain heavy on her spirit for the past two hours.

Rosalie went off, still in tears; and Jeanne waited. Nervously, with a tightness in her chest, she awaited the unknown, that mystery for which her father had so confusedly tried to prepare her, the revelation of the greatest secret of love.

She had heard no footsteps on the stairs, but suddenly three light knocks sounded on her door. She shuddered violently and did not answer. She heard another knock, and then the sound of the handle being turned. She buried her head under the bedclothes as though a thief were breaking in. Footsteps came quickly across the floor; and somebody touched her bed.

She started, uttered a small cry; and when she poked out her head she saw Julien standing beside the bed smiling, looking down at her. 'Oh! how you startled me,' she said.

'Weren't you expecting me?' he answered. She said nothing. He was in full evening dress, with that serious expression which suited his handsome looks; and she felt dreadfully mortified at being in bed in the presence of someone so formally attired.

They did not know what to say or how to behave with each other, hardly dared even to look at each other at that important and decisive moment of their lives, one on which all their future happiness together would depend.

Perhaps he was faintly aware of the dangers in such an encounter, of the self-command and tender lover's wiles that are needed to avoid wounding any of the maidenly delicacy, the infinitely fastidious sensibilities of a virginal spirit nurtured on dreams.

He gently took her hand and kissed it and, kneeling at the bedside as at an altar, he breathed in the lightest whisper: 'Will you love me?' And she, instantly reassured, raised her head in its cloud of lace from the pillow and smiled: 'But I do love you, dear.'

He put his wife's small, slender fingers into his mouth and said in a muffled voice: 'Will you show me that you love me?'

At that she became nervous again and answered without

really thinking what she was saying, only remembering what her father had told her: 'Dear, I belong to you.'

He covered her wrist with moist kisses and raised himself up slowly to kiss her face, which she was now trying to hide again.

Then he abruptly threw one arm across the bed and clasped his wife through the sheets, sliding his other hand under the pillow to lift up her head; and quietly, very quietly, he murmured: 'Then won't you make room for me beside you?'

Instinctively she took fright and whispered: 'Not yet, please not yet.'

He seemed disappointed, a little put out, and as he persisted his tone was still pleading but a little roughened: 'Why not now, as it will come to that anyway in the end?'

The words displeased her; but she repeated, submissive and resigned: 'I belong to you, dear.'

He left her at once and disappeared into his dressing-room; and she could hear his movements plainly, the rustle of garments being unfastened, the chink of coins in a pocket, boots being dropped one after the other.

Suddenly he came in again in his socks and underwear and crossed the room quickly to leave his watch on the mantelpiece. Then he rushed back into the small room next door and moved about for a short time, and Jeanne turned over hastily on her other side and closed her eyes when she heard him approach.

She felt a cold, hairy leg against her own, and started up as if to fling herself to the floor; then she covered her face with her hands, hardly able to keep from screaming with fright, and buried herself under the bedclothes.

Immediately he took her in his arms, although she had turned her back to him, and set his lips to her neck, to the floating laces of her cap and the embroidered collar of her nightdress, in a shower of hungry kisses.

She was motionless, rigid with apprehension as she felt a strong hand searching for her breast, which she had clasped between her arms. The rough contact was brutal to her and her breath came fast; and she wanted above everything to escape, to run away through the house, shut herself in somewhere, get away from this man.

He did not move. She felt the warmth of him against her back. Then her panic subsided, and suddenly she realized that she had only to turn round to embrace him.

At last he seemed to lose patience and become discouraged: 'Then you won't be my little wifie?' She whispered through her fingers: 'But I am your wife, am I not?' With a shade of vexation he answered: 'No, my dear, come now, don't make fun of me.'

She was much affected by the displeasure in his tone; and turned to him quickly to beg him to forgive her.

He seized her in a passionate embrace, hungrily, as if to devour her; and with swift, mordant, frenzied kisses his lips moved over the whole of her face and throat until she was numb from his caresses. She had unclasped her hands and lay inert beneath his striving, no longer knowing what she was doing, what he was doing, her mind in too great a turmoil to take it in. Suddenly she felt a rending pain; and she began moaning and writhing in his arms as he took violent possession of her.

What came afterwards? She could scarcely remember, for she had lost her wits; only she seemed aware that a shower of light kisses, kisses of gratitude, rained down on her lips.

After that, surely, he must have spoken to her and she must have answered. Later he renewed his advances, which she repulsed with horror; and she started and pushed him away when she felt coarse hair against her breast, as she had when it first brushed her leg.

At last he grew tired of pleading with her to no avail, and lay still on his back.

Then she too lay quiet, pondering what had happened; her dearest, most private hopes had been betrayed in a disillusion far from the rapture of her dreams, her sweetest expectations crushed, her happiness lay in ruins, and she said to herself in that moment of despair: 'So that is what he calls being his wife; that is what it means, it is that!'

She lay still for a long time in her distress, while her gaze wandered over the tapestries on the walls, the ancient love story that decorated her room.

As Julien did not speak or move she turned at last, slowly, to look at him – and saw that he was asleep! He was sleeping with his mouth open and a serene look on his face! Asleep!

Incredulous, she felt more deeply humiliated and outraged by his sleeping than by his treating her so roughly, as though she had been the first to hand. How could he sleep on this of all nights? Was there nothing unusual in what had happened between them? Oh! She would have preferred him to strike her, violate her again, bruise her with odious caresses until she lost her senses.

She propped herself on one elbow and, leaning towards him, listened without moving to the light breath from his lips which at times came close to being a snore.

The day broke leaden at first, then lightened to rose and finally to a brilliant dawn. Julien opened his eyes, yawned, stretched his arms, looked at his wife, smiled and asked her:

'Did you sleep well, my darling?'

She noticed that he now said '*tu*' to her and, somewhat taken aback, she answered: 'Oh, yes. And you?' – using the formal '*vous*'. 'Oh, I slept very well myself,' he said, turning to kiss her, and then calmly began talking. He expounded his ideas on their style of living, his plans for economizing; this was a word which kept recurring in his conversation and gave Jeanne some surprise. She listened without really taking in the meaning of his words, looking at him, as a thousand things passed through her mind no more than skimming the surface.

Eight o'clock struck. 'Well, it's time to get up,' he said. 'We shall look foolish if we lie in bed too long,' and he stepped out of bed first. When he was dressed he good-naturedly helped his wife with all the small details of her toilet, and would not allow her to call Rosalie.

He stopped and held her back as they were leaving the room. 'You know, we can call each other "*tu*" and "*toi*" when we're alone, but it's better to wait a little before we talk like that in front of your parents. It will come quite naturally when we return from our wedding trip.'

She did not appear until luncheon. And so the day passed as usual, as though nothing out of the way had happened. There was merely one more man in the house.

5

FOUR DAYS LATER THE CARRIAGE ARRIVED TO take them to Marseilles.

After all that she had suffered that first night Jeanne had soon grown accustomed to Julien's touch, his kisses and caresses, although she recoiled no less from their more intimate embraces.

She loved him; she found him attractive; she was happy and high-spirited again, as she had been before.

Their farewells were brief and without regret. Only the baroness betrayed emotion, and just as the carriage was about to depart she put a large purse into her daughter's hand, as heavy as lead: 'Here is a little pocket-money for a young wife,' she said.

Jeanne put it in her pocket; and the horses set off.

Julien said to her later in the day: 'How much is there in that purse your mother gave you?' She had not given it a thought, and she poured out the contents into her lap. There was a stream of gold coins: two thousand francs. She clapped her hands, crying: 'Now I can be madly extravagant,' and shut the purse again.

After a week of travelling in blazing heat they arrived in Marseilles.

Next day the *Roi-Louis*, a small packet-boat bound for Naples and calling at Ajaccio, carried them to Corsica.

Corsica! the maquis! bandits! mountains! Napoleon's

native land! It seemed to Jeanne that she was stepping wide awake out of reality into a dream.

Standing together on deck they watched the cliffs of Provence disappear from view. There was no movement in the deep azure sea. Opaque and polished like a vessel fired in the sun, the great expanse of water under the boundless sky was an almost unreal blue.

'Do you remember going out in old Lastique's boat?' she asked him.

He dropped a brief kiss on her ear by way of reply.

The steamer's paddles thrashed their way through the sea, disturbing its heavy slumbers; and a wide creamy trail of foam on the churned-up water, bubbling like champagne, stretched out in a straight line in the wake of the vessel as far as the eye could see.

Suddenly only a short distance ahead a huge fish, a dolphin, leaped out of the water, plunged in again head first and disappeared. Jeanne uttered a little cry of alarm and clung to Julien's breast. Then she began laughing at her own fright and watched eagerly to see the creature come into view again. It shot up after a few seconds like a great mechanical toy. It dropped back, re-emerged; then there were two of them, then three, then six, gambolling about round the heavy boat, forming an escort for their monster of a brother, the wooden fish with iron fins. They swam from one side of the boat to the other and flung themselves into the air, now all together, now one after another as in a game, a merry chase, bounding through the air in a wide arc and diving back in procession into the sea.

Jeanne clapped her hands in delight each time the huge, supple swimmers reappeared. Her heart leaped, as they leaped from the water, with the carefree pleasure of a child.

They vanished without warning. When they came into sight again they were far away, out in the open sea; then they disappeared altogether, and Jeanne felt a moment's sadness at their going.

The evening was calm and mild, and the clear air radiated a

sense of peace and contentment. Not a tremor in the air, nor a ripple on the water; and that infinite repose of sea and sky was reflected in the torpor of minds which not a ripple disturbed.

The sun went slowly down in the direction of an invisible Africa, and they could almost believe they already felt the heat from that burning land; but when the daystar had vanished from sight their faces were brushed by a sort of cool caress, barely even the suggestion of a breeze.

They did not care to return to their cabin which was redolent of all the unpleasant odours of a steamer; and they both wrapped themselves in their cloaks and lay down beside each other on the deck. Julien fell asleep at once; but Jeanne lay open-eyed, unsettled by the journey in which so much was unfamiliar. The monotonous turning of the paddles soothed her; and she gazed up at the legions of brilliant stars, which shone in the pure southern sky as clear and sparkling as though they had been newly washed.

She grew drowsy at last towards morning. She was wakened by sundry sounds and voices. The sailors were singing as they dressed the ship for the day. She shook her husband, who had not stirred, and they both rose to their feet.

She exulted in the salt savour of the spray, which seemed to penetrate right to her finger-tips. There was sea all round them. In the distance ahead, however, a greyish mass, indistinct in the early dawn, seemed to be lying on the waves like a pile of clouds heaped together, pointed, chiselled into curious shapes.

Then it came more clearly into view; the outline stood out more sharply against the lightening sky; a line of tall, oddly shaped mountain peaks rose up out of the sea: Corsica, shrouded in a filmy veil.

Behind it the sun rose, drawing a line of black shadow round the mountain crests; then all the peaks were lighted up while the rest of the island lay wreathed in mist.

The captain came up on deck, a tanned, desiccated old man, small and shrunken, shrivelled by the strong salt winds; in a voice hoarse from thirty years of command, worn with shouting through rain and storm, he said to Jeanne:

'D'you get the smell of her, that jade over yonder?'

She did indeed catch a curious, pungent scent, an aroma of wild plants.

The captain went on: 'That's Corsica out there, Madame, Corsica in flower: a lovely woman with a perfume all her own. I'd know it again after twenty years, five miles out at sea. It's where I come from. The man over on St Helena, he's always talking about it, they say, the scent of his native land. He comes from my family.'

The captain took off his hat and bowed towards Corsica, bowed to the great Emperor away across the ocean who came from his family.

Jeanne was moved almost to tears.

Then the sailor pointed to the horizon: 'Les Sanguinaires!' he said.

Julien, who was standing beside his wife, put his arm round her waist and they both gazed into the distance where the captain was pointing.

At last they made out a group of rocks shaped like pyramids, which the ship soon rounded to enter a large, calm bay, surrounded by mountains rising in a host of tall peaks, their lower slopes clothed in moss-like greenery.

The captain pointed to this and said: 'The maquis.'

The ring of mountains seemed to close in behind the vessel as she moved forward, swimming slowly through a lake of blue water so transparent that they could often see to the bottom.

At the head of the bay the town came suddenly into view, a cluster of white buildings lying between the edge of the waves and the foot of the mountains.

A few Italian boats lay at anchor in the harbour. Four or five small craft came out and circled round the *Roi-Louis* to take her passengers ashore.

Julien said to his wife in a low voice as he collected their luggage: 'Twenty sous is enough to give the steward, isn't it?'

He had asked her the same question repeatedly all that

week, and it had vexed her each time. She replied somewhat impatiently: 'If one is not sure how much to give, then it's best to give too much.'

He was always haggling, with waiters, head waiters, coachmen, everyone with something to sell, and when after prolonged bargaining he had brought down the price he said to Jeanne, rubbing his hands: 'I don't like being swindled.'

She shuddered at the sight of a reckoning, anticipating the remarks he would make about each item, humiliated by his haggling, blushing to the roots of her hair at the sneering glances of servants after her husband had left them a paltry tip.

There was yet another dispute with the boatman who set them ashore.

The first tree she saw was a palm!

They arrived at a big, empty hotel in a corner of a spacious square, and ordered luncheon.

After dessert, when Jeanne was rising from table to go out and wander about the town, Julien put his arm round her and murmured fondly in her ear: 'Shall we rest a little, puss?'

'Rest? But I don't feel tired,' she said in surprise.

He held her close. 'I want you. Understand? It's two days since . . . !'

Blushing crimson with shame, she faltered: 'Oh! now? But what would people say? What would they think? How can you ask for a room in broad daylight like this? Oh, Julien, please.'

But he cut her short: 'Really, I'm not concerned about what hotel servants say or think. You'll soon see how much I care about that.'

He rang the bell.

She said nothing more, but waited with eyes downcast, revolted body and soul by this continual desire of the male, submitting only with distaste, resigned but humiliated, for to her there was something bestial and degrading in it, indeed something obscene.

Her senses still slept; yet her husband treated her now as though she shared his ardour.

When the waiter came, Julien asked him to show them to their room. The man was a real Corsican, hirsute to the eyeballs, who did not understand what Julien wanted and told them that the apartment would be ready by the evening.

Julien explained with impatience: 'No, we want a room now; we're tired after the journey and would like to rest.'

Then the gleam of a smile showed through the man's beard, and Jeanne wished she could make her escape.

When they came downstairs again an hour later she was afraid to face the people they encountered, convinced that everyone would laugh and whisper when her back was turned. At heart she was angry with Julien for not understanding, for having none of the fine sensibilities of natural modesty; and she felt that there was a veil, a barrier, between them, as she became aware for the first time that two people can never penetrate into each other's souls, into their inmost thoughts; and that even when they are together, side by side, sometimes interlaced, still they cannot intermingle, and the moral being of each one of us remains eternally separate and alone throughout our lives.

They stayed three days in the little town that nestled in the curve of the blue bay, where the air was as hot as a furnace within the screen of mountains into which no breath of wind could find its way.

At the end of that time they drew up an itinerary for the whole of their journey, and in case the way should prove too rough in parts for a carriage they thought it best to hire saddle-horses. One morning at dawn they set out on a pair of small Corsican stallions, fiery-eyed, thin and tireless. A guide went with them on a mule and carried their provisions, for inns are unheard-of in that wild country.

The road first took them round the shore of the bay, then dipped into a shallow valley leading in to the high mountains. The river-beds they crossed were often almost dry; a thin trickle of water still moving under the stones like a hidden beast, with a faint gurgling sound.

The land was uncultivated and seemed to be entirely

barren. The mountainsides were covered with tall grasses, yellow in the heat of high summer. From time to time they met with a mountain dweller, either on foot or riding a small horse, or astride a donkey no bigger than a dog. And every one had a loaded gun on his back; rusty old weapons – but formidable in their hands.

The air seemed heavy with the sharp scent of the aromatic plants growing over the whole island; and the track led slowly upwards through long clefts in the mountains.

Crags of granite, rose or blue in colour, gave the vast scene a fairy-tale look; and the rocks of that country had been flung up in undulations so immense that the forests of tall chestnut trees on the lower mountain slopes looked in their greenery no bigger than bushes.

At times the guide pointed to the high escarpments and pronounced a name. Jeanne and Julien followed his pointing finger but could see nothing at first, then made out something grey like a heap of stones tumbled down from the summit. It was a village, a little hamlet of granite hanging there, clinging like a bird's nest and almost invisible on the great mountain.

Jeanne became impatient of travelling so long at a walking pace. 'Let's canter on,' she said. And she urged her horse forward. She turned soon to look back when she did not hear her husband gallop up behind her, and burst out laughing when she saw him jolting up and down in the oddest fashion, white in the face and holding on to his animal's mane. As he was usually so debonair, the 'gay cavalier', it was the more comical to see him so awkward and scared.

They slackened their pace to a slow trot. The track ran now through an interminable mass of brushwood which spread like a cloak over the whole mountainside.

This was the maquis, the impenetrable maquis, compounded of holm oak, juniper, strawberry and gum trees, buckthorn, heather, wild laurel, myrtle and box, bound together and interlaced like heads of tangled hair with twining clematis, giant ferns, honeysuckle and bushes of cistus, rosemary, lavender and thorn, throwing a compact, indivisible fleece over the shoulders of the mountains.

They began to feel hungry. Their guide caught up with them and led the way to one of those delightful springs so often found on precipitous slopes, a fine round thread of icy water issuing from a small hole in the rock and running off the tip of a chestnut leaf which a passer-by had put there to guide the thin jet to a thirsty person's mouth.

Jeanne was so happy that she could hardly stop herself crying out for joy.

They started off again, and now began the descent on a path leading round the bay of Sagone.

It was almost dark when they passed through Cargese, the Greek village founded long ago by a colony of refugees who had been forced to leave their country. Beside a fountain there was a group of tall and beautiful girls, singularly graceful, with elegant hips, long hands and slender waists. Julien called out a 'Good evening' to them, and they answered in lilting voices in the sweet-sounding tongue of the country their forebears had left.

When the young couple arrived at Piana they had to ask hospitality as people used to do in the old days in out-of-the-way places. Julien knocked on a door, and Jeanne felt a slight tremor of pleasure as they waited for it to open. Oh! this was real travelling! meeting the unexpected, the untrodden path!

It turned out that they had chosen a young married couple. They were given the kind of reception that might have been accorded by the Patriarchs to a guest sent from God, sleeping on a straw mattress in the old house whose timber frame, pitted and infested by the shipworms that devour wooden beams, rustled and sighed as though it were alive.

They left at sunrise and presently came to a halt at the edge of a forest, a forest of purple granite. There were peaks and pillars, turrets and many fantastic forms modelled by time, by the biting winds and salt mists from the sea.

These astounding rock formations rose to a height of three hundred metres, tall and slender, rounded, crooked and hooked, distorted, unexpected and fantastic, appearing like trees, plants, animals, buildings, men, robed monks, horned devils, enormous birds – a whole monstrous population, a nightmare menagerie petrified at the will of some capricious god.

Jeanne was silent, her heart too full for words, and she gripped Julien's hand tightly in a sudden need for love, at the sight of such grandeur in nature.

Leaving that scene of petrified chaos they presently foun themselves in another bay completely enclosed by ramparts of blood-red granite. The scarlet cliffs were reflected in the blue sea below.

Jeanne murmured: 'Oh! Julien!' finding no other words to express her emotion, breathless with wonder; and tears came into her eyes. He looked at her in surprise and asked her: 'What's wrong, puss?'

She dried her eyes, smiled and said in a rather shaky voice:

'Nothing . . . only . . . it's so exciting . . . I was simply overwhelmed. I'm so happy that the least thing makes my heart turn over.'

He did not understand feminine weaknesses of that sort at all, the delicate feelings of those sensitive creatures who are distracted at a trifle, moved as deeply by enthusiasm as by disaster, thrown into panic, rapture or despair by some indefinable sensation. Jeanne's tears seemed to him ridiculous, and as the path was uneven and demanded all his attention he said: 'You had better keep an eye on your horse.'

They rode down an almost impassable track towards the bay, then turned to the right to ascend the sombre vale of Ota.

They soon found, however, that the track was very rough. 'Shall we go up on foot?' Julien suggested. She asked nothing better and was overjoyed at the prospect of walking beside him, the two of them alone together, after her recent emotion.

The guide went on ahead with the mule and horses and they followed on foot, taking short steps.

The cleft in the mountain, from the summit to the foot, opened up as they advanced. The path leads down to the bottom of the ravine. There it continues between immense walls of rock; and a stream hurls itself in a torrent through the gorge. The air is ice-cold, the granite cliffs look black and the glimpse of blue sky far above is unexpected and vertiginous.

Jeanne was startled by a sudden sound. She looked upwards; a huge bird flew out from a hole. It was an eagle. Its outspread wings seemed to touch both sides of the ravine as it rose into the blue and disappeared from sight.

Higher up, the fissure in the mountain divides in two; the path continues in sharp zigzags between two ravines. Light-footed and carried away by excitement, Jeanne went on ahead, scattering stones under her feet and leaning fearlessly towards the abyss on each side. Julien followed her, a little breathless, keeping his eyes on the ground for fear of vertigo.

All at once they were bathed in sunlight; they felt as though they had risen out of hell. They were thirsty, and a trail of moisture guided them through tumbled stones to a tiny spring where the water had been channelled through a hollowed stick for goatherds to drink. There was a carpet of moss all around. Jeanne knelt down to drink; and Julien did the same.

As she was savouring the coolness of the water he took her by the waist and tried to steal her place at the end of the wooden pipe. She held firm; their lips collided, met, they pushed each other away. Each of them in turn seized the narrow end of the tube between their teeth, to keep hold of it in their struggles. The thread of cold water was lost and recaptured again and again, broken off and renewed, splashing their faces and necks, their clothes, their hands. Tiny droplets glittered in their hair like pearls. And through the running water ran a stream of kisses. Love gave Jeanne a sudden inspiration. She filled her mouth with the pure liquid, blew out her cheeks like wineskins and made Julien understand that she wished to put her lips to his to quench his thirst.

He smiled, opened his mouth and threw back his head, holding out his arms; and drank from that spring in the living flesh a single draught which entered into him in a stream of burning desire.

Jeanne leaned over him with unaccustomed tenderness; her heart was hammering; her breasts lifted; her eyes were soft and moist. She murmured in a low voice: 'Julien . . . I love you!' and then, in her turn drawing him towards her, she fell back and hid her face in her hands, crimson with shame.

He threw himself on her and clasped her in a transport of passion. Her breath came fast in nervous expectation; with a shock like a thunder-clap she felt the sensation she had invited, and uttered a sharp cry.

Her heart beat so hard and she walked so stiffly that they were long in reaching the summit of the mountain and did not arrive until evening at Evisa, where they were to stay with a relative of their guide, Paoli Palabretti.

He was a tall man with a slight stoop and the dejected air of a consumptive. He showed them to their room, a gloomy chamber with bare stone walls, but a splendid one for that country where all refinement is unknown; and he was expressing his pleasure at receiving them in his own language – a Corsican dialect with touches of French and Italian – when a crisp voice interrupted him. A little brown woman with large dark eyes, a sun-warmed skin and narrow waist, her teeth always showing as she laughed continually, darted forward to embrace Jeanne and shake Julien by the hand, saying: 'Good day, Madame, good day, Monsieur, how do you do?'

She took their hats and shawls and gathered them all up with one hand, for she had the other arm in a sling; then she sent everyone outside, saying to her husband: 'Take them for a walk until dinner time.'

Monsieur Palabretti obeyed her instantly, placing himself between the two young people and taking them off to see the village. He dragged his steps and his speech also, repeating after every fit of coughing: 'It's the cold air in the valley, gets on my chest.'

He led them by a roundabout path under immensely tall chestnut trees. Presently he stopped and said, in his toneless voice: 'It was here that Mathieu Lori killed my cousin Jean Rinaldi. I was there, you know, right at Jean's side, when Mathieu showed himself ten paces away. "Jean," he shouted, "don't you go to Albertacce; don't go over there, I say, I'll kill you if you do."

'I grabbed Jean's arm: "Don't go, Jean, he would, he'd do it."

'It was about a girl they were both after, Paulina Sinacoupi.

'But Jean started shouting: "I will go, Mathieu; you're not going to stop me."

'Then Mathieu levelled his gun before I had time to take aim, and fired.

'Jean leapt up, both feet in the air, like a child skipping, aye, Monsieur, and he came down on me with all his weight; that made me let go of my gun and it rolled away right to that big chestnut over there.

'Jean had his mouth wide open but he never spoke a word more; he was dead.'

The young people stared in astonishment at this calm witness of a crime. 'What happened to the murderer?' Jeanne inquired.

After a long fit of coughing Paoli Palabretti answered: 'He took to the mountains. It was my brother who killed him, the year after. You know my brother, Philippi Palabretti, the bandit.'

Jeanne shuddered. 'Your brother? A bandit?'

The quiet Corsican's eyes flashed with pride. 'Aye, Madame, he was famous, he was. He brought down six policemen. He died alongside Nicolas Morali in the Niolo, after they'd been fighting for six days and nearly starved to death; they were surrounded.'

He added, with an air of resignation: 'That's the way of things, with us,' in the same tone of voice in which he said: 'It's the cold air in the valley.'

They went in to dinner then, and the little Corsican woman behaved as though she had known them for twenty years.

Something was troubling Jeanne, however. When she was in Julien's arms again, would she experience the same strange, intense shock to her senses that she had had on the moss beside the spring?

When they were alone in their room she trembled with anxiety that she might be unmoved by his embraces, as she had been before. However, she was quickly reassured, and that night was her first night of love.

Next day when it was time for them to continue their journey she was reluctant to leave that humble dwelling where, as she imagined, she had entered a new domain of happiness.

She drew her host's wife into her bedchamber and, after making it plain that she was not intending to give her a present, she proposed – insisting even with impatience – to send her a souvenir from Paris immediately on their return, a memento of their stay to which she attached an almost superstitious importance.

At first the young Corsican woman did not wish to accept such a present, and demurred for a long time. Finally however she consented. 'Very well,' she said, 'send me a pistol, a very small one.'

Jeanne stared at her wide-eyed. The other added in a whisper close to her ear, confiding as it were a sweet, intimate secret: 'It is to kill my brother-in-law.' With a smile, she swiftly unrolled the bandages from her injured arm and showed Jeanne the white, rounded flesh scarred by an almost healed stiletto wound: 'He would have killed me if I hadn't been as strong as he is. My husband isn't jealous, he knows me; and then he's ill, you know; and that cools his blood. Besides, I'm a decent woman, Madame; but my brother-in-law believes everything he's told. He's jealous on my husband's account; and he's sure to try again. So if I had a little pistol I'd be easy in my mind, knowing I could get my revenge.'

Jeanne promised to send her a weapon, kissed her new friend affectionately, and she and Julien went on their way.

The remainder of the journey was nothing but a dream, an unending embrace, an intoxication of caresses. She saw nothing of the scenery, the people or the places where they stayed. She had eyes for nothing but Julien.

Then there began a childlike, charming intimacy, the foolish trifling of love, with absurd delightful phrases and pet names for every part of their bodies, every mound and hollow where their lips took pleasure.

Jeanne slept on her right side, so that her left nipple was often uncovered when she awoke. When Julien observed this he named it 'Monsieur the sleeper-out' and the other 'Monsieur in love', because the pink flower at the tip seemed more responsive to his kisses.

There was 'dear Mama's walk', the passage between them where he went so continually to and fro; and another, more secret still, they named 'the road to Damascus' in memory of the vale of Ota.

They arrived in Bastia, and now the guide had to be paid. Julien searched his pockets. Unable to find what was needed, he said to Jeanne: 'As you're not spending the two thousand francs your mother gave you, you'd better let me take charge of them. They will be safer carried in my belt; and I shall not have to find change.'

She handed him her purse.

They travelled to Leghorn, visited Florence, Genoa and the whole of the Corniche.

They arrived back in Marseilles on a day when the mistral was blowing. Two months had passed since they left Les Peuples. It was now the fifteenth of October.

The cold wind that blew so strongly seemed to Jeanne to come straight from her home, from faraway Normandy, and her spirits sank. Julien seemed to have changed lately; he appeared tired and indifferent; and she felt apprehensive, without knowing the reason.

She postponed their departure for four days, unable to bring herself to leave that sunny clime. It was as if her happiness had come full circle.

At last they left Marseilles.

They were to buy everything in Paris that they needed for their establishment at Les Peuples; and Jeanne, with dear Mama's present to spend, was looking forward to taking home some treasures; but she thought first of all of the pistol she had promised to the young Corsican woman in Evisa.

She said to Julien the day after they arrived:

'Darling, will you give me Mama's money now, so that I can buy some things?'

He turned and asked her, with a look of displeasure: 'How much do you need?'

She was surprised and said hesitantly: 'Why . . . whatever you like.'

He answered: 'I will give you a hundred francs; be sure not to waste it.'

She was taken aback, so bewildered that at first she could think of nothing to say.

At last she stammered: 'But . . . I . . . I gave you that money to – '

He interrupted her.

'Yes, exactly. We share what we have, and so it doesn't matter whether the money is in your pocket or mine. It's not as if I'm refusing it to you – I'm giving you a hundred francs.'

She took the five gold pieces in silence but never dared to ask him for more, and she bought nothing besides the pistol.

A week later they set out on the return journey to Les Peuples.

6

THE FAMILY AND SERVANTS WERE WAITING AT the white gate with the brick pillars. When the post-chaise drew up there were prolonged greetings and embraces. Dear Mama wept; Jeanne also wiped away a tear or two; Papa strode impatiently to and fro.

They went into the drawing-room, where a fire was burning, and while the luggage was being unloaded the young couple described their journey. Words poured from Jeanne's mouth in a torrent; and everything was recounted, all in half-an-hour, although a few small details may have been omitted from that rapid recital.

Then Jeanne went off to unpack her belongings. Rosalie too was in a state of great excitement as she assisted her. When all was done and the lingerie, the gowns and various toilet articles had been put away, the maid left her mistress alone; and Jeanne, feeling somewhat weary, dropped into a chair.

She wondered what to do now, seeking something to occupy her mind, something she could do with her hands. She did not in the least wish to go down to the drawing-room again and sit with her mother, who was sleeping; and she thought of going for a walk; but the country had such a dismal look that even a glance out of the window seemed to weigh her spirits down with gloom.

It was then that it came home to her that she no longer had anything to do, and never would have anything again. As a young girl at the convent she had spent all her time thinking and wondering about the future, occupied herself in dreaming. The hours had been filled by the continual stirring of hopes and expectations, so that she took no account of their passing. Next, she had no sooner emerged from those austere walls which had seen the birth of her illusions, than her dreams of love had been immediately realized. The man whom she had hoped to find, whom she had met, loved and married all within a few weeks, as marriages do follow on such swift decisions, had carried her off in his arms without giving her time to reflect.

Now, however, the reality of those first days with all its charm was to become the reality of every day, closing the door on hopes never defined, on the delicious uncertainties of the unknown. Indeed, the time of waiting was at an end.

There was nothing more, then, to occupy her today, or

tomorrow, or ever again. A vague sense of disillusion, of dreams faded and lost, brought the prospect home to her.

She rose and went to the window, pressing her forehead against the cold pane. After a moment or two, watching the sombre clouds as they rolled across the sky, she decided to go out of doors.

Could it be the same countryside, the same grass and trees that had been there in May? What had become of the sunlit dancing leaves and the lawn, a poem in green with its flaming dandelions, blood-red poppies and gleaming daisies, the capricious yellow butterflies quivering as though attached to invisible threads? And the air, intoxicating with vibrant life, all the scents and seeds of fruitfulness – that was gone.

The paths were muddy from the continual autumn rains and covered with a thick carpet of dead leaves, while the shivering poplars above them were now almost stripped of their foliage. The slender branches trembled in the wind, shaking their few remaining leaves which would soon fly off into space. All day long, like an incessant shower of rain as sorrowful as falling tears, those last leaves, yellow now like large gold coins, detached themselves and spun round and round as they fluttered and fell.

She walked on to the copse. That was as gloomy as a death chamber. The wall of greenery which had separated the little winding walks and given them a screen of intimacy was now sparse and bare. The bushes, intertwined like a fine lace-work of wood, were tapping their meagre branches together; and the murmur of dead leaves, which the wind rustled and stirred and piled up in occasional heaps, was like the distress-ful sighs of the dying.

Tiny birds hopped about in search of shelter, and in their shrill notes could be heard a shiver of cold.

The linden and the plane-tree, however, were defended against the winds from the sea by a vanguard formed by the dense screen of elms and still wore their summer finery, one apparelled in red velvet, the other in orange silk, the first cold spell drawing different colours from their sap.

Jeanne walked slowly up and down dear Mama's avenue along the side of the Couillards' farm. She was in low spirits, a presage perhaps of the long hours of tedium in the monotonous life that was opening out before her.

After a time she sat down on the bank where Julien had first spoken to her of love; and there she remained while scarcely a thought passed through her mind, scarcely even a dream, overcome by a profound lassitude so that she longed to lie down, to sleep, to escape from the melancholy of that day.

Suddenly she saw a seagull flying across the sky, borne on a gust of wind; and she remembered the eagle she had seen out in Corsica, in the gloomy vale of Ota. She felt the pang that comes with the memory of some good thing which has drawn to a close; and she saw again briefly in her mind that radiant island with its strange scents, its orange and citron trees ripening under the sun, rose-crested mountains and azure bays, ravines and waterfalls.

As she surveyed the landscape that surrounded her on every side, rain-sodden, austere, dismal with the gloom of falling leaves and a stormy grey sky, such a wave of desolation broke over her that she returned to the house, afraid that she would burst into tears.

Dear Mama had been too long accustomed to the gloom of such days to pay attention to it, and drowsed in a state of torpor beside the fire. Papa and Julien had gone for a walk, discussing their business affairs. Night fell, spreading sombre shadows about the big drawing-room, which the fire lit up with an occasional flare.

There was light enough still to see the cheerless spectacle outside of the dying year, with an overcast sky reflecting the muddy tints of the earth below.

After a short time, the baron reappeared, followed by Julien; as soon as he entered the room, which was growing dark, he rang and called: 'Quickly, bring the lamps! How gloomy it is in here.'

He seated himself beside the fire. His wet feet steamed in

the heat, the mud soon dried and fell from his shoes, and he rubbed his hands together cheerfully: 'I believe it's going to freeze,' he said; 'the sky is light in the north; there's a full moon; yes, I think it will set hard tonight.'

Then he turned to his daughter: 'Well, little one, are you glad to be back in your own country, in your own home with the old folks again?'

The simple question was too much for Jeanne. Tears came into her eyes and she flung herself into her father's arms, embracing him with emotion as if she were asking to be forgiven; for, though she had striven to appear in good spirits, she had felt almost faint with sadness. She recalled how much she had looked forward to seeing her parents again and was astonished to find herself so cold-hearted that even her love for them was numbed, as sometimes happens when we meet again those we love after long absence. It is as if once the habit of seeing them daily has been broken there is also a break in one's affection, until the common interests of daily life make it whole again.

Dinner was a lengthy meal; there was little conversation. Julien appeared to have forgotten his wife's existence.

Afterwards in the drawing-room she allowed herself to doze beside the fire, opposite dear Mama who had fallen asleep; and when the men's voices roused her for a moment, raised in argument, she wondered, as she tried to shake off her lethargy, whether she too would be entirely overcome by the inertia of uninterrupted habit.

The fire in the hearth, which burned low and red in the daytime, crackled and blazed into life. The flames lit up the faded tapestry of the armchairs, and the fox and the stork, the melancholy heron, the grasshopper and the ant gleamed in the sudden flare.

The baron smiled as he came over and stretched out his hands to the blaze: 'Aha! the fire's burning well this evening. It's freezing, children, it's freezing.' He put his hand on Jeanne's shoulder, pointed to the fire and said: 'You see, little girl, that's the best sight in the world: a fire in the hearth, and your family gathered round. There's nothing like it. But what about going up now? You children must be worn out.'

When the young woman was in her room again, she wondered how on two separate occasions she could feel so differently on returning to the place she thought she loved. Why did she now feel wounded and bruised, why did this house, the countryside she loved so well and everything that used to make her heart leap with joy, have such a heart-rending effect on her today?

But suddenly her glance lighted on her clock. The little bee still fluttered above the scarlet flowers with the same rapid, continuous movement, left right, right left. She was overcome with a sudden burst of affection, moved to tears at the sight of the small mechanism singing out the hours, throbbing like a living breast.

She had certainly not been so deeply affected when she kissed her father and mother. The heart has its mysteries which reason cannot penetrate.

For the first time since she was married she retired to a solitary bed, Julien excusing himself on the plea of fatigue and going to another room. It had been agreed between them from the first that they should have separate rooms.

It was a long time before she fell asleep, for it seemed strange now not to feel a body pressed against her own; she had become unused to sleeping alone, and the north wind kept her wakeful as it howled and raged over the rooftops.

She was wakened in the morning by a shaft of bright light painting her bed blood-red; and the rime-encrusted window panes were glowing as though the whole horizon were on fire.

She put on a thick dressing-gown, ran over to the window and flung it open.

A cold breeze rushed into the room, keen and wholesome, stinging and sharp on her skin, bringing tears to her eyes; and in the empurpled sky a large sun, ruddy and swollen like the face of a drunkard, could be seen behind the trees. White frost lay hard and dry on the earth and rang under the peasants' feet. In that one night the poplars' branches had been stripped of the last of their leaves; and out beyond the heath the long greenish line of the waves was flecked with white.

The squalls of wind soon left the plane-tree and the linden bare. With every icy gust, leaves torn off by the sudden frost were scattered in the air in whirls like a flight of birds. Jeanne dressed and went out of doors, and for want of anything else to do visited the farmers.

The Martins threw up their hands, and the farmer's wife kissed her on both cheeks; she was pressed to take a small glass of walnut liqueur. After this she went on to the other farm. The Couillards threw up their arms, the farmer's wife gave her a peck on the ear and she was obliged to drink a small glass of black-currant wine.

Then she went back to breakfast.

That day passed like the one before it, cold rather than wet. The remaining days of the week were like those two; and the weeks of the month were like the first.

Gradually however she came to yearn less for foreign climes. Habit spread a layer of resignation over her life, like the lime deposit sometimes left by water. She began to interest herself again in the hundred small details of everyday existence, in simple, modest occupations. A sort of meditative melancholy grew up in her, a vague disenchantment with life. What did she need? What did she wish for? She did not know. She had no worldly needs: no thirst for pleasure, no impulse towards new experiences; and what, indeed, could those be? Like the old, faded tapestries in the drawing-room, everything was losing its colour in her eyes, becoming effaced, taking on a pale, drab shade.

Her relations with Julien had completely changed. He seemed altogether different since they had returned from their wedding trip, like an actor who has played his part and now puts on again his everyday countenance. He paid scarcely any attention to her, seldom even spoke to her; all signs of love had vanished abruptly; and the nights when he came to her room were few and far between.

He had taken over the management of the household and estate, revising the leases, harassing the peasants, reducing expenditure; and as he adopted the style of a gentleman farmer he increasingly lost the polish and elegance which had characterised him in the days of their engagement.

He always wore an old, brass-buttoned, velvet shooting jacket from his younger days, spotted and stained, which he had found in his wardrobe; and had so taken to neglecting his appearance, as people do when they no longer feel the need to please, that he had given up shaving, and his long, ill-trimmed beard made him look singularly gross. He took no care of his hands; and he drank four or five small glasses of brandy after every meal.

When Jeanne essayed a fond, gentle reproach he answered so roughly, 'Leave me alone, will you?' that she did not venture to offer more advice.

She was surprised herself at the extent to which she became resigned to these changes. He had turned into a stranger, a stranger whose mind and heart were closed to her. She often reflected on this, wondering how it could happen that after meeting and falling in love, and marrying on a surge of tender feeling, they had suddenly become almost as unknown to each other as though they had never shared a bed.

How was it, besides, that she did not suffer more at his desertion? Was life to be always like this? Had they been mistaken? Did the future hold nothing more for her?

If Julien were still handsome and well-groomed, debonair and charming, would she not then be suffering deeply?

It had been agreed that after New Year's Day the newly married pair should be left to themselves; Papa and dear Mama would return to their house in Rouen for several months. The young people would not leave Les Peuples that winter, and so would be able to complete all their arrangements in the château, when they would feel at home there and enjoy being in the place where all their lives were to be spent. There were, besides, a few families in the neighbourhood to whom Julien would introduce his wife. These were the Brisevilles, the Couteliers and the Fourvilles.

The young couple had not yet been able to pay any calls, however, because it had been impossible until then to arrange for the painter to come to change the coat of arms on the carriage.

The baron had, in fact, given over the old family conveyance to his son-in-law; and not for the world would Julien have consented to call at the neighbouring châteaux until the arms of the Lamares had been quartered with those of the Le Perthuis des Vauds.

There was only one painter in the district who was a specialist in heraldic ornament, a man from Bolbec by the name of Bataille, who was summoned to each of the Norman châteaux in turn to emblazon the prized insignia on the doors of their carriages.

At last one morning in December as they sat at luncheon they saw somebody open the gate and walk straight up the drive. He carried a box slung on his back. It was Bataille.

He was shown into the house and served at table as though he had been a gentleman, because his particular skill, his continuous relations with all the noble families in the *département*, his knowledge of armorial bearings and crests and the terms sacred to heraldry used to describe them had all made of him a sort of human coat of arms with whom noblemen did not disdain to shake hands.

A pencil and paper were immediately forthcoming, and while he was at table the baron and Julien made sketches of their escutcheons with all the quarterings. The baroness took a lively interest in these matters and exerted herself to offer suggestions; and Jeanne also joined in the discussion with suddenly awakened curiosity.

Bataille expressed opinions while he ate, and took up the pencil from time to time to draw a line, quoted instances, described the carriages of all the aristocracy in the district, and seemed to carry an atmosphere of nobility about with him in his mind, even in his accent.

He was a small man with close-cropped grey hair and paint-stained hands smelling of turpentine. He was said to have been involved in a serious offence, a public scandal, at some time in the past; but he was generally held in such high regard by all the titled families that the stain of this had long been effaced.

As soon as he had drunk his coffee he was taken out to the coach-house, and the oilcloth cover was removed from the carriage. Bataille examined it and then stated with deliberation the measurements he thought suitable for the shield; and, after a further exchange of views, applied himself to his task.

In spite of the cold, the baroness had a chair brought out so that she could sit and watch him at work; then her feet grew chilled and she called for a foot-warmer; and she began placidly talking to the painter, questioning him about marriages that were news to her and about recent births and deaths, bringing up to date from what he was able to tell her the genealogical trees that she carried in her mind.

Julien sat astride a chair beside his mother-in-law. He smoked his pipe, spat, listened to the conversation and kept an eye on the recording of his lineage in paint.

Before long old Simon, with a spade over his shoulder, passed by on his way to the kitchen garden and stopped to look at the work in progress; the news of Bataille's arrival had reached both farms, and the two farmers' wives lost no time in making their appearance. They stood spellbound, one on each side of the baroness: 'That's a tidy bit of work, that is, wants a neat hand to do a job like that.'

The coats of arms on the two carriage doors could not be finished before eleven the next morning. Everybody was present at that hour; and the carriage was pulled out of the coach-house so that it could more easily be seen and admired.

It was perfect. Bataille was complimented and went off with his box slung on his back. The baron, his wife, Jeanne and Julien all agreed that the painter was a very talented fellow who would certainly have become an artist if circumstances had permitted.

Julien had introduced reforms, by way of economy, which in turn made other changes necessary.

The old coachman was now the gardener, since the viscount had sold the carriage horses to save the cost of their upkeep and proposed to drive himself.

Then, as somebody was needed to hold the horses when their masters descended from the carriage, he had turned a young cowherd named Marius into an under-servant.

Finally, he arranged to provide himself with horses by inserting a special clause into the Couillards' and the Martins' leases by which the two farmers were bound each to furnish a horse for one day in every month, the date to be appointed by himself, in return for which they would be exempted from supplying poultry.

In consequence of this arrangement the Couillards had brought out a big chestnut hack and the Martins a small animal with a shaggy grey coat – the two beasts were put in double harness; and Marius, his small figure submerged in an old livery of Simon's, drew up the conveyance in front of the château steps.

Julien, freshly attired, was standing erect with something of his former style, though his long beard made him look common.

He inspected the horses, the carriage and their small attendant and judged them satisfactory, for the newly painted coats of arms were the only points of any importance to him.

The baroness, who had come downstairs on her husband's arm, climbed painfully into the carriage and took her seat, leaning back on a heap of cushions. Jeanne appeared next. At first she laughed at the pair of horses, for the grey, she said, must be the grandson of the chestnut; then when Marius caught her eye, with the top of his face hidden by the cockaded hat which had slipped down to rest on his nose, his hands invisible in the depths of his sleeves, the tails of the livery hanging round his legs like petticoats and his feet poking out oddly in enormous shoes; and when she saw him tip his head back in order to see, raise his knee to step forward as though he were taking a river in his stride, and flounder about like a blind man to carry out his orders, utterly lost, swallowed up in his voluminous garments, she broke into peals of uncontrollable laughter.

The baron turned round, and when he saw the little fellow in such confusion he too found the sight irresistible and began to laugh, calling on his wife to look, speechless with mirth.

'L-l-look at Ma-Ma-Marius! He's so droll! Upon my soul, what a s-sight.'

At that, the baroness leaned out of her window to regard him, and was promptly overcome by such a fit of merriment that the carriage rebounded on its springs as though somebody were shaking it.

Julien was white in the face: 'What has come over you, laughing like that? You must be mad!'

Jeanne sat down on the steps of the house, almost ill with laughing, unable to stop. The baron did the same; and the sound of convulsive sneezing, a sort of continuous clucking from within the carriage, indicated that the baroness was choking with laughter. Suddenly Marius' frock-coat began to shake. No doubt he too had seen the joke, for inside his headgear he was laughing fit to burst.

Julien flew into a rage. With one blow he separated the lad's head from the outsize hat, which rolled away over the lawn; then, turning to his father-in-law, he brought out in a voice that trembled with fury: 'It's hardly for you to laugh, is it? We should never have come to this if you had not squandered your fortune and run through your estates. Whose fault is it if you are ruined?'

Their merriment froze, stopped dead. No one spoke. Jeanne was almost in tears as she silently took her seat beside her mother in the carriage. The baron seated himself opposite the two women, shocked and speechless; and Julien mounted the box, dragging the snivelling boy, whose cheek was beginning to swell, up beside him.

The road was dull, and they found it long. There was no conversation inside the carriage. All three were dismayed and embarrassed by what had happened, but unwilling to confess to it. They knew that it would be impossible to engage on any other topic of conversation, for their minds were full of the painful little scene and they thought it better to preserve silence than to speak of it.

As the carriage, drawn by the two beasts trotting unevenly together, went past the farms, black hens scattered in panic and dived out of sight into the hedgerows, and sometimes a wolf-hound galloped after them yelping, then ran bristling back to its kennel and turned to bark again at the carriage. A lad in muddy sabots walking with a long-legged, leisurely stride, his hands in his pockets and his blue smock puffed out by the wind, stood back to let the carriage pass and awkwardly took off his cap, revealing his hair pasted flat on his head.

There were farms scattered widely over the plains that stretched away into the distance.

Finally they turned off the highway into a great avenue of pines. The ruts in the drive were deep and muddy and the carriage swayed from side to side, at which dear Mama uttered cries of alarm. The white gate at the end of the avenue was shut; Marius ran to open it, and a circular sweep rounding an extensive lawn led them to a tall, vast, gloomy-looking edifice with closed shutters.

The central door opened; an elderly, rheumatic manservant wearing a red and black striped waistcoat partly covered by a working apron came sideways down the steps from the entrance. He asked the visitors their names and conducted them to a spacious drawing-room, where he managed with difficulty to open the Venetian shutters. The furniture was shrouded in dust-sheets, the clock and candelabra swathed in white linen; and a smell of mould, the cold, damp atmosphere of bygone days, seemed to infuse the lungs, heart and skin with melancholy.

They all seated themselves and waited. There was a sound of footsteps in the corridor above suggesting unaccustomed haste. The master and mistress of the house had been taken by surprise, and were dressing as quickly as they could. It was a lengthy process. A bell rang several times. Other steps could be heard descending a staircase, then going upstairs again.

The cold was penetrating; the baroness felt it and succumbed to an attack of sneezing. Julien paced to and fro. Jeanne sat dejectedly beside her mother. The baron stood with his back to the marble mantelpiece, with lowered gaze.

One of the tall doors opened at last, to reveal the Viscount and Viscountess de Briseville. They were both small and spare, staccato in their movements, of uncertain age, ceremonious and ill at ease. The viscountess, who wore a flowered silk gown and small dowager's cap with ribbons, spoke quickly in a rather sharp voice.

Her husband, clad in a formal frock-coat, bowed with slightly flexed knees. His nose, eyes and loose teeth, his hair gleaming as though polished with beeswax and his splendid ceremonial attire all had the sheen of things well cared for.

After the first greetings and neighbourly courtesies had been exchanged, no one could think of anything more to say. Meaningless phrases of congratulation were exchanged. Hopes were expressed on both sides that these excellent relations would continue. It was agreeable to pay calls when one lived all the year round in the country.

In the meantime the icy air in the room was chilling them to the bone, making their voices hoarse. The baroness had begun to cough, while her bout of sneezing still continued. The baron gave the signal for their departure. The Brisevilles pressed them to stay: 'What, so soon? Do, pray do remain a little longer.' Jeanne had risen, however, although Julien thought the call too short and was making signs to her.

Their host went to ring for the servant to order the carriage, but the bell was out of order. He hastened away, and returned to inform them that the horses had been taken out of harness.

They were obliged to wait. Everyone tried to think of something to say. They talked about the wet winter. With involuntary shudders of apprehension Jeanne asked what their hosts found to occupy them, alone together the whole of the year.

But the Brisevilles were surprised at the question; they were never without occupation, writing to their highborn relations in every part of France, spending their days absorbed in small details, as ceremonious with each other as they were with strangers and conversing in a stately fashion on the most trivial subjects.

Beneath the high, blackened ceiling of the great drawing-room, a room in disuse where everything was parcelled up in linen, the two small figures so spruce and correct gave Jeanne the impression of preserved specimens of nobility.

At last the carriage with its two ill-matched nags appeared outside the windows. Marius, however, had disappeared. No doubt he had supposed that he was free until the evening, and taken himself off to find entertainment.

Julien was angry when he heard this, and requested that the lad should be sent home on foot; and after many civilities on both sides they started out on the road back to Les Peuples.

Although the memory of Julien's brutish behaviour still remained with them, no sooner were they inside the carriage than Jeanne and her father began laughing and imitating the Brisevilles' accents and gestures. The baron played the husband, Jeanne the wife, but the baroness's sense of propriety was slightly offended and she said: 'It's wrong to make fun of them, they are very well-bred people and come from extremely good families.' Papa and Jeanne desisted, not wishing to upset dear Mama, but from time to time nonetheless they exchanged a glance which set them off again. He made a formal bow and adopted a solemn tone of voice: 'Your château at Les Peuples must be very cold, Madame, with the strong sea winds blowing all the time?' She put on a prim expression and simpered, with a little wriggle of the head like a duck in the water: 'Oh! Monsieur, there is enough to occupy me the whole year round. We have so many relations, so much correspondence. And Monsieur de Briseville leaves everything to me. He is engaged in scholarly research with Father Pelle. They are working together on a religious history of Normandy.'

The baroness smiled in her turn, a little put out, and

repeated good-temperedly: 'It's not right to laugh at people of our own class.'

The carriage came to an abrupt halt; and Julien called out to someone behind. Jeanne and the baron leaned out and beheld a remarkable object advancing towards them. With his legs entangled in the floating skirts of his livery, blinded by his headgear which continually capsized, shaking his sleeves like the sails of a windmill, floundering frantically through large puddles, stumbling over every stone in the road, rushing headlong in leaps and bounds and covered with mud, Marius was following the carriage as fast as his legs would carry him.

As soon as he came up with them Julien leaned out and seized him by the collar, pulled him up onto the box and, letting go of the reins, proceeded to pound the hat with his fist until it collapsed on the lad's shoulders with a noise like a drum. Marius howled inside it and tried to escape and jump to the ground, while his master held him with one hand and rained blows on him with the other.

Jeanne cried, horrified: 'Papa . . . Oh! Papa!' and the baroness was roused and seized her husband's arm in indignation: 'Do stop him, Jacques.' The baron quickly lowered the window in front and grasped his son-in-law by the sleeve: 'Will you stop striking the child?' His voice trembled as he uttered the words.

Julien turned round in astonishment: 'Look at the state he's got his livery in, the little wretch.'

But the baron interposed his head between them: 'Well, that's of no importance! No need to be so rough with him.' This only infuriated Julien anew: 'It's nothing to do with you, leave me alone,' and he raised his hand again. But his father-in-law promptly took hold of it and brought it down with so much force that he banged it on the wooden seat, and shouted in such an angry tone: 'If you don't stop, I'll get down myself and make you!' that the viscount abruptly subsided, shrugged his shoulders without replying and whipped up the horses into a smart trot.

The two women remained perfectly still, ashen pale, and the thudding of the baron's heart could be distinctly heard.

At dinner Julien was more agreeable than usual, as though nothing had happened. Jeanne, her father and Madame Adélaïde, easy-going by temperament, were quick to forget the incident in their relief at seeing him in such good humour, and allowed their spirits to rise with the sense of well-being of convalescents; and when Jeanne mentioned the Brisevilles again her husband joined her in joking about them, although he was quick to add: 'All the same, they are persons of great distinction.'

They paid no further calls, for they were all afraid to revive the subject of Marius. It was decided simply to send New Year cards to the neighbouring houses, and to postpone visiting them until the following spring and the warmer weather.

Christmas came. The priest was invited to dinner, and also the mayor and his wife. They were asked again on New Year's Day. These were the only distractions to break the monotonous succession of their days.

Papa and dear Mama were to leave Les Peuples on the 9th of January; Jeanne wanted them to stay, but Julien did not encourage it, and in the face of his son-in-law's increasing coolness towards him, the baron sent for a post-chaise from Rouen.

The day before their departure was bright and frosty, and since the packing was finished Jeanne and her father decided to go down to Yport, which they had not visited since her return from Corsica.

They went through the wood where she had walked on her wedding day, where she had felt so close to the man whose companion she was to be for the rest of her life, where she had received her first caress and thrilled with the first tremor in a foretaste of that sensual love that she was only to experience to the full in the wild vale of Ota, beside the spring where they had mingled their kisses with the water as they drank.

There were no leaves left on the trees, no creepers, nothing but the sound of the branches and the dry rustling of brushwood stripped bare in winter.

They walked through the little village. The empty, silent streets still smelt of brine, seaweed and fish. The great brown nets were hung out to dry outside the doors or spread on the shingle. The tide was on the ebb and the grey, cold sea with its ceaseless booming and its endless line of surf laid bare the greenish rocks at the foot of the cliffs towards Fécamp. The big boats grounded along the shelving beach looked like huge dead fish. Darkness was falling, and groups of fishermen came down to the beach, treading heavily in their big seaboots, woollen mufflers round their necks, a bottle of brandy in one hand and a boat-lantern in the other. For a long time they circulated about the boats which were lying heeled over; with Norman deliberation they stowed their nets on board, their buoys, a large roll of bread, a pot of butter, a glass and the bottle of rough brandy. When that was done they heaved each boat up on its keel and pushed it down with a great clatter over the shingle into the water until it cleft the surf, rose on a wave and swung there for a moment or two, then spread its brown wings and vanished into the night with a small light shining at the masthead.

The seamen's wives were big women, with hard bodies projecting in outline under their flimsy clothes, who had waited until the last of the fishermen sailed away and now went back to the hushed village, their strident voices shattering the quiet of the sleeping streets.

The baron and Jeanne stood still, watching the men go out into the darkness as they went out every night, men who risked their lives not to starve and yet were so wretchedly poor that they never tasted meat.

The baron was exalted, carried away by the view of the sea: 'It is terrible, yet beautiful as well. How splendid it is, the sea at night, with so many lives on it in peril! Don't you find it so, Jeannette?'

She smiled without warmth as she replied: 'It is not half as lovely as the Mediterranean.' But her father was indignant:

'The Mediterranean! oil, syrup, blue water like a wash-tub. Look at that sea, what a terrifying sight it is with those foaming crests! And think of all those men out there, out of sight already.'

Jeanne agreed with a sigh: 'Yes, perhaps so.' But that word 'Mediterranean' as she spoke it had cast its spell on her heart anew, and her thoughts sped back to those far-off lands where her dreams came to rest.

The father and daughter did not return through the woods, but walked up to the road and slowly ascended the slope. They spoke little, saddened by the prospect of parting.

Sometimes as they passed the dykes beside the farms they encountered a strong smell of crushed apples in the air, the smell of fresh cider which seems to hover over the whole Normandy countryside at that time of year; and at times there was a greasy farmyard odour, the good warm stench of cattle dung. A small lighted window down in a farmyard showed where the farmhouse stood.

Jeanne had the sensation that her spirit swelled and grew until it understood unseen things; and those occasional gleams of light in the fields gave her a vivid impression of the isolation of all beings, which everything tends to sunder, to separate, to drag away from their desires.

She said then in a tone of resignation: 'Life is not all roses.'

The baron sighed: 'Well, little girl, that's something we cannot help.'

The next day, after Papa and dear Mama had gone, Jeanne and Julien were alone.

7

CARDS NOW BEGAN TO PLAY A PART IN THE YOUNG couple's life together. Every day after luncheon Julien smoked a pipe and wet his throat with brandy, increasing the dose to six or eight glasses, and played a few games of bezique with his wife. After this she went up to her room, where she sat at the window and picked up a piece of embroidery or trimmed a petticoat, while the rain beat on the windows and they rattled in the wind. Sometimes when she grew tired of sewing she raised her head and looked out into the distance where the sombre sea was flecked with white horses. After gazing at it vaguely for a minute or two she took up her work again.

She had no other occupation, since Julien had taken charge of all the household affairs to satisfy his need for authority and his passion for economizing. He proved to be extremely miserly, never gave a tip, and kept them on short rations; when Jeanne first came to Les Peuples she ordered a small Normandy cake every day from the baker, but he put an end to that extravagance and made her eat toast instead.

She did not protest, for she wished to avoid any sort of disagreement or quarrel; but she suffered a pang at every instance of her husband's meanness. To her this was something base and detestable, brought up as she had been in a family where money was of small account. How often had she heard dear Mama say: 'But money is made to be spent.' Now Julien was always repeating: 'Will you never learn not to throw money out of the window?' Whenever he had reduced somebody's wages or cut down a bill to save a few pence he would smile as he slipped the money into his pocket and say: 'Small streams make great rivers.'

There were days, however, when Jeanne would revert to daydreaming. She would slowly come to a pause in her work, letting her hands fall limp on her lap, while her eyes clouded as she recalled some childhood story and floated off on a delightful adventure. But the sound of Julien's voice as he gave an order to old Simon would wrench her abruptly back out of the soothing reverie; and she would take up her patient work again and tell herself: 'That's all over'; and a tear would fall on her fingers as they plied the needle.

Rosalie, who had always been so merry and given to singing, had also changed. Her plump cheeks had lost their high colour and were now almost hollow, looking sometimes as though they had been daubed with earth.

Jeanne often asked her: 'Are you ill, child?' The maid always answered: 'No, Madame.' Then a slight colour came into her face and she quickly made her escape.

She no longer ran to and fro, but moved with painful slowness and showed none of her old coquetry, buying nothing from the pedlars, who displayed their silken ribbons, corsets and toilet articles in vain for her to see.

The big, gloomy house, its walls stained with long grey streaks of rain, seemed to give out a hollow sound.

The end of January brought the first snow. Heavy clouds from the north could be seen far away over the dark sea, and white flakes began to fall. In one night the whole plain was buried, and in the morning the trees wore a foamy covering of frost.

Julien, topbooted and shaggy, passed his time watching for migrant birds, in ambush behind the dyke between the copse and the heath. From time to time a shot broke the frozen silence of the fields; and a flock of frightened black crows rose out of the tall trees and whirled away into the sky.

Sometimes in an access of boredom Jeanne descended the steps to the drive. Sounds of life reached her from a distance, reverberating from the somnolent calm of the dull, leaden pall that lay over the earth.

Then she heard nothing more, nothing but the snoring of the distant waves and the faint, unceasing susurration of the cloud of frozen waterdrops floating down.

The level of the snow continued to rise as that dense, light foam continuously fell.

On one of those white mornings Jeanne was in her room, sitting quietly warming her feet at the fire while Rosalie, whose looks were changing daily, laboriously made the bed. All at once Jeanne heard a piteous sigh behind her. She asked, without turning her head: 'What is the matter with you?'

The maid answered as usual: 'Nothing, Madame'; but her voice sounded broken and exhausted.

Jeanne had begun thinking of something else, when she was aware that she could no longer hear the girl moving about. She called: 'Rosalie!' There was no sound. She supposed then that the maid had left the room without her hearing and called again, raising her voice: 'Rosalie!' and was about to put out her hand to ring when a deep moan somewhere close by made her start in alarm.

The maid was sitting on the floor with ashen face and staring eyes, her legs stretched out, her back against the wooden bedstead.

Jeanne ran across the room: 'What is it, what is it?'

The girl did not speak or move; she stared wildly at her mistress, gasping as though she were rent by a fearful pain. Suddenly she arched her whole body and slipped down on her back, clenching her teeth to stifle a cry of agony.

Her legs were parted, her dress clung to them and something moved beneath its folds. Just then a curious gurgling sound came from the same place, a choking breath; it was followed immediately by a long-drawn-out wail like a cat mewing, a feeble plaint distressing to hear, the first cry of pain of an infant coming into the world.

Suddenly Jeanne understood, and ran in a panic to the head of the stairs, calling: 'Julien! Julien!'

He called up from below: 'What do you want?'

She could scarcely utter the words: 'It's . . . it's Rosalie, she . . .'

Julien ran headlong up the stairs, taking them two at a time, burst into the room and in one movement pulled up the maid's skirts, to reveal a horrid little bundle of flesh, crumpled and contorted, slimy all over, moaning as it stirred feebly between two bare legs.

He was scowling as he stood up again, and pushed his bewildered wife out of the room. 'This doesn't concern you. Go away. Send Ludivine up here, and Simon.'

Jeanne went down to the kitchen, trembling from head to foot; then, as she dared not go upstairs again, she entered the drawing-room where the fire had not been lit since her parents' departure, and waited anxiously for news.

After a few moments she saw the servant running out of the house. He returned five minutes later accompanied by the widow Dentu, the local midwife.

A great commotion ensued on the staircase, as though a wounded person were being carried down; and Julien came to tell Jeanne that she could go up to her room again.

She was shivering as though she had just been at the scene of a terrible accident. She sat down again in front of her fire, then asked him: 'How is she?'

Julien strode up and down, preoccupied and irritable; he seemed greatly put out, and did not answer at first; then after a few moments he stood still and said: 'What do you propose to do with that girl?'

She did not understand, and stared at her husband: 'What? What do you mean? I don't know.'

He shouted in sudden anger: 'Well, we can't keep a bastard in the house.'

Jeanne was greatly perplexed. After a long pause, she said: 'But, my dear, could it not be put out to nurse?'

He did not let her finish. 'And who is going to pay for it? You, I suppose?'

She thought it over for a long time, wondering what could be done; then she said: 'But the father will take charge of the child; and if he marries Rosalie there will be no more difficulty.'

Julien, apparently at the end of his patience, replied angrily: 'The father! . . . the father! . . . do you know who he is . . . the father? You don't, do you? Well, then? . . .'

Jeanne's emotions were aroused. 'But surely he will not abandon the girl like that. It would be shameful! We'll ask who it is, and go and see him, and he'll have to explain himself.'

Julien was calmer now and had resumed his pacing up and down. 'My dear, she'll not say who the man is; she'll not tell you, any more than she would tell me . . . and suppose he doesn't want anything more to do with her? . . . We can't keep an unmarried mother and her bastard under our roof, can we?'

But Jeanne was determined: 'Well, the man must be a scoundrel; but we shall have to find out who it is; and then he will have us to deal with.'

Julien had turned very red and said impatiently: 'Well, but . . . in the meantime . . . ?'

She did not know what to say, and asked him: 'What do you suggest yourself?'

He was ready with an answer: 'Oh! it seems very simple to me. I'd give her some money and tell her to go to the devil with her brat.'

The young woman turned on him in indignation. 'We could never do such a thing. That girl and I are foster-sisters; we have grown up together. She's done wrong, more's the pity; but I'm not going to turn her out because of that; and if necessary I will bring up the child myself.'

Julien burst out: 'We'll have a fine reputation, won't we, with our name and family connections! Everyone will say that we harbour vice here, giving a home to whores; decent people won't want to set foot in our house again. What are you thinking of? You must be mad!'

She was unmoved. 'I am not going to let Rosalie be turned out. If you won't keep her, my mother will take her back – we shall find out who the child's father is, sooner or later.'

Upon that he flung out of the room in exasperation, banging the door and shouting: 'How stupid women are! The notions they get in their heads!'

In the afternoon Jeanne went up to see the young mother. The maid was lying quite still in bed, with her eyes open, while the widow Dentu who was looking after her rocked the newborn baby in her arms.

Immediately Rosalie saw her mistress she hid her face in the sheets in despair and burst into a storm of weeping. Jeanne attempted to kiss her, but she kept her face covered and resisted. Then the nurse intervened and pulled the sheet away; she offered no more resistance, and her sobs became quieter.

A small fire was burning in the grate. It was cold; the baby was crying. Jeanne did not dare to say anything about the child for fear of bringing on another flood of tears; but she held her maid's hand and repeated mechanically: 'It will be all right, it will be all right.' The unhappy girl stole glances at the nurse, shuddering at the little creature's cries; and from time to time as her convulsions of woe died down a strangled sob was forced from her, emerging with a gurgling sound as she gulped back her tears.

Jeanne kissed her again and whispered very softly in her ear: 'We'll take good care of it, never fear.' Then she made a hasty escape as a fresh burst of weeping began.

She visited Rosalie every day, and each time the maid burst into tears when her mistress appeared.

The baby was put out to nurse with a woman who lived nearby.

In all that time Julien spoke scarcely a word to his wife, and seemed to have harboured a deep resentment against her since her refusal to dismiss her maid. One day he raised the subject again, but Jeanne pulled a letter from her mother out of her pocket, in which the baroness asked that the girl should be sent to her if she were not to be kept on at Les Peuples. Julien was furious at this, and cried: 'Your mother is mad, just as you are.' But he did not pursue the matter further.

Two weeks later the young mother was able to get up and resume her duties.

Then one morning Jeanne made her sit down, took her hands in her own, looked at her steadily and said: 'Come now, child, tell me all about it.'

Rosalie began trembling and faltered: 'What, Madame?'

'Whose child is it?'

The question threw the maid into a paroxysm of despair; she tried frantically to free her hands and cover her face.

Jeanne kissed her in spite of herself, however, and consoled her: 'It's a misfortune, my girl, of course. You were weak;

but it often happens. If the father marries you, no one will think any more about it; and we can take him into our service with you.'

Rosalie groaned as though she were in torment and jerked at her hands, trying to release herself and run away.

Jeanne went on: 'I can understand very well that you feel ashamed; but, as you see, I'm not angry, I'm talking to you gently. If I ask the man's name it's for your own sake, because when I see how unhappy you are I think he must be deserting you, and I want to prevent that happening. Julien will go to see him, you know, and we will force him to marry you; then, as we shall keep you both with us, we'll be able to see that he makes you happy into the bargain.'

This time Rosalie jerked her hands so violently that her mistress let go of them, and she rushed wildly out of the room.

Jeanne said to Julien at dinner that evening: 'I've tried to persuade Rosalie to tell me the name of her seducer, with no success. Do try yourself, so that we can make the rascal marry her.'

Julien immediately flew into a passion: 'Now listen to me, I don't want to hear any more about that. You wanted to keep the girl, so keep her, but don't pester me about her again.'

He had been in a worse humour than ever since Rosalie's confinement; and it was now a habit with him to shout at his wife whenever he spoke to her as though he were perpetually in a rage, while she by contrast spoke quietly, constraining herself to be gentle and placatory in manner to avoid all disagreement; but she often wept in bed at night.

In spite of his constant bad temper her husband had resumed his love-making for the first time since they returned from their wedding trip, and rarely three evenings in succession passed without his coming to her room.

Rosalie was soon completely recovered, and less unhappy, although she still seemed to be haunted by some hidden fear.

Twice more she ran away when Jeanne attempted to question her.

Julien's behaviour became unexpectedly more agreeable; vague hopes were re-awakened in the young wife and she became gay and lively again, although she suffered at times from a strange malaise, which she mentioned to no one. There was no sign of a thaw and for nearly five weeks the vast expanse of the sky, clear crystal blue by day and at night frosted with stars, spread out as austere and glittering as the smooth, hard sheets of snow beneath it.

Isolated homesteads in their square courtyards behind screens of tall trees powdered with rime looked like beings sleeping in white chemises. No one, man or beast, ventured out of doors any more; the only signs of life within were thin threads of smoke rising from the cottage chimneys straight up into the glacial air.

The plain, the hedges, the rows of elms all looked lifeless, killed by the cold. Occasionally the trees could be heard to crack, as though their wooden limbs had broken under the bark; and sometimes a big branch would tear away and fall, as the relentless frost petrified the sap and snapped the fibres.

Jeanne looked forward eagerly to the return of warmer days, attributing all the vague discomforts she was feeling to the exceptionally severe weather.

At times she had a distaste for all kinds of food and could eat nothing; at times her pulse was faint; at times her scanty meals gave her nausea and indigestion; her nerves were taut, perpetually on edge, and she was unbearably restless, in a state of constant agitation.

One evening the thermometer fell even lower, and Julien shivered as they left the table – he insisted on economizing on firewood, and the room was never adequately heated. He rubbed his hands and murmured: 'It will be good to sleep together tonight, eh, puss?'

He laughed in his old, boyish way and Jeanne flung her arms round his neck; but she was feeling particularly unwell that evening, full of aches and pains and in such a nervous state that she kissed him on the lips and begged him in a whisper to let her sleep alone. She explained in a few words: 'Please, my darling; I am really not at all well. I expect I shall feel better tomorrow.'

He did not press her: 'Just as you like, my dear; you must take care of yourself.'

They talked of other things.

She retired early to her room. Julien, unusually for him, had had a fire lit in his own. As soon as he was informed that it was 'burning up nicely' he kissed his wife on the forehead and went off.

The cold seemed to penetrate the whole house; it pierced the walls, which made small noises as though they were shivering, and Jeanne shivered in her bed.

She rose twice to put more wood on the fire and to look for gowns, skirts, old clothes to heap on her bed. Nothing could warm her; her feet were numb, while tremors ran through her legs up to her thighs making her restless, and she turned continually from side to side in a state of nervous exhaustion.

Soon her teeth were chattering; her hands shook; her chest felt constricted; her heart beat slowly with dull, heavy thuds and sometimes seemed to stop; and she gasped for air as though she could not breathe.

A sudden mental anguish came over her at the moment when the cold carried its irresistible attack to the very marrow of her bones. She had known nothing like it before, as though life itself had forsaken her and she were about to breathe her last.

The thought came into her head: 'I'm going to die . . . I am dying . . .'

She sprang out of bed in terror and rang for Rosalie, waited, rang again, waited again, ice-cold and shivering.

The maid did not come. Probably she was asleep, in that first deep sleep that nothing can penetrate, and Jeanne ran barefoot in panic to the foot of the stairs.

She groped her way up without a sound, found the door and opened it, called: 'Rosalie!' went in, bumped against the bed, ran her hands over it and realized that it was empty. It was empty and quite cold, as though no one had been there.

She said to herself in surprise: 'Well, to think of her running wild in weather like this!'

Now her heart was beating wildly, leaping and throbbing, nearly suffocating her, and with her legs almost giving way she went down the stairs again to wake Julien.

She burst into his room, convinced that she was at death's door, impelled by the desire to see him before she lost consciousness.

In the flickering firelight she saw two heads on the pillow, Rosalie's head beside her husband's.

She screamed, and they both sat upright. For a moment in the shock of discovery she stood still, without moving. Then she fled, running back to her own room; and when Julien called frantically: 'Jeanne!' she was filled with a terrible dread of seeing him and hearing his voice, his explanations and lies, meeting him face to face; and she rushed out of her room and ran downstairs.

It was dark, and in her haste she was in danger of falling down the stairs and breaking her limbs on the stone. She went on, however, driven by an imperative need to get away, know nothing more, see no one.

When she reached the bottom she sank down on one of the stairs, still barefoot, with nothing on but her nightdress; quite distraught, she did not move.

Julien had jumped out of bed and was dressing in haste. She heard him moving, walking about. She stood up, ready to run away. Now he was coming downstairs, calling her: 'Jeanne, listen!'

No, she would not listen, she would not let him touch her; and she ran into the dining-room as though she were escaping from a murderer. She sought a way out, a hiding-place or dark corner, somewhere she could avoid him. She hid under the table. But now he was opening the door, with a lamp in his hand, calling again: 'Jeanne!' and she was off again like a hare, rushing into the kitchen where she ran twice round the room like a cornered animal, and when he caught up with her she jerked the garden door open and fled out of doors.

The snow was knee-deep in places, and its icy touch on her bare legs spurred her to a new, desperate effort. Although she had nothing to protect her from the cold, she did not feel it; her body was numb with shock, so that she no longer had any sensation in it as she fled, white as the ground under her feet.

She ran down the main avenue and through the copse, then crossed the dyke and struck out over the heath.

There was no moon; the stars glittered like seeds of fire scattered over the blackness of the sky; yet the plain was light, white without lustre, in fixed immobility and infinite silence.

Jeanne rushed on, hardly drawing breath, unaware, unthinking. Suddenly she was at the edge of the cliff. By instinct she stopped dead and crouched down, utterly void of thought and will.

In the dark abyss before her the mute, invisible sea gave off the salt smell of seaweed at low tide.

She remained there a long time, inert in mind and body; then suddenly a fit of shivering came over her, a violent shaking like a sail flapping in the wind. An irresistible force agitated her arms, hands and feet, which vibrated in abrupt, jerky movements; and she woke with a start to a clear and piercing sense of reality.

She had visions of scenes from the past: sailing with him in old Lastique's boat, their conversation, her awakening love, the boat being baptised; and before that, the night when she first arrived at Les Peuples, when she had been cradled in dreams. And now! now! Oh! her life was in ruins, all happiness at an end, all hope vain; and a terrible future lay ahead, full of agony, betrayal and despair. It were best that she should die and end it all forthwith.

A voice was calling in the distance: 'This way, here are her footprints; quickly, quickly, this way!' It was Julien, out searching for her.

Oh! she had no wish to see him again. Now she could hear a

faint sound in the depths before her, the sound of the sea sliding over the rocks.

She stood up, and, roused to the point of being ready to hurl herself down, uttered the farewell to life of the despairing, the last moan of the dying, the last word of young soldiers mortally wounded in battle: 'Mother!'

Immediately the thought of dear Mama came into her mind; she pictured her in tears; she saw her father kneeling beside her own drowned body, and experienced in one second all the anguish of their grief.

She fell back limply into the snow, and did not try to escape again when Julien and old Simon came up to her, followed by Marius with a lantern, and took hold of her arms to pull her back from the very edge of the cliff.

They had no difficulty in lifting her, she could no longer move at all. She felt herself being carried along, laid down in a bed, massaged with hot linen cloths; then memory faded as she lost consciousness altogether.

Presently a nightmare – was it a nightmare? – possessed her. She was in bed in her room. It was daylight, but she could not get up. Why? She did not know. She heard a small sound, a sort of scratching and rustling, on the floor and suddenly a mouse, a little grey mouse ran swiftly over the sheet. It was followed immediately by another, then a third, trotting with quick, tiny steps towards her breast. Jeanne was not afraid; she put out her hand and tried to catch the little creature, but failed.

Then more mice, ten, twenty, hundreds, thousands of them sprang up from all directions. They swarmed up the bed-posts and ran over the hangings, over the whole bed. Soon they were inside the bedclothes; Jeanne felt them slipping over her skin, tickling her legs, running up and down all over her body. She saw them come up from the foot of the bed, to run past her throat and find their way between the sheets; and she struggled to catch one, putting out her hands and closing them on empty air.

Then she tried frantically to escape and called out, with the feeling that she was being held down so that she could not move, that strong arms were round her in a paralysing grip; but she could see no one.

She had no sense of time. It must have lasted a long while, very long.

She awoke at last to aching fatigue and at the same time a pleasant sensation. She felt weak, so weak . . . She opened her eyes, and was not surprised to see dear Mama sitting in her room, with a big man she had never seen before.

How old was she? She had no idea, and imagined herself a little girl. Moreover, she had entirely lost her memory.

The big man said: 'Look, she's coming round.' And dear Mama began weeping. The man went on: 'Now, Baroness, calm yourself, you may rest at ease, I assure you. Only don't talk to her about anything, anything at all. Let her sleep.'

It seemed to Jeanne that she again spent a very long time drowsing, falling into a heavy sleep whenever she tried to think; and she made no effort to remember anything, as though at the back of her mind she were afraid of the reality that recollection would bring back.

A time came when she awoke to see Julien beside her, alone; and immediately everything came back to her, as though a curtain over her past had been raised.

She felt a sharp pain in her heart, and again attempted to run away. She threw back the sheets, sprang to the floor and fell down, her legs too weak to support her.

Julien rushed to her side, and she screamed at him not to touch her. She twisted and turned. The door opened. Aunt Lison came hurrying in, followed by the widow Dentu, the baron and lastly dear Mama, panting and distraught.

She was put to bed again, and cunningly she closed her eyes immediately so that she would not have to talk, she would have leisure to think.

While her mother and aunt were tending her they earnestly begged her to speak, asking: 'Can you hear us now, Jeanne, my little Jeanne?'

She pretended not to hear, and did not answer; and she was

perfectly aware that the day was drawing to a close. It was growing dark. A nurse was brought in to sit with her, who gave her a drink from time to time.

She drank without speaking, but she did not sleep again; she found it difficult to think as she tried to recollect things which eluded her, as though there were gaps in her memory, large blank spaces in which no events were recorded.

Little by little, after much effort, she did succeed in recapturing all the facts.

She considered them steadily, with determination.

Dear Mama, Aunt Lison and the baron had come back to her, therefore she must have been very ill. But what of Julien? What had he said? Did her parents know? And Rosalie? Where was she? And what was she herself to do? What was she to do? It came to her in a flash – she would go back to Rouen with Papa and dear Mama, and everything would be as it used to be. She would be a widow; that was all.

She waited, listening to all that was said round her, giving no sign of how well she understood but glad to have recovered her reason, patient and cunning.

At last in the evening she was alone with the baroness, and whispered to her: 'Dear Mama!' Her own voice surprised her, seemed to her altered. The baroness seized her hands: 'My child! My darling Jeanne! Do you know who I am?'

'I do, dear Mama, but you really mustn't cry; we have so much to talk about. Has Julien told you why I ran away, out into the snow?'

'Yes, my precious, you had a high fever, it was very dangerous.'

'It's not that, Mama. I had the fever afterwards; but did he tell you what caused it and why I ran away?'

'No, my darling.'

'It was because I found Rosalie in his bed.'

The baroness thought she was still delirious, and caressed and soothed her. 'There now, my precious, compose yourself, try to sleep.'

But Jeanne persisted: 'I am quite clear-headed now, dear

Mama, not talking wildly as I must have done these last few days. One night I felt ill, and I went to find Julien. Rosalie was in bed with him. I was out of my mind with grief, and I ran out into the snow to throw myself over the cliff.'

The baroness, however, only repeated: 'Yes, my precious, you have been very ill, very ill.'

'It's not that, Mama; I found Rosalie in Julien's bed, and I will not stay with him any longer. You must take me to Rouen, as you used to do.'

The doctor had warned the baroness not to oppose Jeanne in anything and she answered: 'Yes, my precious.'

The sick woman grew impatient: 'I can see you do not believe me. Go and fetch dear Papa, he will understand.'

Dear Mama rose painfully to her feet, took up her two sticks and went out with dragging steps, to return a few minutes later supported by the baron.

They seated themselves at the bedside and Jeanne at once began to talk. In a weak voice she told them everything, quietly and frankly: Julien's peculiar temperament, his harsh behaviour, his meanness, finally his unfaithfulness.

When she came to the end the baron realized that she was not wandering in her mind, but he did not know what to think, what decision to take or how to answer her.

He took her hand affectionately, as he used to do when he told her stories at bedtime. 'Listen, my darling, we shall have to be prudent. We must do nothing in haste; try to bear with your husband until we have come to a decision about this . . . Promise?' She murmured: 'Very well, but I am not going to stay here when I am well again.'

Then she added very softly: 'Where is Rosalie now?'

The baron answered: 'You won't see her again.' But she repeated with insistence: 'Where is she? I wish to know.' Then he admitted that she had not left the house; but, he said, she would certainly be sent away.

The baron left the patient's room thoroughly incensed and, as a father, wounded to the quick; he sought out Julien and addressed him brusquely, without preamble: 'Sir, I have come to ask you to account for your behaviour towards my daughter. You have deceived her with your own servant; that is doubly shameful.'

Julien played the innocent, however, and vigorously denied it, taking an oath and calling God to witness. Besides, what proof was there? Wasn't Jeanne out of her mind? Hadn't she just had a cerebral fever? Hadn't she run off into the snow one night in a fit of delirium, at the onset of her illness? It was precisely in the middle of that attack, when she was running about the house half naked, that she said she had seen her maidservant in her husband's bed!

He flew into a rage; he threatened legal proceedings; he declared himself insulted. The baron, thrown into confusion, made excuses, apologized and fairly offered his hand, which Julien refused to take.

Jeanne was not angry when she heard what her husband had replied, and merely said: 'He is lying, Papa, but we shall bring it home to him in the end.'

In the next two days she spoke little, withdrawn and pensive.

On the third morning she demanded to see Rosalie. The baron refused to have the maid sent in to her, and said that she had left. Jeanne would not yield, and insisted: 'Then let someone go to her home and bring her here.'

By the time the doctor arrived she was thoroughly wrought up. He had been told everything, to enable him to give an opinion. Jeanne burst into tears, her nerves frayed beyond measure, and almost screamed: 'I want to see Rosalie: I want to see her!'

Upon that the doctor took her hand and said to her in a low voice: 'Do calm yourself, Madame; any excitement may be bad for you because you are with child.'

She was shocked as though he had struck her; and immediately thought she felt something move inside her. Then she was silent, not even hearing what was said to her, deep in thought. She could not sleep that night, kept wakeful by the new and extraordinary knowledge that there was a child, living, in her belly; sad and grieved that it should be Julien's child; anxious, fearing it might resemble its father. When morning came she sent for the baron. 'Dear Papa, I have made my decision; I wish to know everything, now especially; you understand, I do wish it; and you know that in my condition I am not to be refused anything. Now listen. You shall go and fetch the priest. I need him, to make sure that Rosalie tells the truth; as soon as he is here you shall send her up and stay yourself, with dear Mama. Be careful above all not to let Julien suspect anything.'

An hour later the priest entered the room, stouter than ever, panting as heavily as dear Mama. He took an armchair beside her, seated with his legs wide apart and his belly hanging between them; and he opened in humorous vein, mopping his brow as usual with a check handkerchief: 'Well, Baroness, we are getting no slimmer, I see; we make a pair, it seems to me.' Then, turning towards the sickbed: 'Hey! hey! What's this I hear, my dear young lady, shall we be having another baptism soon? Ah! ah! ah! not a boat this time.' In a more serious tone he added: 'This one will be a defender of our country;' then, after a moment's reflection: 'Unless it is a good wife and mother;' and, bowing to the baroness, 'like yourself, Madame.'

The door opened at the end of the room. Rosalie stood clinging to the frame, tearful and distressed and refusing to enter the room, while the baron impelled her forward. He lost patience, and pushed her so hard that she stumbled into the room. She covered her face with her hands and stood there sobbing.

As soon as Jeanne saw her she raised herself up in the bed, whiter than the sheets; and her thin, clinging nightdress rose and fell with the wild beating of her heart. She could scarcely speak, and her breath came with difficulty. At last she uttered a few words in a voice broken with emotion: 'I . . . I . . . have no need . . . to question you . . . It . . . it's enough to see you . . . like this . . . to . . . to see you . . . that you are ashamed . . . now you are with me.'

She paused, breathless, and went on: 'But I wish to know

everything, everything. I have sent for His Reverence so that it shall be like confession, do you understand?'

Rosalie had not moved and was almost sobbing aloud through her fingers.

In an access of fury the baron seized her wrists, pulled them sharply away from her face and flung her to her knees beside the bed: 'Speak, now . . . answer.'

She remained there, kneeling in the attitude in which Mary Magdalene is painted, her cap awry, her apron on the floor and her face once more hidden in her hands, which she had freed.

Then the priest addressed her: 'Come now, my girl, do as you're told and answer. We're not going to do you any harm; but we do need to know what happened.'

Jeanne leaned over the edge of the bed and stared at her maid. 'It's true, isn't it,' she said, 'that you were in Julien's bed when I came in unexpectedly?'

Rosalie groaned through her hands: 'Yes, Madame.'

Then the baroness also burst into tears, with a loud noise as though she were choking; and her convulsive sobs accompanied Rosalie's.

Jeanne, with her eyes fixed on the maid, asked her: 'How long had that been going on?'

Rosalie faltered: 'Ever since he first came.'

Jeanne did not understand. 'Since he came . . . Then . . . since . . . since the spring?'

'Yes, Madame.'

'Since he came to this house?'

'Yes, Madame.'

Jeanne's questions followed all in a rush, as though they had lain heavy on her mind like a weight:

'But how did it happen? How did he ask you? How did he seduce you? What did he say? When and how did you yield? How could you give yourself to him?'

This time Rosalie took her hands away, seized in her turn with a feverish desire to talk, a need to answer.

'I don't know exactly. It was the day when he first came to dinner here, when he came looking for me in my room. He'd hidden himself in the barn. I didn't make a noise, not to make a fuss about it. He slept with me; I hardly knew what I was doing when it happened; he did just what he liked. I didn't say nothing, because I fancied him, see . . .'

Jeanne gave a cry: 'Then, your . . . your baby . . . it's his?'

Rosalie sobbed.

'Yes, Madame.'

They were both silent.

The only sound was that of Rosalie and the baroness weeping.

Under the shock of what she had heard, Jeanne felt her own eyes streaming; and the teardrops ran down her cheeks without a sound.

Her maid's child had the same father as her own! Her anger had subsided. She was now filled with a dull, heavy sense of despair, deep and boundless.

She spoke again at last in an altered voice, the voice of a woman in tears:

'When we came back from . . . from abroad . . . after the journey . . . when did he start again?'

The maid, now in a state of collapse, blurted out: 'It was the . . . the first night, he came.'

Every word wrung Jeanne's heart. That first night, then, the night of their return to Les Peuples, he had left her to go to this girl. That was why he had let her sleep alone!

She knew enough now, she had no desire to hear more; she cried out: 'Go away, go away!' When Rosalie, prostrate, could scarcely move, Jeanne called to her father: 'Take her away, out of this room.' But the priest who had said nothing until then, judged the moment opportune to interpose a short sermon.

'What you have done is very wrong, my daughter, very wrong indeed; and it will be some little time before the good God will pardon you. Think of the hell that awaits you if you do not behave yourself in future. Now that you have a child, you must mend your ways. No doubt the baroness will do something for you, and we'll find you a husband . . .'

He would have gone on for a long time if the baron had not grasped Rosalie again by the shoulders, raised her up and dragged her to the door, and thrown her out into the corridor like a parcel.

When he returned, paler even than his daughter, the priest continued: 'What can one do? They are all the same round here. It is deplorable, but one can't change them, and one must show a little indulgence towards these human failings. They never marry until they're in the family way, never, Madame.' He added with a smile: 'You might say it's a local custom.' Then, with indignation: 'Even children go in for it. Didn't I come across two of them last year in the cemetery, Catechism pupils, a boy and a girl! I told the parents! D'you know what they said to me? "What can we do, Your Reverence, it's not us that's taught them those nasty ways, we can't do nothing about it." You see, Monsieur, your servant has only behaved as the others do.'

The baron interrupted him, trembling with vexation: 'The girl? She doesn't concern me! It's Julien's behaviour that I find shocking. What he's done is disgraceful and I shall take my daughter away.'

He strode to and fro in mounting fury: 'It is shameful to have betrayed my daughter like that, shameful! The man's a blackguard, miserable scum; and I'll tell him as much, I'll strike him with my cane, I'll kill him!'

The priest, who was taking a leisurely pinch of snuff at the side of the weeping baroness, made an attempt to fulfil his mission as a peacemaker and replied: 'Come now, Baron, between ourselves, he's only done what everybody does. Do you know many men who are faithful to their wives?' And with sly familiarity he added: 'Now, I'll wager you yourself have sown your wild oats. Tell me, with your hand on your heart, isn't that so?' The baron had stopped dead in front of the priest, who went on: 'Oh! yes, you've done as they all do. You may even have had a girl like that yourself once, who knows? I tell you, everyone does it. Your wife has been no less happy, has she, no less beloved?'

The baron was dumbfounded, and stood motionless.

It was true, by Jove! he had done the same, and more than once too, as often as he could; nor had the conjugal home been sacred – he'd never hesitated to seduce his wife's maidservants if they were pretty! Was he a blackguard on that account? Why did he judge Julien's conduct so severely when it had never even occurred to him that he might have been blamed for his own?

The baroness, whose sobs had again left her short of breath, had the trace of a smile on her lips at the thought of her husband's early peccadilloes, for she belonged to that sentimental, tender-hearted breed, easily affected, to whom amorous adventures are a part of life.

Jeanne was in a state of collapse, staring straight in front of her, lying on her back with her arms limp at her sides, miserably brooding. A phrase of Rosalie's came back to her and wounded her to the quick, piercing her heart like a gimlet: 'I didn't say nothing because I fancied him.'

She too had 'fancied him'; and it was for that, and for nothing else, that she had given herself, bound herself for life and abandoned all her other hopes, all her half-formed plans, all the unknown tomorrows. She had let herself slip into marriage as into a yawning pit, only to emerge into this state of grief and despair, because like Rosalie she had 'fancied him'!

The door was pushed violently open. Julien appeared, wearing a savage expression. He had found Rosalie moaning on the stairs and realized that she must have been talking and that some plan would be devised, and came in to find out what was afoot. The sight of the priest nailed him to the spot.

His voice was calm, although a little uncertain, as he asked: 'What is it? What's happened?' The baron, who had been fulminating a few minutes earlier, dared not speak now for fear that the priest might repeat his argument, and his son-in-law in consequence invoke the baron himself as an example. Dear Mama's sobs grew louder; but Jeanne had raised herself on her arms, her breath coming fast, and was staring at the one who had made her suffer so cruelly. She poured it all out:

'What has happened is that we know it all, we know how shamefully you have behaved ever since . . . since the first day you came to this house . . . we know that that servant-girl's child is yours, as . . . as mine is . . . they will be brothers . . .' Overcome by excess of grief at the thought, she fell back on the pillows in a frenzied fit of weeping.

He stood gaping, not knowing what to say or do. The priest once more intervened.

'Come, come, we mustn't take on like this, my dear young lady, let's be sensible.' He rose, went to the bed and placed his warm hand on the forehead of the despairing woman. The simple contact was curiously soothing; she had an immediate sense of relief, as though the touch of that rough fellow's strong hand, so well used to the gestures of absolving and consoling, had brought her a mysterious appeasement.

The good man, who had remained on his feet, continued: 'Madame, one must always forgive. This is a great misfortune which has come upon us; but God in His mercy has set against it a great joy, for you are to be a mother. This child will be a consolation to you. It is in his name that I beg you, I implore you to pardon Monsieur Julien's fault. Then there will be a new bond between you, a pledge of his faithfulness in the future. Can you remain estranged in your heart from him whose child you carry in your womb?'

She was exhausted now, bruised and grieved, without the strength even to be angry or bitter, and she made no answer. She felt her nerves go slack as though they had been gently severed, as though she were scarcely alive.

The baroness, who appeared as incapable of harbouring resentment as she was of any prolonged exertion, murmured: 'Come now, Jeanne.'

The priest drew the young man close to the bed, took his hand and placed it in that of his wife. He tapped it lightly as if to give their union a definite form; abandoning his professional preacher's voice, he said with a contented air: 'There now: believe me, it's better like this.'

The two hands parted immediately after their moment of

contact. Julien, not daring to kiss Jeanne, kissed his mother-in-law on the forehead, turned on his heel and took the arm of the baron, who at heart was glad that the matter had been thus settled and did not resist; they went out together to smoke a cigar.

Then the patient, lying prostrate, fell into a light sleep while the priest and dear Mama conversed quietly in low voices.

The good father talked, explained, expounded his ideas; and the baroness inclined her head in agreement. He said in conclusion: 'That's settled, then; you will give the Barville farm to this girl, and I will undertake to find her a husband, a nice decent fellow. Oh! with a fortune of twenty thousand francs we shall not lack suitors. Our only difficulty will be in making a choice.'

Now the baroness was smiling and happy, with two tears still trickling down her cheeks but the traces already almost dry.

She went on: 'It's agreed then, Barville is worth at least twenty thousand francs; but the property will be in the child's name. The parents will enjoy the income from it during their lifetime.'

The priest rose and pressed dear Mama's hand: 'Do not disturb yourself, Baroness, don't move at all; I know what it costs to take one step.'

As he went out he met Aunt Lison coming to visit her patient. She remarked nothing; she was told nothing; and, as usual, she knew nothing.

8

ROSALIE HAD GONE, AND JEANNE'S UNHAPPY pregnancy was nearing its term. She had suffered too much to take any pleasure in the thought of motherhood. She awaited the birth of her child without interest, still haunted by vague fears of some undefined calamity.

Spring had come soft-footed. The naked trees shivered in winds that still held a chill, but through the damp grass and decaying autumn leaves in the ditches yellow primroses were peeping out. A humid smell, like the odour of fermentation, rose from all over the plain, from farmyards and sodden fields. And a mass of tiny green spikes pushed up out of the brown earth and glittered in the sunlight.

A woman massive in build as a fortress came to take Rosalie's place and supported the baroness in her monotonous walks from one end to the other of her avenue, where a line of continually wet and muddy footprints was left by her uneven tread.

Dear Papa gave his arm to Jeanne, who was heavy now and always ailing; and Aunt Lison, anxiously fussing over the coming event, held her hand on the other side, deeply stirred in the presence of a mystery that she herself would never experience.

They walked together for hours, seldom speaking, while Julien who had acquired a sudden taste for horsemanship rode about the countryside.

Nothing new occurred to disturb their dull existence. The baron, his wife and the viscount paid a call on the Fourvilles, with whom Julien already seemed to have a close acquaintance, although no one knew how this had developed. Another formal call was exchanged with the Brisevilles, still hidden away in their sleeping manor-house.

At about four o'clock one afternoon a man and woman on horseback came trotting up the drive to the château, and Julien came into Jeanne's room in great excitement. 'Make haste! come down at once. The Fourvilles are here. It's just a friendly call, quite informal, as they know about your condition. Tell them that I am out but shall be coming in soon. I'm going to tidy myself up a little.'

Jeanne was surprised at this, and went downstairs. A pale, pretty young woman with a sad face and a look of exaltation in her eyes, with fair hair dull as though no sunbeam had ever caressed it, quietly introduced her husband, a species of giant, an ogre with bristling auburn moustaches. Then she went on: 'We have met Monsieur de Lamare on several occasions. We heard from him how unwell you have been; and, as your neighbours, did not wish to wait any longer before paying you an informal call. As you see, we have come on horseback. I had the pleasure the other day of receiving a call from your mother and the baron.'

She spoke without constraint, well-bred and perfectly at ease. Jeanne was enchanted and adored her at once. 'This is a friend,' she thought.

Count de Fourville, by contrast, was like a bear in a drawing-room. When he seated himself he put his hat on the chair beside him, hesitated some time as to what to do with his hands, placed them on his knees, then on the arms of his chair, and finally linked his fingers as though in prayer.

Presently Julien entered the room. Jeanne, astonished, hardly recognised him. He had shaved. He was as handsome, debonair and charming as he had been when they were engaged. He shook the hairy paw of the count, who seemed to wake up at his appearance, and kissed the countess's hand, at which her ivory cheeks took on a tinge of rose and her eyelids quivered.

He talked. He was engaging, as he used to be. His large eyes, mirrors of love, had their old caressing glance; brushing and perfumed oil had restored his hair, which lately had been so dull and coarse, to its former smooth, shining waves.

The countess turned to him and said, as they were leaving: 'Will you come riding on Thursday, my dear Viscount?'

As he bowed and murmured, 'Indeed I will, Madame,' she took Jeanne's hand and said in a bright, affectionate tone with a friendly smile: 'Oh! when you are well again, we will all three gallop across country. That will be delightful, don't you think?'

With a casual movement she took up the skirt of her habit; then she was in the saddle, light as a bird, while her husband made a clumsy bow and then bestrode his great Norman beast, so erect that man and horse together were like a centaur.

Julien seemed to be greatly taken with them, and exclaimed as they disappeared through the gate: 'What delightful people! It will be useful for us to have their acquaintance.'

Jeanne too was pleased, she hardly knew why, and replied: 'The little countess is charming; I'm sure I shall like her; but the husband looks rather a boor. Where did you meet them?'

He rubbed his hands cheerfully: 'I met them by chance at the Brisevilles's. The husband does seem a little uncouth. He has a mania for sport, but the man's a real aristocrat.'

Dinner was almost a gay meal, as though some secret happiness had stolen into the house.

Nothing further occurred until the end of July.

One Tuesday evening as they were sitting under the plane-tree, round a wooden table with two glasses on it and a decanter of brandy, Jeanne suddenly uttered a cry, turned very pale and pressed both hands to her side. A swift, sharp pain had shot through her, then died away.

Ten minutes later she had another attack of pain, longer although less acute. She reached the house with great difficulty, half carried by her father and husband. The short distance from the plane-tree to her room seemed interminable; and she groaned in spite of herself, begging to stop, to sit down, with an intolerable sensation of weight in her belly.

The child was not expected until September, and this was before her time, so since there was fear of a mishap the trap was brought out, and old Simon went off at a gallop to fetch the doctor.

He arrived about midnight, and at first glance recognized the signs of a premature birth.

In bed, Jeanne's pains had abated slightly, but she now had an agonizing sensation, an almost despairing weakness of her whole being, as though it were a presentiment, a mysterious touch of death. There are moments when it brushes us so close that its breath is chill on the heart.

The room was full of people. Dear Mama had sunk panting

into an armchair. The baron's hands trembled as he rushed to and fro, fetching and carrying, questioning the doctor, losing his head. Julien paced up and down, composed but wearing an expression of concern; and the widow Dentu stood at the foot of the bed with the demeanour appropriate to a woman of experience whom nothing can surprise. Nurse, midwife and watcher by the dead, she received newcomers into this world, heard their first cry, bathed the newborn body for the first time, wrapped it in its first linen cloth; then with the same calmness listened to the last words, the death rattle and the final throes of the dying and dressed them in their last garment, sponging the worn-out body with vinegar and wrapping it in the winding-sheet. Thus she had acquired an unshakeable indifference to all the accidents of birth and death.

Ludivine the cook and Aunt Lison waited discreetly out of sight by the door in the hall.

From time to time the patient uttered a feeble cry.

For two hours it appeared likely that the event would be long in coming; but at daybreak the pains suddenly recommenced, violent at first and soon becoming agonizing.

Jeanne, often scarcely able to stifle a cry between her clenched teeth, thought constantly of Rosalie who had not suffered at all, had uttered hardly a groan when her child, a bastard, had arrived so easily, almost without pain.

Unhappy as she was and confused in mind, she made endless comparisons between the two of them; and she railed against God, whom until then she had believed to be just; she was indignant at the shameless favouritism of fate, and the criminal lies of those who preach honesty and goodness.

At times the spasms of pain were so violent that she was unable to think at all. She no longer had strength, spirit or consciousness for anything but pain.

In the intervals of relief she could not take her eyes away from Julien; and another kind of pain, a pain of the spirit, took possession of her when she remembered how her maidservant had collapsed at the foot of this same bed with her baby between her legs, brother to the little being who was tearing so cruelly at her entrails. Clearly as in the light of noon she recalled her husband's gestures, looks and words as he stood facing that girl lying on the floor; and now she could read him as though his thoughts were recorded in the way he moved, and she observed the same boredom, the same indifference to her as he had shown to the other, the lack of concern of an egoist irritated at being a father.

A terrible convulsion seized her, a spasm of pain so acute that she thought: 'I am going to die. I'm dying!' Then she revolted furiously, inwardly cursing with rage the man who had ruined her life and the unknown child who was killing her.

She made a supreme effort, straining to rid herself of her burden. In a moment she felt her whole womb empty itself; and her pain subsided.

The nurse and the doctor were bending over her, pressing and pulling. They took something away; and presently she was startled to hear a muffled sound, one that she had heard before; and that sad little cry, the faint mewing of a newborn child, penetrated her soul, her heart, her whole exhausted body. With an instinctive movement she tried to hold out her arms.

She was filled with joy, her spirit soared to embrace this happiness newly come into being. In one instant she was released, at peace, and happy as she had never been before. She thrilled in body and soul at the knowledge that she was a mother!

She wanted to see her child! It had no hair or nails, since it was premature; but when she saw that larva move, open its mouth and utter wailing cries, when she touched that crumpled, grimacing, living, puny little creature, she was flooded with intense joy and realized that she was secure now from all despair since she had a love that would occupy her entire being.

From that time she had only one thought: her child. In a single moment she became a fanatical mother, the more so since she had been disappointed in her love and deceived in her hopes. She insisted on having the cradle beside her bed, and as soon as she was able to get up she spent whole days seated at the window, rocking the light crib.

She was jealous of the wet-nurse: when the thirsty little creature put out its hands to the heavy, blue-veined breast and fastened its greedy lips on the brown, wrinkled button of flesh, when she watched the sturdy, calm peasant woman she longed, white and trembling, to tear her son away, to strike and rend with her nails that breast from which he drank so greedily.

She was determined to embroider fine, elaborate garments for him herself. He was swathed in a cloud of lace, and had magnificent bonnets. She talked of nothing else, interrupted conversations to invite people to admire a beautifully worked shawl, a bib or piece of ribbon, hearing nothing of what was said round her, enthusing over scraps of linen as she held them up and turned them round and round to display them; then all at once she would ask: 'Do you think he will look nice in this?'

The baron and dear Mama only smiled at these fond raptures; but Julien, whose everyday habits were interrupted, whose authority and consequence were diminished by the arrival of this squalling, all-powerful tyrant, in unconscious jealousy of this morsel of flesh who was robbing him of his place in the household, exclaimed repeatedly with annoyance: 'How tiresome she is with her brat!'

She soon became so obsessed with the baby that she spent whole nights sitting beside the cradle, watching him as he slept. This passionate absorption was unhealthy and exhausting, and since she now took no rest and was growing weak and thin and starting to cough, the doctor ordered her son to be taken away from her.

She raged, wept, entreated; but her pleading fell on deaf ears. He was left with his nurse at night, and every night his mother rose and went barefoot to listen at the keyhole to hear whether he was sleeping peacefully, or whether he was wakeful and wanted something.

Once Julien found her there when he came home late after dining with the Fourvilles; and after that she was locked in her room so that she would be obliged to go to bed.

The christening took place towards the end of August. The baron was godfather and Aunt Lison godmother. The child was given the names of Pierre Simon Paul; he was to be known as Paul.

Aunt Lison departed without ado at the beginning of September, and her absence, like her presence, went unremarked.

One evening after dinner the priest appeared at the château. He seemed somewhat embarrassed, as though he came with a secret burden, and after a number of insignificant remarks he asked the baroness and her husband to grant him a few minutes' private interview.

The three walked slowly to the end of the main avenue in animated conversation, while Julien, left alone with Jeanne, was surprised, nervous and put out by this secrecy.

He wished to accompany the priest when he took his leave, and they went off together in the direction of the church, where the angelus was ringing.

It was chilly, almost cold, and after a short time the others went back into the drawing-room. They were all half asleep when Julien entered abruptly, red-faced and indignant.

He called out to his parents-in-law from the doorway, without noticing that Jeanne was in the room: 'Have you lost your heads? What the deuce are you thinking of, throwing away twenty thousand on that girl?'

They were too astonished to answer. He went on, bellowing with rage: 'It's perfectly ridiculous; do you mean to leave us without a penny?'

The baron regained his countenance and attempted to check him: 'Be quiet! Remember your wife is present.'

But he stamped his foot in exasperation: 'Upon my soul, I don't give a fig for that; she knows about it, anyway. It's robbery, and she'll be the one to lose by it.'

Jeanne stared at them both in amazement, not understanding. 'What's this about?' she asked.

Then Julien turned to her and called her to witness, as a fellow beneficiary whose interest was affected like his own. He gave her a brief account of the plot to marry off Rosalie with the Barville land as a dowry, worth at least twenty thousand francs. He protested: 'But your parents are mad, my dear, they ought to be restrained! twenty thousand francs! twenty thousand francs! they've taken leave of their senses! twenty thousand francs for a bastard!'

Jeanne listened without emotion, feeling no anger and surprised that she should be so calm, so indifferent now to everything but her child.

The baron was at a loss for words. At last he burst out, tapping his foot: 'Consider what you are saying, it's outrageous. Whose fault is it that this girl-mother needs a dowry? Whose child is it? You'd have been willing to abandon her!'

Julien stared at the baron, astonished by the strength of his feeling. He went on more quietly: 'But fifteen hundred would have been enough. They all have children before they marry. And when they do, it's of no consequence who the man is. If you give away one of your farms to the value of twenty thousand francs, you will not only be depriving us, you will be announcing to all the world what has happened; you ought at least to consider our name and position.'

His tone was severe, as that of a man who takes a firm stand on the justice of his case and the logic of his reasoning. The baron gaped at him, taken aback by this unexpected argument. Then Julien sensed his advantage and stated his conclusions: 'Luckily nothing has been done as yet; I know the lad who is going to marry her, he's a very decent fellow, and we can come to an arrangement with him. I will see to it myself.'

Upon that he left the room, no doubt dreading a prolonged discussion and thankfully taking the general silence to imply consent.

As soon as he had gone the baron, who was trembling with outrage, exclaimed: 'It's too bad, it's too bad!'

But when Jeanne looked up to see her father's shocked

expression she burst out laughing in her old light-hearted way, as she used to laugh at anything she found absurd.

'Oh, Father,' she said to him, 'did you hear how he said it: twenty thousand francs?'

Dear Mama, always as ready to laugh as to cry, was delighted at Jeanne's high spirits and shook with merriment, gasping for breath until tears came into her eyes, at the thought of her son-in-law's furious face, his indignant exclamations and emphatic refusal to allow money which was not his own to go to the girl he had seduced. Her gaiety was infectious and set the baron off in his turn; and all three made themselves almost ill with laughing, as they used to in the old happy days.

When they were somewhat quieter, Jeanne said in surprise: 'It is strange, I don't care about it any more. He's like a stranger to me now. I can't believe that I'm his wife. You see, I find his . . . his want of subtlety . . . amusing.'

For no particular reason they embraced and smiled at each other affectionately.

Two days later after luncheon, just after Julien had set out on horseback, a tall fellow of between twenty-two and twenty-five, wearing a new blue smock still creased at the folds with balloon sleeves buttoned at the wrists, came through the gate as slyly as though he had spent all the morning there in hiding, crept along the Couillards' dyke and round the château, and hesitantly approached the baron and the two women who were still sitting under the plane-tree.

He removed his cap when he saw them and came forward, bowing with an embarrassed air.

As soon as he was close enough to make himself heard he blurted out: 'Your servant, Monsieur le Baron, Madame and company.' Then, as no one spoke, he announced: 'Désiré Lecoq's the name.'

The baron was none the wiser, and asked the visitor: 'What do you want?'

The youth became greatly agitated at the need to explain himself. He looked down and up again several times, from the cap in his hands to the top of the château roof: 'It's His Reverence that dropped a word to me on the subject . . .' He stopped there, in the fear of saying too much and spoiling his chances.

The baron did not understand, and asked: 'On what subject? I know nothing about it.'

Then the other made up his mind and said, speaking more quietly: 'It's about your servant-girl . . . that Rosalie . . .'

Jeanne, who had guessed the reason for his visit, rose with the baby in her arms and left them. The baron pointed to the chair his daughter had occupied and said: 'Come here.'

The peasant sat down at once, murmuring: 'Good of you, I'm sure.' Then he waited as though he had nothing more to say. After a long pause he at last brought himself to speak, and looked up at the blue sky: 'Nice weather for time of year. Good for land, it is, good for seed in the ground.' And he fell silent again.

The baron grew impatient; he broached the subject abruptly, his tone dry:

'So it's you who are going to marry Rosalie?'

The youth, with the habitual deviousness of the Norman, was instantly on his guard. His voice was sharper as he replied with caution: 'That's as maybe; maybe aye, maybe nay; it's as maybe.'

But the baron cut short these tergiversations: 'Confound it! answer me, yes or no: isn't that what you've come to see me about? Will you take her, yes or no?'

The youth looked down at his feet in embarrassment: 'If it's like His Reverence says, I'll take her; but if it's like M'sieur Julien says, I won't.'

'What did Monsieur Julien say to you?'

'He told me I'd get fifteen hundred francs; but His Reverence said it'd be twenty thousand; I'll take her for twenty thousand, but fifteen hundred, that's no use to me.'

The baroness in the depths of her armchair began to shake with breathless laughter at the peasant's anxiety. He glanced at her sidelong, uneasy, not knowing what could have caused such mirth, and waited.

The baron was displeased by this haggling, and put an end to it: 'I have told His Reverence that you'll have the farm of Barville during your lifetime, to revert to the child after your death. It's worth twenty thousand francs. I have only one thing more to say. Do you agree, yes or no?'

The man smiled, humble and contented now, and became suddenly loquacious: 'Oh! well now, I won't say nay to that. There wasn't nothing against it but that. When His Reverence dropped the word to me I'd have agreed there and then, dang me if I wouldn't. "Only too pleased to do a favour for M'sieur le Baron, he'll make it worth my while," I said to myself. That's a fact, isn't it, you do somebody a favour and it always pays you back in the end; it's made up to you somehow. Only when M'sieur Julien came to see me, he said it was only fifteen hundred. I said to myself, "Got to get to the bottom of this," and I came to you. Not to say I didn't trust you, only I had to know. Fair reckonings make good friends, isn't that so, M'sieur le Baron . . .'

He had to be cut short; the baron asked him:

'When is the wedding to be?'

The man became suddenly shy again, overcome with embarrassment. At last he said hesitantly: 'I'll have a bit of paper first, eh?'

This time the baron lost his temper: 'Hang it, man, you'll have your marriage lines. You can't have a better paper than that.'

The peasant persisted: 'A bit of paper, now, to be going on with, there won't be no harm in that.'

The baron stood up, to put an end to it: 'Answer me at once, yes or no. If you don't want it, I know somebody else who will.'

The prospect of a rival worried the crafty Norman and he took fright. He came to a decision, and held out his hand as though to settle the purchase of a cow. 'There's my hand on it, M'sieur le Baron. No going back now.'

The baron shook hands with him, then called: 'Ludivine!' The cook put her head out of the window: 'Bring a bottle of wine.' They clinked glasses and drank to their agreement – and the peasant stepped more lightly as he went away.

Julien was told nothing of his visit. The marriage contract was drawn up in great secrecy, and after the banns had been published the wedding took place on a Monday morning.

A woman neighbour carried the baby to church, following the bridal couple, like an omen of certain good fortune. No one in the neighbourhood showed surprise; people only envied Désiré Lecoq. He was born with a silver spoon in his mouth, they said with knowing grins and entirely without ill feeling.

Julien made a terrible scene, which cut short the stay of his parents-in-law at Les Peuples. Jeanne watched them leave without great regret, for Paul had grown to be an inexhaustible source of happiness to her.

9

WHEN JEANNE HAD FULLY RECOVERED FROM HER confinement, they thought it time to return the Fourvilles' call and also to call on the Marquis de Coutelier.

Julien had just bought a new phaeton at a public auction, choosing a one-horse carriage so that he would be able to drive out twice a month.

The horse was put in harness one fine day in December, and after driving for two hours along the highway across the Normandy plains they came down into a small valley with wooded sides and cultivated land at the bottom.

The ploughed fields soon gave place to meadows, and the meadows to a tract of marsh covered with tall reeds, dry at that time of the year, when the long leaves rustled like yellow streamers.

The road through the valley took a sharp turn, bringing the château of La Vrillette into view, with one wall abutting on the wooded hillside and the whole of the opposite wall standing in a large lake, which extended to the forest of tall fir trees climbing up the further side of the valley.

They drove on over an ancient drawbridge and through a huge Louis XIII portal, to enter the great courtyard of a graceful manor-house of the same period, with brick window frames flanked by slated turrets.

Julien described every part of the building to Jeanne, in the manner of a frequent visitor who knew it well. He did the honours with enthusiasm, going into ecstasies over its beauty: 'Look at that gateway! Isn't it splendid, a mansion like this? The whole of the other façade is on the lake with a ceremonial flight of steps down to the water; and there are four boats moored at the bottom, two for the count and two for the countess. The end of the lake is over there on the right, where you see that screen of poplars; that is where the river rises that runs out to Fécamp. It's full of waterfowl, this place. The count adores shooting over it. This is a real manor-house.'

The entrance door stood open and the countess, pallid and smiling, came out to greet her visitors dressed in a trailing robe like a châtelaine of old times. She looked, indeed, like the lovely Lady of the Lake, born for this fairy-tale manor.

The drawing-room had eight windows, four of which looked out over the water and the sombre firs that scaled the opposite slope.

The dark tones of the green foliage made the lake appear deep, forbidding and gloomy; and when the wind blew the moaning in the trees was like a voice from the marsh.

The countess took Jeanne's hands as though they had been childhood friends, made her be seated and took a low chair beside her while Julien, in whom all his former style had revived in the last five months, smiled and chatted in gentle tones, very much at home.

The countess and he talked of their rides. She lightly mocked his style of horsemanship, calling him 'the stumbling cavalier', and he laughed with her, christening her 'the Amazon queen'. Jeanne was startled by a gunshot under the windows, and gave a little cry. It was the count bringing down a teal.

His wife immediately called to him. They heard the sound of oars, the bump of a boat against stone, and he came into sight, an enormous booted figure followed by two wet dogs, reddish in colour like himself, who lay down on the carpet in front of the door.

He appeared more at ease in his own house, and delighted to have visitors. He had more wood put on the fire, ordered madeira and biscuits to be brought; and suddenly said: 'You will dine with us, of course.' Jeanne, who was always thinking of her child, refused; he insisted, and when she still would not accept Julien made a brusque gesture of impatience. Then she was afraid of provoking him again to an ugly, quarrelsome mood; and although the thought of not seeing Paul until the next day was agony to her, she consented to stay.

They passed a delightful afternoon. First they went to see the springs; these gushed out from the foot of a moss-covered rock into a basin of clear water that bubbled perpetually as though on the boil. Then they were taken in a boat along waterways that were actual paths cut through a forest of dry reeds. The count rowed, seated between his two dogs who sniffed the air; and every stroke of his oars lifted the big boat and sent it flying along. Jeanne dipped her hand in the cold water from time to time and enjoyed the icy chill that ran through her fingers up to her heart. Julien and the countess sat right back in the stern, wrapped in shawls, smiling all the time as people do when they are happy and their contentment needs no expression.

Evening came shivering on icy breezes from the north blowing through the dried-up reeds. The sun had sunk behind the fir trees; and the very look of the red sky, studded with quaint little scarlet clouds, made them feel cold.

They returned to the vast drawing-room where a huge fire was blazing. A pleasant sensation of warmth greeted them as soon as they entered the room. The count was in merry mood, and he picked up his wife in his athlete's arms and lifted her up as though she were a child until her face was level with his own, then planted two fat, contented kisses on her cheeks.

Jeanne smiled as she regarded this kindly giant, who might have been taken for an ogre simply on account of his moustaches; and she thought: 'How mistaken one is, every day, about everybody.' Then her eyes turned almost involuntarily to Julien and she saw him standing in the doorway, deathly pale, staring at the count. In alarm, she went to her husband and asked him in a whisper: 'Are you ill? What's the matter?' He answered angrily: 'Nothing, leave me alone. I was cold.'

When they went into the dining-room the count asked if he might be permitted to have his dogs in; they came at once, to squat on their haunches one each side of their master. He gave them titbits every few minutes, caressing their long silky ears. The animals stretched their necks, wagged their tails and wriggled with contentment.

Jeanne and Julien were preparing to leave after dinner, when Monsieur de Fourville insisted that they should stay to watch fishing by torchlight.

He assigned them their posts, with the countess, on the steps down to the water, and stepped into his boat followed by a manservant holding a net and a lighted torch. It was a clear, sharp night under a gold-studded sky.

The torch sent strange, exciting trails of fire creeping over the water, threw dancing gleams on the reeds, lit up the great curtain of firs. Suddenly the boat came round and a colossal, fantastic shadow the shadow of a man, rose up against the illuminated border of the woods. The head was above the trees, disappearing in the sky, and the feet sank into the lake. Then the enormous apparition raised its arms as though it would lay hold of the stars. They rose swiftly, those huge arms, then dropped again; and at the same moment there was the sound of churned-up water.

When the boat had quietly come round again the prodigious phantom seemed to be running along the woods as the torchlight fell on them, moving with the boat; then it sank into the horizon out of sight, only to reappear with its singular movements, not so large but sharper in outline, on the façade of the château.

A loud shout was heard from the count: 'Gilberte, I've caught eight!'

The oars beat the water. The enormous shadow now rested motionless on the wall, gradually diminishing in height and breadth; its head seemed to fall, its body to grow thin; and when Monsieur de Fourville mounted the steps again, still followed by his servant holding the torch, it was reduced to the proportion of his person and reproduced all his movements.

There were eight big fish thrashing about in the net.

When Jeanne and Julien were on the road, well wrapped up in the coats and rugs which had been lent to them, Jeanne said almost absently: 'What a splendid man he is, that giant!' And Julien, who was driving, replied: 'Yes, but his manners are sometimes too free in company.'

A week later they went to call on the Couteliers, who were regarded as being chief among the provincial nobility. Their estate, Reminil, adjoined the big town of Cany. The new château, built in the reign of Louis XIV, was hidden from view within a magnificent walled park. The ruins of the ancient castle could be seen on a hill nearby. Liveried footmen showed the visitors in to a large, imposing apartment. A Sèvres chalice rested on a sort of pedestal in the middle, with an autographed letter from the king in a crystal case let into the base, inviting the Marquis Léopold-Hervé-Joseph-Germer de Varneville, de Rollebosc de Coutelier to accept this present from the sovereign.

Jeanne and Julien were inspecting this royal gift when the marquis entered with his wife. She was powdered, agreeable as her position required her to be, and affected in manner from a desire to show condescension. The marquis, who was heavily built, with white hair standing stiffly erect, imbued his gestures, voice and whole manner with a haughtiness which announced him as a person of consequence.

They were people who conducted their lives according to

etiquette and seemed to think, feel and speak always on stilts.

They conversed in a monologue, smiling with an air of detachment, as though the function imposed on them by their birth was to spend their lives being pleasant to the lesser gentry of the neighbourhood.

Jeanne and Julien, who were tongue-tied, did their best to please. They felt they should not prolong the call but did not quite know how to bring it to an end; however, their hostess herself did so in the most natural manner, simply by stopping the conversation at the right moment like a queen graciously dismissing them.

As they drove home, Julien said: 'We'll make that the last of our calls, if you don't mind; the Fourvilles will be enough for me.' And Jeanne was of the same opinion.

December, the dark month like a black hole in the bottom of the year, passed slowly. They began to live an indoor existence as they had the year before. Jeanne, however, was continually occupied with Paul and did not find it at all tedious, while Julien eyed the child askance, restless and discontented.

Often when his mother held him in her arms, caressing him in one of those frenzies of tenderness that women have for their children, she would hold him out to his father and say: 'Do give him a kiss; anyone would think you don't love him.' With an air of disgust he brushed the little creature's smooth brow with his lips, arching his body as if to avoid touching the tiny, shrivelled, clawing hands. Then he promptly left the room, as if it was repulsion that drove him away.

The mayor, the doctor and the priest dined with them from time to time; sometimes the Fourvilles came, with whom they were becoming more and more friendly.

The count seemed to adore Paul. He would hold him on his lap all the time when they called, even throughout an afternoon. He handled him delicately with his great giant's hands, tickled the end of his nose with the ends of his long moustache and then in a burst of emotion covered him with kisses like a mother. It was a constant grief to him that there were no children of his marriage.

The weather in March was clear, dry and mild. Countess Gilberte repeated her earlier suggestion that the four of them should ride together. Jeanne, growing a little weary of the long evenings, long nights and long days all monotonously alike, was pleased at the prospect and readily agreed; she passed a pleasurable week in making her riding-habit ready.

Then their outings began. They always rode two by two, the countess and Julien in front, the count and Jeanne a hundred paces behind them. These two conversed tranquilly, like friends, and indeed they came together naturally in friendship, having the same upright natures and simplicity of heart; the leading pair often talked in low voices, occasionally bursting into peals of laughter, exchanging swift glances as though they had to say with their eyes what their lips could not utter; and they would suddenly break into a gallop on an impulse to escape, to fly far, far into the distance.

Then, as it seemed, Gilberte became ill-humoured. Gusts of wind sometimes carried her sharp voice back to the two slower riders in the rear. The count would smile and say to Jeanne: 'My wife is not always in the best of moods.'

One evening as they were riding home the countess was goading her mare, spurring it on and then pulling it back with a jerk of the reins, when they heard Julien say several times: 'Take care, do take care, she'll bolt with you.' She retorted: 'So? It's no concern of yours,' in such a shrill, harsh tone that the words rang out distinctly over the countryside as though they remained suspended in the air.

The animal reared, bucked, foamed at the mouth. A sudden shout of alarm came from the count's powerful lungs: 'Do be careful, Gilberte!' Then, as though in defiance, in one of those feminine bouts of nerves that nothing can control, she struck her mount brutally on the head with her whip and it reared in fury, pawed the air, dropped its forelegs to the ground again and took off with a tremendous bound, galloping over the plain at breakneck speed.

First it covered a stretch of grassland, then plunged on through ploughed fields, churning up the rich moist soil into a cloud of dust and going so fast that mount and rider could hardly be distinguished apart.

Julien stayed where he was, stupefied, shouting in desperation: 'Madame! Madame!'

The count uttered a sort of groan, bent over the neck of his powerful steed and drove it forward with the full weight of his body; and he impelled it to move so fast, urging, pressing, goading it with voice, gesture and spur, that the big cavalier seemed to be carrying the heavy brute between his legs, lifting it up as though they were rising into the air. They covered the ground at incredible speed, hurling themselves forward in an undeviating line; and Jeanne could see the two silhouettes, husband and wife, flying, flying into the distance and growing smaller until they were lost to sight, just as one often sees a pair of birds chasing each other, losing their way and disappearing towards the horizon.

Then Julien rode up at a walk, and muttered angrily: 'She's in a wild mood today.'

They set off together in pursuit of their friends, who were now out of sight in a depression in the plain.

After a quarter of an hour they saw them coming back; and soon they had joined them.

The count was red-faced and perspiring, laughing, pleased, triumphant, and held the rein of his wife's quivering horse in a firm grip. She was pale, and looked unhappy and overwrought; and she supported herself with a hand on her husband's shoulder as though she were on the verge of collapse.

Jeanne realized that day that the count was passionately in love.

For a month afterwards the countess appeared to be happy as she had never been before. She visited Les Peuples more often, was always laughing, embracing Jeanne in sudden bursts of affection. It was as though some mysterious, ecstatic joy had entered her life. Her husband too was happy, his eyes never left her, and he was always seeking to touch her hand or her dress as his passionate love grew stronger.

He said to Jeanne one evening: 'It's a happy time for us just now. Gilberte has never been sweet-tempered like this before. She's never out of humour any longer, never angry. I believe she does love me. I've never been sure of it until now.'

Julien too seemed to be changed, in better spirits, with none of his old impatience, as though the friendship between the two families had brought peace and happiness to both.

Spring was unusually early and warm.

From the mild mornings to the calm evenings the whole surface of the earth germinated in the warm sunshine. All kinds of seeds burgeoned at once with sudden vigour, the sap rising unchecked in that passion for rebirth that nature occasionally manifests in a favoured year, as though the world has rediscovered its youth.

Jeanne found the ferment of life all round her obscurely disturbing. She would feel a sudden languor at the sight of a small wild flower, fall into a delicious melancholy and spend hours in idle reverie.

Then she was filled with fond memories of the early days of her love; not that she felt any renewal of her feeling for Julien: that was over and done with, finished for ever; but her whole body, caressed by the warm air and permeated with the scents of spring, stirred as if in response to a sweet, invisible summons.

She liked to be alone, to revel unrestrained in the warmth of the sun while obscure, peaceful sensations of pleasure transfused her being without prompting her to thought.

She was idling a morning away in this fashion when a vision flashed briefly into her mind of the sunlit gap in the dark foliage of the little wood near Etretat. It was there that she had felt the first tremor at the nearness of the young man who was in love with her; it was there that he had spoken shyly, for the first time, of his heart's desire; there, too, she had believed she was entering the radiant future of her dreams.

She wished to see that place again, to make a sort of

sentimental, superstitious pilgrimage to it, as though to return there would change something in the course of her life.

Julien had set out at dawn; she did not know where he had gone. She ordered the Martins' small grey horse, which she sometimes rode, to be saddled for her; and started off.

It was one of those days so still that there is no movement anywhere, not a blade of grass, not a leaf; it seems that nothing will move again until the end of time, as though the wind had died. Even the insects seem to have disappeared.

A burning, sovereign calm descended from the sun imperceptibly, in a golden haze; and Jeanne, soothed and contented, allowed her nag to go at its own pace. She looked up now and then at a tiny white cloud no bigger than a pinch of cotton wool, a flake of vapour hanging forgotten up there all alone in the middle of the blue sky.

She rode down into the valley which descends to fling itself into the sea through the high arches in the cliff known as the Gates of Etretat, and without haste entered the wood. A shower of light streamed down through the branches, which as yet were hardly in leaf. She wandered along various paths searching for the place, but did not find it.

She was crossing a long ride when she saw two horses at the far end tethered to a tree, and recognized them immediately; they were those of Gilberte and Julien. The solitude was beginning to oppress her; she was glad of this unexpected encounter, and put her horse into a trot.

She rode up to the two animals, which were standing patiently as though accustomed to long waiting, and called out. No one answered.

A woman's glove and two whips lay on the trampled earth. So they had sat there and then gone further away, leaving their horses.

After a quarter of an hour had passed, then twenty minutes, she began to feel surprised and wondered what they could be doing. She had dismounted, and was leaning against a tree, standing without moving, when two small birds flew down and landed on the grass nearby without seeing her. One of them fluttered about, hopping round the other with its wings outspread and quivering, jerking its head and chirruping; and suddenly they coupled.

Jeanne was taken aback, surprised as though she had never known this fact of life; then she said to herself: 'Of course, it's spring;' upon that another thought occurred to her, a suspicion. She looked again at the glove, the whips, the two horses left under the tree; and sprang up to mount her own horse with an overwhelming desire to flee.

She rode back to Les Peuples at a gallop. Her mind was active, reasoning, bringing facts together, assembling circumstances. Why hadn't she guessed before? Why had she seen nothing? How could she have failed to understand Julien's absences, the return to his former elegance, the improvement in his temper? She called to mind also Gilberte's nervous brusqueries, her gushing affection, her recent almost beatific state which so delighted the count.

She reined in her horse to a walk, for she wished to think seriously, and a fast pace made it difficult.

After the shock of discovery her heart quietened until it was almost calm and she felt neither jealousy nor hatred, only a stirring of contempt. She scarcely thought of Julien; nothing in him could surprise her any longer; but she was outraged by the double treachery of the countess, her friend. Everyone, then, was faithless, lying, false. Tears came into her eyes. We sometimes mourn a lost illusion as deeply as we mourn the dead.

She decided however to feign ignorance, close her mind to Julien's present attachment and love no one but Paul and her parents; and to bear with the others, keeping a serene countenance.

As soon as she was in the house again she snatched up her son, bore him off into her room and covered him with distracted kisses for an hour on end.

Julien came home to dinner, all charm, smiles and good intentions. He inquired: 'Are Papa and dear Mama not coming to us this year?'

She was so grateful to him for showing her such consideration that she almost forgave him for what she had discovered in the wood; and since she now passionately longed to see as soon as possible the two beings she loved most after Paul, she passed the whole evening in writing to them to hasten their arrival.

They were proposing to return to Les Peuples on May 20th. It was then the 7th of the month.

She awaited them with growing impatience as though she felt a new need even beyond her filial love for them, the need of her heart to be in contact with hearts that were sound and true, the need to converse openly and without reserve with clean-living people free from all that was ignoble, whose lives had been always upright in thought, deed and desire.

She felt now that her conscience stood in a sort of isolation among all the others that had given way. Although she had quickly learnt to dissimulate, and although she welcomed the countess with outstretched hand and smiling lips, the sensation of emptiness, of contempt for people, seemed increasingly to take possession of her; and every day the small items of local news filled her with greater distaste, a loftier disdain for humankind.

The Couillards' daughter had just had a child and the marriage was about to take place. The Martins' servantgirl, an orphan, was in the family way; a little neighbour of fifteen also; and a widow, a poor, wretched, lame woman of such foul condition that she was known as the Cowpat, even she was with child.

Every minute brought news of another pregnancy or else of an escapade by some girl, by the mother of a family even, or a wealthy and respected farmer.

In the ardour of that spring the sap seemed to be stirring in men as well as in plants.

Jeanne, whose dulled senses were no longer aroused, whose bruised heart and sentimental soul seemed to respond only to the warm breath of fecundity, who was a rapt and impassioned dreamer empty of desire and dead to the needs of the flesh – she was astounded by this bestiality, filled with a repugnance for it which turned to loathing.

The coupling of creatures shocked her now as though it were something unnatural; and if she held anything against Gilberte it was not in the least that she had taken her own husband away, but simply that she too had let herself fall into that universal mire.

The countess was by no means a woman of peasant stock, of those in whom the lower instincts are dominant. How could she have yielded herself like one of the brute creation?

On the very day when Jeanne's parents were to arrive, Julien again made her recoil by relating to her gaily, as something quite natural and amusing, how the baker had heard a slight noise from his oven the day before, which was not a baking day. Expecting to catch a thieving cat, he opened the door and found his wife inside, and she 'was not putting bread in the oven'.

He added: 'The baker stopped up the opening; they were nearly suffocated in there; it was the baker's little boy who told the neighbours; he had seen his mother going in with the blacksmith.'

Julien laughed as he said: 'They'd make us eat the bread of love, those clowns. It's a real La Fontaine tale.'

After that Jeanne shrank from touching bread.

When the post-chaise pulled up in the drive with the baron's cheerful face at the window a profound emotion welled up in the young woman's breast, a passionate surge of affection such as she had never felt before.

She was shocked almost to fainting, however, when she saw dear Mama. In those six months of winter the baroness had aged ten years. Her large, flabby, drooping cheeks were purple as if swollen with blood; her eyes were dull; she could move only with support under both arms; her breath came with a painful wheeze, and with such difficulty that it was distressing to come near her.

The baron, who saw her every day, had not remarked this change in her; and when she complained of her constant shortness of breath and increasing weight he only said in reply: 'No, no, my dear, you have been the same ever since I have known you.'

After Jeanne had taken them to their room she retired to her own and wept, troubled and bewildered. Then she went to her father again and threw herself on his breast, her eyes still full of tears: 'Oh! How Mother has changed! What is the matter with her, tell me, what is it?' He was greatly surprised, and replied: 'Has she? Do you think so? I can't agree with you. I have never left her side, and I assure you I see nothing wrong, she is just the same as usual.'

Julien said to his wife that evening: 'Your mother is in a bad way. I think there's something seriously wrong with her,' whereupon Jeanne burst into tears and he lost patience: 'Oh, come now, I am not saying there's no hope. You always rush to conclusions. She's changed, that's all, it's her age.'

After a week she thought no more about it and became accustomed to her mother's altered features, suppressing her fears perhaps in the way that some egoistic instinct always leads us to reject or suppress any apprehension or anxiety which threatens our peace of mind.

The baroness could scarcely walk, and her daily outing was no longer than half an hour. After she had walked once to the end of 'her' avenue she could not move again, and demanded to rest on 'her' seat. When she felt unable to complete the full length she would say: 'Let us stop now: my hypertrophy is too much for my legs today.'

She laughed seldom now, merely smiling at things which a year ago would have made her shake all over with mirth. Her sight remained excellent, however, and she spent days rereading *Corinne* or Lamartine's *Meditations*; then she asked for the 'souvenir drawer' to be brought to her. She would empty the old, cherished letters into her lap, place the drawer on a chair beside her and replace her 'relics' in it one by one after slowly looking at each. When she was alone, quite alone, she kissed one or two, as one drops a secret kiss on the hair of a loved one who has died.

Sometimes Jeanne would come in unexpectedly and find her mother in tears, tears of sorrow. She would ask: 'What is it, dear Mama?' And the baroness would reply after a long sigh: 'It is my relics. They make me remember things, good things of the past which are over now! And then, there are people you seldom think of any more, and suddenly they are with you again. You think you see them and hear them, and it is dreadfully affecting. You'll find that out for yourself one day.'

When the baron entered the room on one of these melancholy occasions, he whispered to Jeanne: 'Jeanne, my dearest, if you'll listen to me you will burn your letters, all your letters, your mother's, mine, all of them. There's nothing worse than dipping into one's youth again when one is old.' But Jeanne too was keeping her correspondence, preparing her 'box of relics'. Unlike her mother though she was in all respects, in this she obeyed a sort of inherited instinct of dreamy sentimentality.

A few days later the baron was called away on business.

The weather was magnificent. Mild starry nights followed calm evenings, serene evenings succeeded to brilliant days and glorious days to dazzling dawns. Dear Mama soon felt better; and Jeanne forgot about Julien's amours and Gilberte's perfidy and was happy, with scarcely a care in her head. The whole countryside was fragrant with blossom; and the wide, tranquil sea glittered under the sun from dawn until dusk.

One afternoon Jeanne took Paul in her arms and went out into the meadows. She gazed at her son, then at the grass by the roadside flecked with flowers, and her spirit seemed to dissolve in infinite bliss. She kissed the child every other moment, clasping him passionately to her breast; and turned faint at a whiff of some pungent country odour, with a sense of boundless well-being. Then she fell to dreaming about his future. What would that be? At times she wished for him to be great, famous, powerful. On the other hand she would like him to live modestly, staying at her side, devoted and affectionate, his arms always open to mama. When she loved him selfishly, as a mother, she wished for him to remain her son, nothing more than her son; but in the light of reason she was passionately ambitious for him to make his mark in the world.

She sat down by the wayside and regarded him. She felt that she had never seen him, actually seen him, before. It came to her with a shock of surprise that one day that tiny creature would be grown up, walk with a firm step, grow hair on his face and speak in a deep voice.

Somebody was calling to her from a distance. She looked up. It was Marius, running towards her. She supposed there must be someone come to pay a call and rose to her feet, vexed at being disturbed. The lad was running as fast as he could, and as soon as he was close enough to be heard he called out: 'Madame, it's Madame la Baronne, she's been taken bad.'

It was like drops of cold water trickling down her spine; her thoughts raced, her mind was in chaos, and she started back to the house with long strides.

From a distance she saw people in a group under the plane-tree. She hastened forward, they made way for her and she beheld her mother lying on the ground, her head raised on two pillows. Her face had darkened, her eyes were closed, her breast was motionless after twenty years of gasping for breath. The baby's nurse took her charge from the young woman's arms and bore it away.

Wildly, Jeanne asked: 'What has happened? How did she fall? Send for the doctor.' She turned and saw the priest; he had heard what had happened, how, no one knew. He rolled up the sleeves of his cassock and zealously offered his services. Vinegar, eau de Cologne and chafing had no effect. 'She should be undressed and put to bed,' the good father advised.

Farmer Joseph Couillard was there, with old Simon and Ludivine. With Father Picot's help they tried to lift the baroness; but when they raised her up her head fell back and her dress tore in their grasp, her huge body was so heavy and difficult to move. Jeanne exclaimed in protest. The big, soft body was laid on the ground again.

A chair had to be fetched from the drawing-room; and after she had been seated in it they found it possible to lift her. Step by step they mounted the flight at the entrance, then the stairway; they carried her into her room and laid her down on the bed.

While the cook was taking an interminable time to undress her the widow Dentu arrived, like the priest appearing suddenly at precisely the right moment, as though they had both 'smelt a death' as the servants say.

Joseph Couillard rode off at full gallop to call the doctor; when the priest was about to go and bring the holy oil, the nurse whispered in his ear: 'Don't trouble yourself, Your Reverence, I understand these things – she's passed away.'

Jeanne pleaded with them, distraught, not knowing what to do, what treatment or remedy to apply. The priest thought it best, in the circumstances, to pronounce absolution.

They waited two hours beside the empurpled, lifeless body. Jeanne had fallen to her knees and was sobbing her heart out with anguish and grief.

When the door opened and the doctor came in she expected to see salvation, consolation and hope enter with him; she hastened to meet him, pouring out all that she knew of the accident: 'She was walking as she does every day . . . she was quite well . . . very well, even . . . she had taken some soup and two eggs at luncheon . . . suddenly she fell down . . . she turned black, as you see . . . never moved again . . . we tried everything to revive her . . . everything . . .' She stopped, as the nurse made a discreet sign to the doctor to convey that it was over, all over. Refusing to understand, she repeated anxiously: 'Is it serious? Do you think it is serious?'

At last he said: 'I am very much afraid that it is . . . that it is . . . over. You must be brave, very brave.'

Jeanne put out her arms and flung herself on her mother.

Julien returned. He looked astonished, visibly put out, and did not exclaim or give any sign of grief; he had been taken too suddenly unawares to arrange his features and assume an expression proper to the occasion. He murmured: 'I was expecting this, I knew it must be the end.' He pulled out a handkerchief and wiped his eyes, knelt, crossed himself, muttered something and rose to his feet again, then tried to raise his wife also. She was clasping the corpse in her arms and kissing it, almost lying on it. She had to be taken away. It was as though she were out of her mind.

After an hour she was allowed to return. No hope remained. The apartment had been turned into a mortuary chamber. Julien and the priest were talking in low voices at a window. The widow Dentu was seated comfortably in an armchair, as a woman who is accustomed to keeping vigil and feels at home in a house which death has visited; she appeared to be already half asleep.

Darkness fell. Father Picot went to Jeanne, took her hands and spoke some words of encouragement, pouring on that inconsolable heart a smooth-flowing wave of priestly consolation. He praised the dead woman in the language of his office and, assuming the hypocritical grief of a parish priest who stands to gain from a death, he offered to pass the night in prayer beside the body.

But Jeanne, in convulsions of sobs, refused. She wished to be alone, entirely alone for that night of farewell. Julien came forward: 'But you cannot do that, we'll stay here together.' She could not speak, but shook her head in refusal. At last she managed to say: 'She's my mother, my mother. I want to be alone to watch with her.' The doctor whispered: 'Let her do as she wishes, the nurse can stay in the next room.'

The priest and Julien agreed, thinking of their beds. Then Father Picot knelt and prayed, rose again and went out, saying: 'She was a saint,' in the same way as he would have said '*Domine vobiscum.*'

Then the viscount asked in his ordinary voice: 'Will you take a little food?' Jeanne did not realize that he was speaking to her, and made no answer. He went on: 'It would be better perhaps if you could eat something, to sustain you.' She answered distractedly: 'Do send for Papa, send for him immediately.' And he went out to order somebody to ride to Rouen.

She remained motionless, sunk in grief, as though she had waited to be alone with her mother for the last time before abandoning herself to a rising tide of despairing regret.

Darkness had come into the room, veiling the dead woman in shadows. The widow Dentu began moving about with her light step, picking up and tidying away invisible objects with the soundless movements of a nurse. Then she lit a pair of candles and quietly placed them on the table covered with a white cloth at the head of the bed.

Jeanne appeared to see nothing, feel nothing, take nothing in. She was waiting to be alone. Julien returned; he had dined; again he asked her: 'Won't you take anything?' His wife simply shook her head.

He took a chair, looking resigned rather than sorrowful, and did not speak.

They sat motionless, all three, a little apart from each other.

Occasionally the nurse fell asleep and began to snore, then awoke with a start.

At last Julien rose and went to Jeanne: 'Would you like to be alone?' She took his hand in an impulsive gesture: 'Yes, I should, do let me.'

He kissed her on the forehead, murmuring: 'I'll come to see you now and again.' He went out with the widow Dentu, who pushed her armchair into the adjoining room.

Jeanne shut the door, then went to fling open both windows. The warm caress of an evening after haymaking met her full in the face. The lawn had been mown the day before, and the cut grass lay out in the moonlight.

That sweet breath of the night was hurtful, wounding as though it mocked her.

She turned back to the bed, took one of the cold inert hands in hers and began to think about her mother.

The flesh was no longer swollen as it had been at the time of the attack; the baroness seemed to be sleeping more peacefully now than ever before, and the pale candle flames, wavering in occasional puffs of wind, kept the shadows on her face in continual movement so that she seemed to be alive, as though she herself had moved.

Jeanne gazed earnestly at her; and a host of memories came tumbling up from the depths of her childhood.

She recalled dear Mama's visits to the convent parlour, the way in which she had held out a paper bag full of cakes, a hundred small details and facts, little endearments, words, inflections, familiar gestures, the wrinkles round her eyes when she laughed and her deep gasping sigh as she sank into a chair.

She remained there deep in thought, repeating in a sort of daze 'She is dead'; and the full horror of that word was revealed to her.

She who lay there – Mama – dear Mama – Madame Adélaïde, was dead. She would never move or speak again, never laugh again or sit opposite dear Papa at dinner; she would never again say: 'Good morning, Jeannette.' She was dead!

She would be nailed down in a box and buried, and that would be the end. They would never see her again. Was it possible? She would no longer have a mother? That dear familiar face that she had seen when she opened her eyes for the first time, loved since she first held out her arms, that outlet for so much tender feeling, that unique being, the mother, who means more to us at heart than anyone on earth – she had gone. No more than a few hours remained to look on that face, motionless now and void of thought; and then nothing, nothing ever again but a memory.

She fell on her knees in a terrible access of despair; clutching and twisting the sheet in her hands, with her mouth pressed to the bed she cried out in a rending voice muffled by the sheets: 'Oh! Mama, dearest Mama, Mama!'

She felt as though she were going mad, mad as she had been that night when she fled through the snow; and she rose and ran to the window to gain relief, to drink in fresh air away from that bed, not the air of death.

The mown grass, the trees, the heath and the sea in the distance lay peaceful in repose, silently sleeping under the moon's gentle spell. A little of that soothing calm entered Jeanne's spirit and tears came slowly into her eyes.

Then she returned to sit by the bed, taking dear Mama's hand in her own as though she were watching by her mother's sickbed.

A large insect had flown into the room, attracted by the candle-light. It beat against the walls like a ball, flying from one end of the room to the other. The humming sound disturbed Jeanne and she turned to look at it; but she never saw anything but a shadow straying over the white ceiling.

She soon ceased to hear it. Then she became aware of the soft ticking of the clock and another, tiny sound, a hardly perceptible rustling. Dear Mama's watch, which had been left in her dress on a chair at the foot of the bed, was still going. Suddenly a vague association between the dead woman and the still-moving mechanism reawakened the pain in Jeanne's heart.

She looked at the time. It was not yet half past ten; and panic seized her at the thought of passing the whole night in that room.

Other memories came back to her: those of her own life – Rosalie, Gilberte – her moments of bitter disillusion. There was nothing, then, but sorrow, calamity and death. All things betrayed, all things lied and brought one to suffering and tears. Where could one find a little rest, a little happiness? In another life, perhaps! when the soul was delivered from the ordeals of this earth. The soul! She began to ponder that unfathomable mystery, eagerly seizing on poetic ideas which other theories no less vague promptly overthrew. Where, then, was her mother's soul now? the soul of that rigid, immobile body? Possibly a long way away. Somewhere in space? But where? Evaporated like the scent of a dried flower? or wandering about like an invisible bird escaped from its cage?

Recalled to God? or dispersed at random among newly created things, mingled with seeds about to germinate?

Very close, perhaps? In this room, near the inanimate flesh from which it had just departed! At that moment Jeanne thought she felt something brush lightly against her, a breath, a phantom touch. It frightened her! She was in such terror that she no longer dared to move or breathe, or turn to look behind her. Her heart beat wildly.

The invisible insect suddenly resumed its flight, dashing itself against the walls as it whirled round and round. She shuddered from head to foot, then realized with relief it was the winged creature humming, and rose and turned round. Her eyes came to rest on the writing desk with the sphinx heads, the piece of furniture which contained the relics.

A curious, fond thought occurred to her; during this last vigil she would read, as she would a sacred book, those old letters that the dead woman had cherished. By doing this, it seemed to her, she would be performing a delicate, sacred and truly filial task, one that would give pleasure to dear Mama in the other world.

It was the old correspondence of her grandfather and grandmother, whom she had never known. She would have liked to hold out her arms to them over their daughter's body, to go to them on that night of mourning as though they were suffering as she was, to form something like a mysterious chain of affection between those who had died long ago, the one who had just departed in her turn, and herself left still on earth.

She rose, pulled down the flap of the writing desk and took out a dozen small packets of yellowed paper from the bottom drawer, tied into neat bundles lying side by side.

She carried them over to the bed and in a refinement of sensibility placed them between the arms of the baroness; then she started to read.

They were old letters of the sort one finds in desks which have been long in the family, letters with the scent of long ago.

The first began: 'My darling.' Another, 'My beautiful grand-daughter', then it was 'My dear little girl' – 'My pet' – 'My beloved daughter' then 'My dear child' – My dear Adélaïde' – 'My dear daughter', according to whether they were addressed to the little girl, the young girl, or, later, the young woman.

They were all full of fond, childish endearments, a hundred intimate trifles, the humdrum yet important family events which have so little importance for those who are not affected by them: 'Papa has influenza; the maid Hortense has burnt her finger; the cat Croquerat is dead; the pine tree on the right-hand side of the gate has been cut down; mother lost her prayer-book on the way back from church, she thinks it was stolen.'

People were mentioned too whom Jeanne did not know, but whose names she vaguely remembered hearing long ago when she was a child.

She was moved by these details, which appeared to her as revelations; she felt that she had entered suddenly into all dear Mama's past, secret life, the life of the heart. She regarded the body lying at rest; and she began to read aloud, reading to the dead woman as though to entertain or console her.

The corpse, immobile, appeared content.

She tossed the letters one by one to the end of the bed, and the thought came to her that they ought to be placed in the coffin, like flowers.

She unfastened another packet. This was in a different handwriting. She began: 'I can no longer live without your caresses. I love you to distraction.'

Nothing more; no name.

She turned the paper over, uncomprehending. It was, indeed, addressed to Madame la Baronne Le Perthuis des Vauds.

She opened the next: 'Come this evening as soon as he has gone out. We'll have an hour together. I adore you.'

In another: 'I have passed a night in delirium, aching for you in vain. I had your body in my arms, your mouth beneath my lips, your eyes gazing into mine. And then I was in such a rage that I could have thrown myself out of the window, to think that at that very hour you were sleeping at his side, that he could possess you at will . . .'

Dumbfounded, Jeanne could not understand.

What did it mean? To whom, for whom, from whom were those words of love?

She went on, coming upon more and more wild protestations, and assignations accompanied by warnings to be prudent, always ending with the words: 'Be sure to burn this letter.'

Finally she opened a banal note in the same handwriting accepting an invitation to dinner, signed: 'Paul d'Ennemare', someone whom the baron called 'poor old Paul' when he spoke of him and whose wife had been the baroness's closest friend.

A suspicion entered Jeanne's mind and immediately became a certainty. He had been her mother's lover.

In the shock of that moment, with her mind in turmoil she pushed the shameful bundles of paper away from her as she would have brushed some poisonous insect from her person, ran to the window and burst into rending sobs that tore at her throat; then she crouched at the foot of the wall in a state of utter collapse, burying her face in the curtain so that no one should hear her moans, and wept in a fathomless abyss of despair.

She might have passed the whole night in that condition; but the sound of footsteps in the next room made her spring to her feet. Perhaps it was her father? Those letters were on the bed and scattered all over the floor! He would need to open only one! Then he would know! He!

She dashed forward and gathered up all the old yellowed papers in handfuls, the grandparents' and the lover's, those she had not unfolded and the others still in bundles in the drawers of the writing-desk, and threw them all into the fireplace in a heap. Then she took one of the candles burning on the night-table and set fire to the pile of letters. A great flame blazed up to throw a bright dancing light over the room, the bed and the corpse, drawing a flickering silhouette in black on the white curtain at the foot of the bed, a shadow of the rigid features and the massive body beneath the sheet.

When nothing was left in the hearth but a heap of ashes she went back to sit by the open window, as though she dared not stay any longer beside the dead woman, and burying her face in her hands she began to weep again, moaning in a heart-broken, desolate lament: 'Oh! poor Mama, oh! poor Mama!'

A terrible thought entered her mind: Suppose it should turn out that dear Mama was not dead but only sleeping heavily, suppose she should suddenly sit up and speak? Would not she love her mother less for knowing that dreadful secret? Would she be able to kiss her as affectionately as before? Would her mother be as sacred to her, would she care for her as dearly, now? No. It was not possible! and the thought of it cut her to the heart.

The night was drawing to an end; the stars were growing dim; it was the cold hour before dawn. The moon descending turned all the surface of the sea to mother-of-pearl as it sank into the waves.

Jeanne was reminded vividly of that night she had passed at the window when she first came to Les Peuples. How far away it seemed, how much everything had changed, how different the future appeared!

Now the sky was turning to rose, a charming and joyful hue, the very hue of love. She marvelled as she gazed at the radiant birth of a day as though it were a remarkable event, and wondered if it were possible that there could be no joy or happiness on an earth where dawns like this were breaking.

A sound at the door startled her. It was Julien. He inquired: 'Well? You are not too tired?'

She murmured, 'No,' glad not to be alone any longer. 'Do go now and rest,' he said. She kissed her mother slowly and sadly, with deep feeling, and returned to her own room.

The day passed in performing those melancholy tasks made necessary by a death. The baron arrived in the evening. He wept copiously.

The funeral took place the next day.

After Jeanne had touched the cold forehead with her lips for the last time, dressed and put the final touches to the corpse and seen it nailed down in the coffin, she retired. Soon the guests would arrive.

Gilberte was the first to come, and flung herself weeping into her friend's arms.

They watched from the window as the carriages turned in at the gate and came on at the trot. Voices resounded in the great hall. Gradually the room filled with women in black whom Jeanne had never met before. The Marquise de Coutelier and the Viscountess de Briseville both kissed her.

Suddenly she saw Aunt Lison making her way to stand behind her. She clasped her affectionately in her arms, at which the spinster almost swooned.

Julien came in, a distinguished figure in deep mourning, full of activity, and gratified by the presence of so much affluence. He spoke to his wife in a low voice, asking her advice on some question. He added in a confidential tone: 'All the nobility have come, it will look very well.' He went out again after making a stately bow to the ladies.

Aunt Lison and Countess Gilberte alone stayed with Jeanne while the funeral ceremony was taking place. The countess embraced her repeatedly, saying over and over again: 'Poor darling, you poor darling!'

When the Count de Fourville came back to fetch his wife, he was weeping as though he had lost his own mother.

10

THE DAYS THAT FOLLOWED WERE SAD, WITH the gloom of a house that seems empty when a familiar presence has gone from it for ever, and when the sight or touch of an object constantly handled by the departed brings a stab of pain. Memories incessantly recur, bringing heartache with them. There is her chair, her parasol still in the hall, her glass that the maid has not put away! Things are left lying about in every room: her scissors, a glove, a volume with pages worn by the increasing weight of her fingers, and a thousand trifles that take on a sad significance because they bring a thousand small incidents back to mind.

Her voice pursues you; you think you hear it; you want to run away, go anywhere to escape the haunting of that house. You are obliged to stay because others do, and they suffer likewise.

Besides, Jeanne was still haunted by her discovery. The thought of it was a burden to her; her crushed spirit would not heal. The horrid secret made her even more lonely than before. With this last betrayal the last of her confidence had gone.

Papa soon began to feel the need to bestir himself, to have a change of air and break out of the black grief into which he was sinking more and more deeply, and he went away.

The big house, which from time to time saw one of its masters disappear in this way, resumed its peaceful, orderly existence.

Then Paul fell ill. Jeanne was out of her mind with anxiety, did not sleep for twelve days and ate scarcely at all.

He recovered; but she was terrified at the thought that he might die. What would she do if that should happen? What would become of her? Gradually, obscurely, she began to feel in her heart the need to have another child. Soon she was dreaming of it, as the old desire came over her to possess two small beings of her own, a boy and a girl. Before long it became an obsession.

Since the affair of Rosalie, however, she and Julien had kept apart. It seemed impossible that they should come together again, situated as they were at present. Julien loved another; Jeanne knew it, and the very thought of submitting to his caresses again made her tremble with revulsion.

Nonetheless she would have resigned herself to it in her ardent desire to become a mother again; but how could they start to embrace each other as they used and renew their old relationship? She would have died of humiliation before revealing her intentions; and he, it appeared, no longer thought of her.

She might perhaps have abandoned the idea; but now she dreamed of a daughter every night; she saw her playing with

Paul under the plane-tree; and sometimes she would feel a restless longing to leave her bed and, without uttering a word, go to her husband in his room. Twice she even crept as far as his door; then quickly returned, her heart beating fast with shame.

The baron had gone away; dear Mama was dead; now there was no one whom Jeanne could consult, to whom she could confide her most intimate secrets.

At last she resolved to go and see Father Picot and under the seal of the confessional tell him her hopes and the difficulties in her way.

She found him reading his breviary in his small orchard.

After they had talked for a few minutes on different subjects she said nervously, blushing: 'I wish to make my confession, Father.'

Astonished, he raised his spectacles to regard her closely; then he burst out laughing. 'But you cannot have any serious sins on your conscience.' She replied, in great confusion: 'No, but I wish to ask your advice, about . . . about something I should find too . . . find it painful to speak of in the ordinary way.'

He instantly abandoned his air of good-fellowship and assumed his priestly manner: 'Very well, my child, I will hear you in the confessional; come along.'

But she kept him back, suddenly hesitant, from a sort of scruple over approaching so indelicate a topic in the quiet of an empty church.

'Or perhaps I will not . . . Father . . . I can . . . I can . . . if you wish . . . tell you now why I have come to see you. Shall we go and sit over there, in your little arbour?'

Slowly they walked over to it. She was trying to find the words to express herself, how to broach the subject. They seated themselves.

She began as though she were making her confession: 'Father . . .' then hesitated, repeated: 'Father . . .' and fell silent, in great confusion.

He waited, his crossed hands resting on his stomach.

Observing her embarrassment, he encouraged her: 'Well, my daughter, it seems you can't bring yourself to do it; come now, take courage.'

She said resolutely, like a coward rushing into danger: 'Father, I wish to have another child.' He did not understand, and said nothing. Nervous and at a loss for words, she tried to explain herself.

'I am alone in the world now; my father and my husband don't get on; my mother is dead; and . . . and . . .' she shuddered as she said very quietly: 'Not long ago I almost lost my son! What should I have done then? . . .'

She was silent. The good man regarded her in perplexity.

'Come now, what is all this about?'

She repeated: 'I wish to have another child.' He smiled at that, accustomed as he was to the coarse jests of peasants who were scarcely ever bashful with him, and answered with a knowing wag of the head:

'Well, I should think that depends only on yourself.'

She raised candid eyes to his, then stammered in confusion: 'But . . . but . . . you see, since . . . since . . . the trouble with that girl . . . my husband and I do not . . . we live . . . we live quite apart from each other.'

The parish priest, with his experience of the promiscuous conduct and lack of dignity in rural life, was astonished by this revelation; then suddenly he thought he could guess what the young woman really desired. He gave her a sidelong glance full of benevolence and sympathy for her distress: 'Yes; I understand perfectly. I can see that your . . . your "widowhood" lies heavy on you. You are young, healthy. Well, it is natural, only too natural.'

He smiled again, broad in speech as he was broad in mind, like many a country priest; he tapped Jeanne's hand gently: 'It is permitted, even sanctioned, in the Commandments: "Thou shalt not desire the fruits of the flesh except in marriage." You are a married woman, are you not? There's nothing to trouble your head about.'

Now it was she who did not immediately understand what

he was hinting; but when his meaning did penetrate to her she blushed crimson, deeply shocked, and tears came to her eyes.

'Oh! Father, what are you saying? and what are you thinking? I swear . . . I swear . . .' And she choked with sobs.

He was surprised; he tried to reassure her: 'Now, now, I didn't mean to upset you. I was only having my little joke; that's not forbidden to honest folk. But leave it to me; you may count on me. I will see Monsieur Julien.'

She did not know what to say. She feared that the priest's intervention might be clumsy and dangerous and would have liked to refuse it, but she did not dare; and after a murmured 'Thank you, Father,' she made her escape.

A week passed. She lived in a fever of anxiety.

One evening at dinner Julien looked at her in a singular fashion, pursing his lips in a smile as she had seen him do when he was in a teasing mood. He even behaved to her with a sort of gallantry that was faintly mocking; and later as they were walking in dear Mama's avenue he whispered in her ear: 'It seems we have made things up.'

She did not answer. She was looking at the trace of a straight line on the ground, almost invisible now that the grass had grown again. It was the imprint of the baroness's footsteps, effaced just as memory is effaced. Jeanne's heart seemed to contract under a wave of sorrow; she felt lost in life, so far away from everyone.

Julien continued: 'There's nothing I should like better myself. I only feared to displease you.'

The sun was declining, the air was mild. Jeanne felt a strong desire to weep, in the need to unburden herself to a sympathetic heart and whisper her woes in the shelter of an embrace. A sob rose to her throat. She held out her arms and flung herself on Julien's breast.

She wept. He looked down at her in surprise, but her face was hidden and he could see nothing but her hair. He thought that she still loved him, and dropped a condescending kiss on her curls.

They went indoors without speaking again. He followed her to her room and they spent the night together.

Thus their former relations recommenced. He played his part as though performing a not unpleasant duty; and she submitted as to a nauseating and painful necessity, one that she was determined to end for ever as soon as she was sure that she was once more with child.

She soon became aware however that her husband's caresses were not the same as they had been before. They had perhaps more finesse, but were less complete. He behaved to her more as a clandestine lover than a settled spouse.

She began, in some surprise, to mark carefully what took place between them and soon realized that his embraces always stopped short of impregnating her.

One night she murmured with her lips close to his: 'Why don't you give yourself to me completely, as you used to do?'

He answered with a snigger: 'Why, dash it, I don't want to put you in the family way.'

She winced at that: 'But why, don't you want more children?'

He was dumbfounded: 'Eh? What do you say? Are you out of your mind? Another child? Never, upon my soul! There's one too many here already, bawling, wasting everyone's time, costing money. Another child! no, thank you!'

She took him in her arms, kissed him, enfolded him in love and whispered: 'Oh! I implore you, make me a mother again!'

He was angry, as though she had actually injured him: 'Really, you're out of your mind. You are talking nonsense – pray spare me any more of it.'

She said no more, but vowed to trick him into giving her the happiness she dreamed of.

She tried after that to prolong her kisses in a make-believe of passionate desire, holding him close with both arms in pretended transports of passion. She employed every ruse, but he remained in control of himself and never once forgot.

Her desire for a child obsessed her more and more until at last, driven to desperation and ready to face anything, dare anything, she went back to Father Picot.

He was finishing luncheon; he was deeply flushed, for he always had palpitations after meals. As soon as he saw her come in he called to her: 'Well?' anxious to know the result of his mediation.

Resolute now and no longer bashful, she answered at once: 'My husband does not wish to have more children.' The father turned towards her, his interest fully aroused, prepared to pry with a priest's curiosity into those mysteries of the bedchamber which made the confessional so agreeable to him. He asked: 'How is that?' Then, in spite of her determination, she found it distressing to explain: 'He refuses to make me a mother.'

The priest understood, he had heard about such things; and he began to question her in precise and minute detail, with the greed of someone fasting.

Then he considered for a few moments, and in a matter-of-fact voice as though he were remarking that the harvest was going well he outlined a cleverly contrived line of conduct for her, settling every point: 'There's only one thing to do, my dear child, and that is to make him believe that you are pregnant. Then he won't be so careful, and you will, in fact, become so.'

She blushed to the roots of her hair; but she persisted, determined to see it through: 'And . . . and suppose he does not believe me?'

The priest well knew the stratagems by which men can be led and held to a course of action: 'Announce your pregnancy to everyone, talk about it everywhere; in the end he will believe it too.'

Then as though to absolve himself from having given this counsel: 'It is your right, for the Church does not tolerate relations between a man and woman except for the purpose of procreation.'

She followed this shrewd advice, and a fortnight later

announced to Julien that she thought she was pregnant. He started in surprise. 'Impossible! it cannot be true.'

She immediately told him the grounds for her suspicion but he dismissed them. 'Pshaw! Wait a little. You will see.'

Then every morning he inquired: 'Well?' And she always answered: 'No, not yet. I am greatly mistaken if I'm not with child.'

Now it was he who was anxious, as angry and perturbed as he was surprised. He kept repeating: 'I can't understand it, can't understand it at all. I'll be hanged if I can see how it happened.'

After a month she announced the news to everyone, except – from a sort of complicated and subtle sense of delicacy – to Countess Gilberte.

Julien did not come near her again for some time after the first shock of her announcement; then, irate, he became resigned: 'That's one we did not ask for.' And he began to visit his wife's room again.

Things fell out exactly as the good father had predicted. She was with child.

Then in a wave of delirious joy she shut her door every night, pledging herself to perpetual chastity in a burst of gratitude to the vague deity she worshipped.

She was almost happy again, astonished that her grief at her mother's death had so soon been assuaged. She had thought herself inconsolable; and now in little more than two months that living wound had closed. There remained now nothing but a tender melancholy, a veil of sadness over her life. Impossible now, it seemed, that anything more should befall her. Her children would grow up and love her; she would be serene and content as she grew old, and would not trouble herself about her husband.

Towards the end of September Father Picot came to pay a formal call, wearing a new cassock with as yet only a week's stains on it; and he presented his successor, Father Tolbiac. The latter was quite young, meagre and very small in stature, emphatic in speech, with deep-set, dark-ringed eyes that betokened a violent disposition.

The older priest had been appointed Superior at Goderville.

Jeanne felt genuine regret at his departure. The good man figured in all the memories of her married life. He had married her, baptised Paul and buried the baroness. She could not imagine Etouvent without Father Picot's paunch advancing before him through the farmyards; and she liked him because he was merry and unaffected.

In spite of his promotion, he did not appear to be in very good spirits. He said to Jeanne: 'It's painful for me, Viscountess, very painful. It's eighteen years now that I've been in this place. Oh, the living does not bring in much, it's not worth anything to speak of. The men are no more religious than they need be, and the women, well, you know, they've hardly any morals. The girls only come to church to get married after they've made a pilgrimage to Our Lady of the Big Belly, and orange blossom doesn't count for much in these parts. All the same, I liked it, myself.'

The new priest was showing signs of impatience and turning red in the face. He said brusquely: 'When I am installed here, that will all have to change.' He had the expression of a bad-tempered child, very frail and thin in his cassock, which was already worn but clean.

Father Picot looked at him askance, as was his way in his lighter moments, and went on: 'If you want to stop all that, you know, Father, you will have to chain up your parishioners; and even that would have no effect.'

The little priest answered in a crisp tone: 'We shall see.' The older one smiled as he took a pinch of snuff: 'Age will calm you, Father, and experience as well; you will drive the last of the faithful out of your church, that's all. The people here are believers, but pigheaded; tread carefully. Bless your heart, when I see a girl come to Mass who looks as if she's in the family way, I say to myself: "That's one more parishioner she's bringing," – and I try to get her married. You'll never stop them going wrong, you know; but you can go and look for the boy and see that he doesn't desert the mother. Marry them, Father, marry them, don't trouble your head about anything else.'

The new priest made a rough retort: 'We see things differently, it's no use going on.' And Father Picot fell to regretting that he must leave his village, leave the sea which was within sight of the presbytery windows, and the little funnel-shaped valleys where he went to recite his breviary, watching the boats go past in the distance.

Both priests then took their leave. The elder embraced Jeanne, who was almost in tears.

Father Tolbiac returned a week later. He spoke of the reforms that he was making, in the manner of a prince taking possession of a kingdom. He asked the viscountess to be sure to attend the Sunday service, and to take the Sacrament on every saint's day. 'You and I,' he said, 'are the head of the parish; we must rule it, and always set an example for others to follow. We must join forces to gain authority and respect. If the church and the château stand together, the villagers will fear and obey us.'

Jeanne's religion was entirely one of sentiment, the sort of dreaming faith a woman always clings to, and if she was for the most part punctual in her observances it was chiefly out of habit formed at the convent, for the baron's Frondist philosophy had long ago broken down her convictions.

Father Picot had contented himself with the little she could give him, and never reproved her. But his successor, having remarked that she was not in church the Sunday before, had come hotfoot to the château in great concern, wearing a stern expression.

She had no wish to break with the presbytery and gave him her promise, with the private reservation that she would be regular in attendance for his first few weeks, to show that she was well disposed towards him.

Gradually however she formed the habit of frequenting the church, and submitted to the influence of this frail priest with his integrity and dominating character. His mystical ardours and transports pleased her. He struck the chord of religious poetry in her that is in every woman's soul. His unbending austerity, his contempt for the world and its sensualities, his distaste for human concerns and his love of God, his untamed youth and inexperience, harsh speech and inflexible will gave Jeanne a conception of the sort of men the martyrs must have been; and she who had suffered and known disillusion allowed herself to be captivated by the rigid fanaticism of this child who was a minister of God.

He led her to the Christ who consoles, showing her how the pious joys of religion could alleviate all her sufferings; and she abased herself in the confessional, feeling small and weak as she knelt before this priest who looked no more than fifteen years old.

Soon however he was detested over the whole countryside.

Inexorably severe with himself, he showed ruthless intolerance to others. One thing above all aroused his wrath and indignation: love. He spoke of it in all his sermons, violently, in the crude terms of ecclesiastical usage, denouncing concupiscence in thundering periods which he hurled at his congregation of rustics; he trembled and stamped his feet with rage and his mind was haunted by the images evoked in his wrath.

The older lads and girls stole sly glances at each other across the church; and their elders, who always enjoyed a jest about such matters, spoke disapprovingly of the little priest's intolerance as they returned to their farms after Mass, together with the son in his blue smock and the farmer's wife in her black mantle. The whole region was in a ferment.

People confided to each other in whispers the severe penances he inflicted on them; they made fun of him when he persisted in refusing absolution to girls whose virtue had been impeached. There was laughter at High Mass on saints' days when some of the young people were observed to keep their seats instead of going up to make their communion with the others.

Soon he began to lie in wait for courting couples to put a stop to their meeting, like a keeper out after poachers. He chased them along ditches and behind barns on moonlit nights and through clumps of gorse on the hillsides.

On one occasion he came upon a couple who did not break away from each other when they saw him; they had their arms round each other's waists and were exchanging kisses on their walk through a stony ravine.

The priest called out: 'Stop that, you wretches!'

The youth turned round and retorted: 'Mind your own business, Your Reverence. This isn't none of yours.'

The priest picked up some stones and threw them at the pair as though he were stoning a dog.

They both ran off laughing; and the following Sunday he denounced them before the whole congregation.

The lads in the neighbourhood all stopped attending divine service.

The priest dined every Thursday at the château, and often called on weekdays to talk to his penitent. She conversed on spiritual themes in a fashion as exalted as his own, bringing into play the whole antiquated, intricate armoury of religious controversy.

They walked together along the baroness's avenue talking of Christ and the Apostles, the Virgin and the Holy Fathers as though they had known them personally. From time to time they would stop to put profound questions to one another which would lead them to diverge into mystic byways, she losing her way in a maze of poetical arguments as high-flown as rockets, while he disputed with more precision, like a monomaniac advocate mathematically demonstrating the squareness of a circle.

Julien held the new parish priest in high regard, and was always saying: 'He suits me, that priest, he does not compromise.' He went willingly to confession and to Mass, freely setting an example.

He visited the Fourvilles now almost every day, shooting with the husband who would not go without him, and riding with the countess in all weathers. The count said: 'This riding is a mania with them, but it does my wife good.'

The baron returned in the middle of November. He had changed, had aged and become lifeless, sunk in sombre grief which affected his whole being. The love which bound him to his daughter seemed suddenly to have increased, as though the few sad months of solitude had given him a more pressing need for affection, trust and tenderness.

Jeanne did not tell him of her new ideas, her religious ardour and her intimacy with Father Tolbiac; nevertheless he felt a strong antagonism to the priest the first time he saw him.

When the young woman asked that evening: 'What do you think of him?' he replied: 'That man is an inquisitor! He could be very dangerous.'

Later, when he learned from peasants who were friends of his of the young priest's rigidity, his outbursts of rage and the sort of persecution that he practised against innate laws and instincts, hatred sprang up in his heart.

He himself belonged to that ancient breed of philosophers who worshipped Nature, and was moved by the sight of a pair of animals coupling; he made obeisance to a sort of pantheistic deity, and his hackles rose at the Catholic conception of a god with a bourgeois disposition, the wrath of a Jesuit and the vengefulness of a tyrant; for God to him was a glimpse of creation in miniature, inevitable, limitless and omnipotent, the creation of life, light, earth, thought, plant, rock, man, air, beast, star, God and insect all simultaneously, creating for the sake of creation, stronger than will, more vast than reasoning, endlessly bringing forth without object or reason in all directions and all forms throughout infinite space, in accordance with necessity as it arises and with the proximity of suns to heat the worlds.

Creation contains the seed of all things, and thought and life develop within it like flowers and fruit on the trees.

Accordingly, reproduction was a general law, a divine act, sacred and praiseworthy, fulfilling the obscure, eternal will of the Universal Being. Going from farm to farm he began a vigorous campaign against the intolerant priest, the persecutor of life.

Jeanne prayed to the Lord in distress and pleaded with her father; but he always answered: 'We must fight against men like that, it is our right and duty. They are not human.' He repeated, shaking his long white locks: 'They are not human: they understand nothing, nothing at all. They live in a dream, a deadly fantasy; they are anti-physical.' He repeated: 'Anti-physical!' as though he had uttered a curse.

The priest was aware that he had an enemy, but since he was anxious to retain his dominance over the château and the young woman he temporized, confident of ultimate victory.

Moreover he was obsessed by one idea: the affair between Julien and Gilberte had chanced to reach his ears, and he was determined to put an end to it any cost.

One day he came to call on Jeanne, and after a lengthy mystical conversation he asked her to join with him to combat and destroy the evil within her own family, to save two souls in peril.

She did not understand and asked him to explain. 'Not now,' he answered, 'the time has not come, but I shall see you again before long.' He departed abruptly.

Winter was almost over, a soft winter as they say on the farms, damp and warm.

The priest returned a few days later and talked in obscure terms about one of those shameful liaisons between people who ought to be above reproach. For anyone who knew of such a situation, he said, it was their duty to put an end to it by any means at hand. He entered into elevated considerations and then, taking Jeanne by the hand, urged her to open her eyes, to understand and help him.

This time she did understand, but she was silent in horror at the thought of how painful this could be for her household, so peaceful at present, and she pretended not to take the priest's meaning. Then he hesitated no longer and spoke out plainly.

'It is a painful duty I have to perform, Viscountess, but I have no choice. I am charged by my ministry not to leave you in ignorance of something you are able to prevent. I must inform you, therefore, that your husband has a guilty relationship with Madame de Fourville.'

She lowered her eyes, resigned, without the strength to answer him.

The priest went on: 'What do you intend to do, after this?'

She said hesitantly: 'What do you wish me to do, Father?'

He replied with violence: 'You must place yourself in the path of this guilty passion.'

She began to weep; and cried in a heartbroken voice: 'But he has deceived me before, with a servant; he does not listen to me; he does not love me any more; he treats me roughly if I say anything to displease him. What can I do?'

The priest did not answer directly, but exclaimed: 'Then you give way to it! You accept it! You consent! Adultery is taking place beneath your roof; and you tolerate it! The crime is committed before your eyes, and you look the other way? Are you a wife? a Christian? a mother?'

She sobbed: 'What do you wish me to do?'

He replied: 'Anything rather than permit this infamy to continue. Anything, I say. Leave him. Fly from this house that has been defiled.'

She said: 'But I have no money, Father; also I have no courage left; and then, how can I leave him without proof? I have not even the right to do that.'

The priest rose, trembling as he said: 'That is cowardice prompting you, Madame. I thought better of you. You are unworthy of God's mercy!'

She fell at his feet: 'Oh! do not abandon me, pray do not, give me counsel!'

His reply was curt: 'Open Monsieur de Fourville's eyes for him. It is he who must put an end to this affair.'

The suggestion horrified her. 'But he would kill them, Father! And I should have informed against them! Oh! not that, never!'

Upon that he raised his hand as though to curse her, quite transported with rage: 'Stay with your shame and your crime;

for you are more guilty than they are. You are the complaisant spouse! I have nothing more to do here.'

And he departed in such fury that he was shaking all over.

She followed him in alarm, prepared to give way, to make promises. But he walked on with rapid steps, still quivering with indignation and angrily shaking the big blue umbrella that was almost as tall as himself.

He caught sight of Julien, who was standing near the gate supervising the pruning of some trees, and turning to the left to cross the Couillards' farm, he said again: 'Leave me alone, Madame, I have nothing more to say to you.'

Immediately in his path, in the middle of the farmyard, several of the children from the estate and from neighbouring farms were crowding round the kennel of the bitch, Mirza, watching something, curious, silent, closely attentive. The baron was standing in their midst with his hands clasped behind his back, also looking on with interest. His attitude was that of a schoolmaster. As soon as he saw the priest in the distance he walked away to avoid meeting him, bowing or speaking.

Jeanne was pleading: 'Let me have a few days, Father, and then come back to the château. I will tell you what I have been able to do, and what I've planned and we will consider.'

They were approaching the group of children at that moment; and the priest went closer to see what interested them so much. It was the bitch, who was whelping. There were five puppies outside the kennel, already crawling about round the mother who was licking them tenderly as she lay full length on her side in labour. Just as the priest bent down the animal, whose body had contracted, stretched out and a sixth puppy appeared. The children all shrieked and clapped their hands with joy: 'There's another, there's another!' It was a game to them, nothing more, a natural game with nothing indecent in it. They watched the puppies being born just as they would have watched apples falling.

Father Tolbiac was at first stupefied; then filled with overmastering rage, he raised his big umbrella and began to hit the crowd of children over the head with all his might. The urchins took to their heels in panic; and he was left confronted with the bitch in labour, who was trying to raise herself up. He did not even let her get on her feet, but lost his head and began beating her mercilessly as hard as he could. She was chained and could not escape, and howled horribly as she struggled to avoid the blows. The umbrella broke in his hands. Then, empty-handed, he trod on her and trampled her in a frenzy, pounding and crushing her. Under the pressure of his feet another little one was squeezed out into the world; and with a frantic kick he finished off the bleeding body still writhing among the newborn puppies as they whined, sightless and heavy-bodied, trying to reach their mother's teats.

Jeanne had run away; but the priest suddenly felt himself seized by the neck; a blow sent his tricorn flying, and the baron, outraged, dragged him to the gate and flung him into the road.

When Monsieur Le Perthuis turned round he saw his daughter sobbing on her knees in the midst of the puppies and picking them up in her skirt. He went back to her with long strides, gesticulating as he shouted: 'There he goes, there he goes, that man in his cassock! Did you see him just now?'

The farmers had come running, and everyone was staring at the disembowelled animal; Mother Couillard exclaimed: 'How could anyone be such a brute!'

Jeanne in the meantime had picked up the seven puppies, intending to rear them herself.

They tried to give them milk; three died the next day. Then old Simon ransacked the neighbourhood to find a bitch in milk. He could not find one, but returned with a cat, which he said would serve their purpose. They killed three more of the puppies and entrusted the last one to this wet-nurse of another race. She adopted it immediately, lay on her side and offered it her teats.

The puppy was weaned a fortnight later so that he should not exhaust his adopted mother, and Jeanne undertook to bring him up herself on the bottle. She had named him Toto.

The baron however asserted his authority and changed the name to Massacre.

The priest did not come back, but the following Sunday he launched a tirade of imprecations, maledictions and threats against the château, declaring that wounds must be cauterized with hot iron, anathematizing the baron – who found it all most diverting – and making a veiled and still tentative allusion to Julien's new amour. The viscount was exceedingly angry, but his ire was tempered by the fear of a serious scandal.

From that day onward the priest continued to threaten vengeance in sermon after sermon, predicting that God's hour would come, when all His enemies would be struck down.

Julien wrote to the Archbishop, respectfully but in strong terms. Father Tolbiac was threatened with suspension and after that he kept silence.

He was to be encountered now on long, solitary walks, striding along with a rapt expression. Gilberte and Julien caught frequent glimpses of him when they were out riding, sometimes as a black speck in the distance far away on a plain or at the edge of the cliffs, sometimes reading his breviary in some narrow vale when they were about to pass through it. On such occasions they would turn back to avoid an encounter with him.

Spring had come, reanimating their love, throwing them into each other's arms every day in one place or another, in any cover that offered in the course of their rides.

As the leaves on the trees were no more than tender green shoots, and the grass was damp, they could not conceal themselves among trees or bushes as they did in the heart of summer, and usually adopted a movable shepherd's hut which had been left on the top of Vaucotte's hill since the autumn before, as a shelter for their embraces.

It stood high on its wheels in an isolated spot five hundred metres from the cliff, at the point where the steep descent into the vale began. Overlooking the plain, it was a place where

they could not be taken by surprise; and their horses, tethered to the shafts, waited for them until they were sated with kisses.

One day however as they were leaving this refuge they caught sight of Father Tolbiac, sitting almost hidden among the gorse on the slope.

'We shall have to leave our horses down in the ravine,' said Julien, 'they could give us away, even from a distance.' And they fell into the habit of tying up the animals in a fold of the valley where the brushwood was thick.

Then as they were both returning to La Vrillette one evening to dine with the count they met the parish priest of Etouvent coming away from the château. He stood back to let them pass; and bowed without meeting their eyes.

They felt a moment's apprehension, which soon passed.

One afternoon when a high wind was blowing (it was the beginning of May) Jeanne was reading by the fire when she saw Count de Fourville arriving on foot, at such a pace that she feared there had been an accident.

She hastened downstairs to receive him, and when they were face to face she thought he had gone mad. He had on a big fur cap that he only wore at home, and his shooting jacket, and was so pale that his auburn moustache, not usually noticeable against his ruddy complexion, looked as though it were on fire.

His eyes rolled wildly in their sockets, empty of expression.

He burst out: 'My wife is here, is she not?' Jeanne's wits deserted her and she replied: 'No, I have not seen her today.'

He sat down as though his legs had given way; he took off his cap and wiped his forehead mechanically several times with a handkerchief, then rose in a single movement and went up to the young woman, stretching out his hands to her with his mouth open about to speak, to confide the news of some dreadful calamity; but he stopped, fixed her with his eyes and said in a sort of frenzy: 'But it is your husband . . . you too . . .' And he rushed away in the direction of the sea.

Jeanne ran out to stop him, calling to him, imploring, her heart shrinking in terror, thinking: 'He knows all! What is he going to do? Oh! if only he doesn't find them!'

But she could not overtake him and he did not hear her. He went straight on, unhesitating, sure of his objective. He crossed the dyke, and went on over the heath with giant strides until he reached the cliff.

Jeanne stood among the trees at the top of the bank and followed him for a long time with her eyes; when he was out of sight she went indoors in an agony of apprehension.

He had turned to the right and broken into a run. The sea was stormy, and the waves had turned to rollers; heavy black clouds were racing past, with others coming up behind them; and each one shook out a furious shower of drops over the hill. The wind whistled, groaned, swept over the grass and flattened the young crops, carried off great white birds like flecks of foam and bore them far away over the countryside.

The squalls blowing over in quick succession whipped the count's face, drenched his cheeks and moustache until they streamed with rain, filled his ears with noise and his heart with uproar.

Ahead of him was the mouth of the deep ravine in the vale of Vaucotte. Between it and himself there was nothing but a shepherd's hut beside an empty sheepfold. Two horses were tethered to the shafts of the movable hut. What was to be feared in such a storm?

As soon as the count saw the horses he crouched on the ground, then crawled forward on hands and knees, like a sort of monster with his big body splashed with mud and his head topped with fur. He crawled up to the solitary cabin and hid beneath it so that he should not be seen through the cracks in the boards.

The horses moved restlessly when they saw him. He cut their reins deliberately with the open knife that he was holding; and as a shower blew up just then the animals ran away, goaded by the hail, which battered the sloping roof of the wooden hut and made it shake on its wheels.

The count rose to his knees, put his eye to the bottom of the door and peered inside.

He did not move; he seemed to be waiting. A fairly long time passed; and suddenly he started to his feet, covered with mud from head to foot. With a violent movement he shot the bolt to secure the door on the outside, took hold of the shafts and began to shake the nesting-box as though he would shatter it to pieces. Suddenly he let go of the shafts and put himself between them like a beast in harness, bending his tall frame and straining desperately, hauling like an ox and gasping for breath. And he dragged the travelling hut and those inside it towards the edge of the steep descent.

They shouted and banged with their fists on the wooden walls, not knowing what was happening to them.

When he came to the top of the incline he let go of the flimsy dwelling, sending it off on a runaway course down the side of the hill.

It hurtled down at a furious pace, faster and faster, leaping and stumbling like an animal, the shafts banging on the ground.

An old beggar who had taken shelter in a ditch saw it go bounding past above his head; and he heard the terrible cries that came from inside the wooden coffer.

An obstacle in its path knocked off one of the wheels, and the hut collapsed on its side and began to roll over and over like a ball, as a house torn from its foundations would tumble from the top of a hill. When it reached the edge of the last gully it left the ground, flew through the air in an arc and fell to the bottom, smashed like an egg.

As soon as it came to rest and lay splintered on the stony ground, the old beggar who had seen it go by picked his way down through the thorn bushes; with the native caution of the peasant he did not venture to approach the shattered hut, but repaired to the nearest farm to tell the news of the accident.

People rushed to the spot; the debris was cleared away; two bodies were found. They were bruised, pounded and bleeding. The man's forehead was split open and his whole face crushed. The woman's jaw was hanging loose, broken by a blow; and their broken limbs were as limp as though there were no bones beneath the flesh.

They were recognizable, however; and a long discussion began as to what could have caused the calamity.

'What were they doing in that there hut?' a woman demanded. Then the old beggar told them that they had apparently taken refuge inside it to shelter from a squall, and the raging tempest must have blown the cabin from its stand and set it in motion. He explained that he had been going to take shelter there himself, when he had seen the horses tied to the shafts and realized there was somebody inside.

He added with satisfaction: 'If it hadn't've been for them, it's me it would've happened to.' A voice said: 'Maybe better if it had!' Then the old fellow flew into a passion: 'What d'you mean, better? Just because I'm poor and them's rich! You look at them now . . .' Trembling, ragged, streaming wet, a squalid figure with his matted beard and long hair straggling from beneath a battered hat, he pointed to the two corpses with the end of his crooked stick; and he announced: 'Them and me's all one when it comes to that.'

Other rustics had come up and were looking on in the background, nervous, cunning, scared, selfish and cowardly. They deliberated as to what should be done; they decided, in the hope of a reward, that the bodies should be carried home to their respective manors. Two carts were fetched. Then a new difficulty arose. Some wanted to have nothing but a layer of straw on the floor of the conveyances; others were of the opinion that it would be proper to have mattresses.

The woman who had spoken earlier called out: 'But they'll be all over blood, them mattresses, they'll have to be washed out in Javel water.'

Then a big, jolly-looking farmer replied: 'They'll pay for them. The better they are, the dearer they come.' This argument was decisive.

The two carts perched high on wheels without springs set

off at a trot, one turning to the right and the other to the left, shaking and tossing about at every jolt in the deep ruts the remains of those two people who had known each other's embraces and were never to meet again.

As soon as the count had seen the cabin rolling down the rough hillside he had run away through the storm as fast as his legs would carry him. He ran for several hours, taking short cuts, leaping over banks, breaking through hedgerows; he arrived at his own house at dusk, without knowing how he had reached it.

The frightened servants were waiting for him, and informed him that the two horses had come back without their riders, Julien's horse following the other.

Then Monsieur de Fourville reeled under the shock; he said brokenly: 'They must have met with an accident in this dreadful weather. Let everyone go out and search for them.'

He set out again himself; but as soon as he was out of sight he concealed himself under a thorn bush, to watch the road by which she whom he still loved wildly and passionately would be brought home dead or dying, or perhaps maimed or disfigured for life.

Soon a cart passed close to him, carrying a strange load.

It stopped in front of the château, then drove through the gate. There it was, yes, it was she; a fearful agony kept him nailed to the spot in dread, in horror of learning the truth; he did not move, but stayed cowering like a hare, quivering at the slightest sound.

He waited an hour, perhaps two. The cart did not come out again. He told himself that his wife was passing away; the thought of seeing her and meeting her eyes filled him with such horror that he was suddenly afraid that he might be discovered in his hiding-place and compelled to go indoors and be with her in that last agony, and he fled again into the middle of the wood. There it suddenly came to his mind that she might be in need of help, that doubtless there was no one to tend her; and he turned and ran wildly towards the house.

As he went through the gate he saw his gardener and called

out: 'Well?' The man dared not answer. Monsieur de Fourville almost bellowed at him: 'Is she dead?' The gardener stammered out: 'Yes, Monsieur.'

He felt an immense relief. A sense of calm instantly flooded his veins and quivering muscles, and he walked up the steps and entered with a firm tread.

The other cart had arrived at Les Peuples. Jeanne saw it from a distance, saw the mattress and guessed that there was a body lying on it, and everything was clear to her. The shock was so great that she fainted.

When she came round, her father was holding her head and dabbing her forehead with vinegar. He asked her hesitantly: 'You have heard?' She whispered: 'Yes, Father.' When she tried to rise, she was in too much pain to stand.

That evening she gave birth to a daughter; the baby was stillborn.

She saw nothing of Julien's burial; she knew nothing about it. She was only aware after a day or two that Aunt Lison had returned; and in the feverish nightmares that haunted her she tried persistently to recall how long it was since the old maid had left Les Peuples, at what time and in what circumstances. She never succeeded, even in her most lucid moments, and could be certain only that she had not seen her aunt since dear Mama's death.

11

FOR THREE MONTHS JEANNE DID NOT LEAVE her room, becoming so weak and wan that it was thought, and even said, there was no hope for her. Then gradually she recovered. Dear Papa and Aunt Lison were both settled now at Les Peuples and never left her side. She suffered from a sort of nervous disorder as a result of shock; she fainted at the slightest sound, and the most trifling occurrence would bring on a long fainting fit.

She had never asked to be told exactly how Julien had died.

What was it to her? Did she not know enough? Everyone supposed his death to have been an accident, but she was not taken in; and she kept the painful secret to herself: the knowledge of his adultery and the remembered picture of the count's sudden terrifying visit on the day of the disaster.

Tender thoughts now filled her mind, sweet, sad memories of the brief joys of love that her husband had given her long ago. These recollections came to her repeatedly, and she trembled when they took her unawares; she saw him as he had been when they were engaged, and also as the cherished figure in the only moments of passion she had ever known, under the blazing Corsican sun. His faults were all attenuated, his callous behaviour effaced, even his infidelities faded into insignificance as his presence receded into the distance of the past. Now after his death Jeanne felt obscurely grateful to the man who had held her in his arms; she forgave him for what she had suffered and remembered only the moments of happiness. Then with the constant march of time the dust of oblivion accumulated month by month over all her recollections, all her woes; and she devoted herself entirely to her son.

He became the idol, the sole concern of the three people round him; and he reigned like a tyrant. A sort of jealousy even began to make itself felt between those three slaves of his, Jeanne watching anxiously as warm kisses were bestowed on the baron after a series of rides on his knee. Aunt Lison, neglected by him as she had always been by everyone, treated sometimes as a maid by that master who as yet could scarcely pronounce a word, went off to her room in tears as she compared the scant caresses that she had to beg for and seldom obtained, with the embraces he reserved for his mother and grandfather.

Two peaceful and uneventful years passed in unceasing preoccupation with the child. At the beginning of the third winter it was decided that they should go to Rouen and stay until the spring; and the whole family migrated. When they arrived at the old house, however, neglected and damp as it was, Paul had such a severe attack of bronchitis that pleurisy was feared; and his three distracted relatives declared that he could not exist without the air of Les Peuples. As soon as he recovered they took him back to the château.

The years that followed passed in pleasant monotony.

The three of them were always gathered round the child, in his room, in the big drawing-room or the garden, rhapsodizing over his lisping speech, his comical expressions and gestures.

His mother's pet name for him was Paulet, and since he could not quite say the word he pronounced it Poulet,* which gave rise to endless peals of laughter. The nickname Poulet remained. He was never called anything else.

As he was growing fast his three attendants, whom the baron called 'his three mothers', became passionately absorbed in measuring his height.

His growth in height was recorded each month by a series of small scratches with a penknife on the frame of the drawing-room door. The set of marks was called 'Poulet's ladder', and had an important place in the lives of everyone round him.

Another individual then came to play a big part in the family; this was the dog Massacre, neglected by Jeanne who took no interest in anything but her son. He was fed by Ludivine and led a solitary life chained up in an old barrel outside the stables.

One morning Paul caught sight of him, and cried to be allowed to go and stroke him. With much trepidation the little boy was led up to the dog. Massacre made a great fuss of the child, who screamed when they were parted. After that the dog was let loose and brought into the house.

He became inseparable from Paul, who was his friend at all times. They tumbled about together and fell asleep side by side on the carpet. Massacre was soon sleeping in the bed of his playmate, who refused to be parted from him. Jeanne was sometimes afraid he might have fleas; and Aunt Lison bore him a grudge for taking such a large share of the little one's affection, stealing it – as she saw it – from the love she hungered for herself.

* Chicken

They exchanged occasional calls with the Brisevilles and the Couteliers. No one but the mayor and the doctor came regularly to disturb the solitude of the old manor-house. After the priest had slaughtered the dog, and aroused Jeanne's suspicions just before Julien and the countess died so horribly, she had become incensed against a god who could employ such a man as his minister, and no longer went to Mass.

From time to time Father Tolbiac would make direct allusions to the château, anathematizing it as haunted by the Spirit of Evil, the Spirit of Eternal Revolt, the Spirit of Error and Lies, the Spirit of Iniquity or the Spirit of Corruption and Impurity. It was in these terms that he designated the baron.

His church was empty now; and when he passed a field where labourers were ploughing the peasants did not stop their work to talk to him, or turn round to call a greeting. Furthermore he was taken for a sorcerer, because he had driven out the devil from a woman who was possessed. It was said that he knew mysterious words to avert spells, which according to him were only a sort of jest of Satan. He laid his hands on cows that gave blue milk or had curly tails, and caused lost objects to be found by uttering a few strange phrases.

With his narrow, fanatical mind he was passionately addicted to the study of religious books giving accounts of the Devil's appearances on earth, the various manifestations of his power, his diverse occult influences and all his resources, as well as the common tricks of his trade. He had learnt all the formulae of exorcism set down in ecclesiastical manuals, because he believed himself especially called to combat that mysterious and fateful Power.

He was for ever thinking he could hear the Evil One wandering about in the shadows; and the Latin phrase was perpetually on his lips: *Sicut leo rugiens circuit quaerens quem devorat.**

After a time fear spread abroad, terror of his hidden power.

* I. Peter V. 8. '. . . as a roaring lion walketh about, seeking whom he may devour.'

Even his fellow clergy, ignorant rustics for whom Beelzebub was an article of faith, who were uneasy at the rites meticulously prescribed in cases of manifestation of his evil power, and had come to confuse religion with magic – even they regarded Father Tolbiac as something of a sorcerer; and they respected him as much for the obscure powers they believed him to possess as for the irreproachable austerity of his life.

He gave Jeanne no greeting when he met her.

This situation disquieted and distressed Aunt Lison, who in her timid spinster's soul could not understand anyone not going to Mass. Doubtless she was devout, doubtless she confessed and took the Sacrament; but no one knew whether she did or not, and no one cared.

When she was alone with Paul, quite alone, she talked to him very quietly about the good God. He listened, more or less, when she related the wonderful stories of olden times; but when she told him that one must love the good God very, very dearly he sometimes answered: 'Where is He, Aunt?' Then she pointed to the sky with her finger: 'Up there, Poulet, but we must not speak of it.' She was afraid of the baron.

One day however Poulet declared: 'The good God is everywhere, but He is not in church.' He had talked to his grandfather about aunt's mysterious revelations.

The child was rising ten years old; his mother looked forty. He was sturdy and boisterous, an intrepid climber of trees, but had little knowledge in his head. He was bored by lessons, and interrupted them as soon as begun. Whenever the baron kept him long at a book Jeanne would be sure to come in and say: 'Do let him go and play now. We must not tire him out, he is so young.' To her he was still only six months or a year old. She scarcely realized that he now walked, ran and talked like a little man; and she lived in constant fear lest he should fall, catch cold, grow overheated with excitement, eat too much for him to digest or too little to make him grow.

When he was twelve a serious difficulty arose: his first communion.

One morning Lison went to find Jeanne and pointed out

that the little boy could not go any longer without religious instruction and without performing his first sacred duties. She produced all sorts of arguments and invoked a number of reasons, the chief of which was the opinion of their acquaintances. The mother hesitated, anxious and undecided, saying that they could wait a little longer.

A month later, however, it happened that when she was calling on Viscountess de Briseville that lady inquired: 'It is this year, is it not, that your Paul will be making his first communion?' Taken by surprise, Jeanne replied: 'Yes, Madame.' That one word decided her, and without saying anything to her father she asked Lison to take the child to classes in the Catechism.

For a month all went well; then Poulet came home one evening with a sore throat. The next day he was coughing. His mother was alarmed and questioned him, at which she discovered that the priest had sent him out to wait at the church door in the draughty porch until the end of the lesson, because he had misbehaved in class.

After that she kept him at home and instructed him herself in the alphabet of her religion. In spite of this, however, and notwithstanding Lison's entreaties, Father Tolbiac refused to accept him among the communicants because he had not been properly prepared.

This happened again the following year. The baron flew into a rage and swore that there was no need for the child to believe in that rubbish, the puerile symbolism of transubstantiation, in order to be a good man, and it was decided that he should be brought up as a Christian, but not as a practising Catholic. When he came of age he should be free to become whatever he pleased.

A short time later, when Jeanne paid a call on the Brisevilles she received no return call. Her neighbours were punctilious in such matters, and she was surprised; but the Marquise de Coutelier explained, in her lofty manner, the reason for their failure to visit her.

The marquise, by virtue of her husband's position as well

as her own fully authentic title and considerable wealth, regarded herself as a sort of queen of the Norman nobility and certainly ruled like one, outspoken, gracious or brusque as occasion demanded, constantly admonishing, correcting, felicitating. Accordingly, when Jeanne went to call on her, this lady stated crisply after a few chilling phrases: 'Society is divided into two classes: those who believe in God and those who do not. The first of these, even the humblest among them, are our friends, our equals; the others mean nothing to us.'

Jeanne, feeling herself under attack, retorted: 'Is it not possible to believe in God without attending Mass?'

The marquise answered: 'No, Madame; the faithful go to the church to pray to God, just as we go to visit people in their own homes.'

Jeanne was nettled, and replied: 'God is everywhere, Madame. For my part, I believe in His goodness from the bottom of my heart, and when certain priests come between Him and me I lose the sense of His presence.'

The marquise rose: 'The priest bears the banner of the Church, Madame; anybody who does not follow it is against Him, and against us.'

Jeanne had also risen to her feet, trembling with indignation: 'You, Madame, believe in the god of a faction. I believe in the god of all who lead a good life.'

She bowed, and took her leave.

The peasants also, among themselves, held her to blame for not having brought Poulet to make his first communion. Either they did not attend the services or receive the sacrament, or in some cases came only at Easter as the rules of the Church prescribed; but with children it was a different matter; they would all have recoiled at the presumptuousness of bringing up a child outside that common law, because Religion, after all, is Religion.

She did not fail to remark their disapproval, and at heart rebelled at all the compromising and compounding with conscience, the universal fear of everything, the craven dread that lies in the depths of everyone's soul and only shows itself under the mask of some convention.

The baron took charge of Paul's studies, and set him to learn Latin. His mother's sole contribution now was to say: 'Above all, do not tire him out;' and she wandered anxiously to and fro outside the classroom, forbidden by dear Papa to enter because she would interrupt the lesson every few minutes to ask: 'Aren't your feet cold, Poulet?' or 'You haven't a headache, Poulet?' or otherwise pull up the tutor: 'Don't make him talk so much, you will make him hoarse.'

As soon as the little boy was at liberty he went out gardening with his mother and aunt. They had a passion at the time for cultivating the land; and the three of them planted young trees in the spring, sowed seeds and eagerly watched them sprout and grow, pruned shrubs and cut flowers to make nosegays.

The young lad was interested chiefly in producing salads. He supervised four large beds in the kitchen-garden, where he took great pains in growing cabbage and Cos lettuces, green and blanched chicory, winter salads and every known species of these edible greenstuffs. He dug and watered, hoed and pricked out with the aid of his two mothers whom he set to work like day labourers. They were to be seen on their knees in the vegetable beds for hours at a time, soiling their hands and clothes, busily inserting the roots of young plants into holes in the earth, which they made with their fingers.

Poulet was growing tall; he would soon be fifteen. Although the scale in the drawing-room was now marked one metre fifty-eight he was still a child at heart, ignorant, foolish, smothered between the two petticoats and the kindly old man who had fallen so far behind the times.

One evening, at last, the baron spoke of college; and Jeanne immediately began to weep. Aunt Lison was alarmed and did not stir from her dark corner of the room.

The mother questioned: 'Why does he need to know so much? We will turn him into a man of outdoor pursuits, a country gentleman. He will cultivate his land, as many noblemen do. He will live and grow old here, live happily in this house where we have been with him and where we shall die. What more is there to be said?'

But the baron was shaking his head. 'How will you answer him if he comes to you when he is twenty-five, and says: "I am nothing, I know nothing, and that is your fault, the fault of your selfishness as a mother. I know I am incapable of working or becoming of any account in the world, yet at the same time I was not made for the obscure, modest, deadly dull existence to which with short-sighted affection you have condemned me." '

She was still weeping, and pleaded with her son: 'Tell me, Poulet, you will never reproach me for loving you too much, will you?'

The big child, surprised, gave his promise: 'No, Mama.'

'You promise?'

'Yes, Mama.'

'You would like to stay here, would you not?'

'Yes, Mama.'

Then the baron spoke out firmly and emphatically: 'Jeanne, you have no right to dispose of that life. What you have just done is shameful, criminal almost; you are sacrificing your child to your own happiness.'

She covered her face with her hands in a sudden burst of sobs, and quavered through her tears: 'I have been so unhappy . . . so unhappy! Now I am having such a peaceful time with him, and he is to be taken away from me . . . What shall I do . . . all alone . . . now?'

Her father rose and went to her, seated himself beside her and took her in his arms. 'What about me, Jeanne?' She flung her arms round his neck in a passionate embrace and then, still stifled with sobs, gasped out: 'Yes. You are right . . . perhaps . . . dear Papa. It was foolish of me, but I have suffered so much. I do agree to his going to college.'

At this point, without understanding very well what was going to be done with him, Poulet began to whimper.

His three mothers kissed him, made much of him and

reassured him. They were all heavy-hearted when they retired and all wept in their beds, even the baron who had kept control of himself until then.

It was decided to send the lad to the college at Le Havre, starting at the beginning of the next term; and all through the summer he was spoilt more than ever.

His mother frequently bewailed the prospect of parting with him. She prepared his outfit as though he were going on a ten-year journey; then one October morning, after a sleepless night, the two women and the baron climbed into the carriage with him and the pair of horses set off at a trot.

A visit had already been made to the college to choose his place in the dormitory and the classroom. Jeanne, with the assistance of Aunt Lison, spent the whole day putting away his clothes in the small chest of drawers. That piece of furniture did not hold a quarter of what they had brought with them, and she went to the headmaster to ask for another. The need for economy was invoked; he pointed out that so much linen and so many personal belongings would be nothing but an inconvenience and never be put to use; and in accordance with the regulations he must refuse to provide a second chest of drawers. The distracted mother thereupon decided to take a room in a small hotel nearby and request the landlord himself to take Poulet anything he might need when the child should ask for it.

Next they took a turn on the pier to watch the ships sailing in and out of harbour.

A dismal twilight descended on the town, and lights appeared one after another. They went to a restaurant to dine; none of them was hungry; they looked at each other moist-eyed, as the dishes were set before them and removed almost untouched.

After dinner they walked slowly back to the college. Children of all sizes were arriving from different directions, brought by their families or servants. Many were in tears. Sounds of weeping could be heard in the dimly lit main courtyard.

Jeanne and Poulet clung to each other in a last embrace. Aunt Lison stayed forgotten in the background, her face buried in her handkerchief. However, the baron, who was also moved by the parting, cut short their farewells and swept his daughter away. The carriage was waiting at the door; they all stepped in and drove back through the night to Les Peuples.

From time to time a loud sob broke out in the darkness.

Jeanne wept all the next day until nightfall. In the morning she ordered the phaeton and set out for Le Havre. Poulet seemed already to have resigned himself to being away from his family. For the first time in his life he had playfellows; he fidgeted on his chair in the parlour, longing to go out and play.

Jeanne visited the school every other day, as well as for the Sunday exeat. She did not know what to do with herself between the hours of recreation and stayed in the parlour, unable to bring herself to stir from the college. The headmaster asked to see her, and requested her not to come so often. She paid no attention to this.

Then he warned her that if she continued to keep her son away from his play during break, and constantly interrupted him in his work, he would have to be sent home; the warning was conveyed to the baron in a note. From that time she was kept like a prisoner at Les Peuples and never let out of sight.

She looked forward to each holiday even more eagerly than her son did.

Her mind was continually agitated, never at rest. She began to wander about alone, going out for whole days at a time taking the dog Massacre with her and daydreaming in the empty expanse of the countryside. She would pass whole afternoons seated on the top of a cliff, gazing out to sea; sometimes she went down through the wood to Yport along the paths where she used to walk, haunted by memories. How distant it was, how remote the time when she had roved about this same countryside as a young girl, intoxicated with her dreams.

Each time she saw her son again it seemed to her that they had been away from each other ten years. From one month to the next he was growing into a man; while she, from month to month, was becoming an old woman. Her father might have been her brother, and Aunt Lison – withered at twenty-five and scarcely aged since – was like an elder sister.

Poulet did hardly any work; he stayed a second year in the fourth form. In the third he did not do too badly; but he had to spend two years in the second; and he was still doing rhetoric when he reached the age of twenty.

He had grown into a tall, blond lad with sideburns already bushing out and a vestigial moustache. Now it was he who visited his family, coming to Les Peuples every Sunday. He had been taking riding lessons for a considerable time, and simply hired a horse to cover the distance in two hours.

Jeanne set out early to meet him with Aunt Lison and the baron, who stooped more and more and walked like a little old man, his hands clasped behind his back as if to save him from falling on his face.

They made slow progress along the highway, stopping sometimes to sit down by the roadside, peering into the distance ahead for a sign of the horseman. As soon as he came into sight, a black speck on the white line of the road, his three relations waved their handkerchiefs; and he put his horse into a gallop to come down on them like a whirlwind, giving Jeanne and Lison palpitations and stirring his grandfather to shouts of 'Bravo!' in impotent enthusiasm.

Although Paul was taller than his mother by a head she still treated him like a child, still asked him: 'Aren't your feet cold, Poulet?' When he was walking past the house after luncheon smoking a cigarette, she would open the window and call out to him: 'Please, Poulet, please do not go out without a hat, you will catch cold in your head.'

She trembled with anxiety when he went off at night on horseback: 'Above everything, do not go too fast, my little Poulet, be careful, think of your poor mother who would be so distressed if anything should happen to you.'

There came a Saturday morning, however, when a letter was brought from Paul to tell her that he would not be coming home the next day, because some of his friends had asked him to go with them on a picnic.

She passed the whole of that Sunday in a state of torment as though some dreadful misfortune threatened; by Thursday she could endure it no longer and set out for Le Havre.

Her son appeared to her changed, in a way that she could not precisely define. His manner was animated, his voice more like a man's. Suddenly, as though it were the most natural thing, he said to her: 'I say, Mama, now that you have come today I will not come out to Les Peuples again next Sunday, because we are having another party.'

Shock took her breath away as though he had announced that he was leaving for the New World; when at last she was able to speak, she cried: 'Oh, Poulet, what is the matter? tell me, what is happening?' He laughed, and kissed her: 'Why nothing in the world, Mama. I am going to amuse myself with my friends, it's what one does at my age.'

She could find no answer, and when she was alone in her carriage strange thoughts came into her mind. She had not recognized her Poulet in him, her own little Poulet of old. Now she realized for the first time that he was grown up, that he no longer belonged to her but was going to live his own life without concern for his elders. In one day – so it seemed to her – this transformation had taken place in him. Why, this was her son, her poor little boy who used to make her prick out vegetables for him, this lusty, bearded youth who was striking out for himself!

For three months Paul paid only occasional visits to his parents, and on those occasions he was restive, plainly impatient to be off again as soon as possible, trying each time to cut the evening short by an hour. This distressed Jeanne, and the baron constantly reiterated to reassure her: 'Let him alone; the boy is twenty now.'

One morning, however, a seedy-looking old man came to inquire for 'Matame la Vicomtesse', speaking French with a

German accent. After much ceremonious bowing and scraping he produced a grubby pocket-book and announced: 'I haf a liddle piece of paper for you.' He unfolded a scrap of greasy paper and held it out to her. She read and re-read it, looked at the Jew, read it once again and asked him: 'What does this mean?'

The man explained in his obsequious manner: 'I vill tell you. Your son haf need of a liddle money, and I know you are a goot mother, I haf lent him zis small sum for his needs.'

She was startled: 'But why did he not come to me?' The Jew embarked on a lengthy explanation involving a gambling debt which would fall due before noon the next day, while Paul being not yet of age could find no one to make him a loan, so that his 'Honour would haf been gompromised' if the money-lender had not 'obliged' him with 'zis small service'.

Jeanne wanted to call the baron but she was rooted to her chair with distress and unable to move. At last she said to the old man: 'Will you be so good as to ring.'

He hesitated, fearing a trick. He muttered: 'If I haf put you to inconvenience, I vill come back another time.' She shook her head to signify 'No'. He rang; and they waited, facing each other, without speaking.

The baron entered the room and took in the situation at a glance. The note was for fifteen hundred francs. He paid the money-lender a thousand, looked him straight in the face and said: 'Do not show yourself here again.' The other thanked him, bowed, and made himself scarce.

The grandfather and the mother left at once for Le Havre; but when they arrived at the college they found that Paul had not been there for a month. The principal had received four letters with Jeanne's signature, notifying him that his pupil was unwell and giving news of his progress. Each letter was accompanied by a doctor's certificate; all, of course, were forgeries. The baron and Jeanne stood staring at each other, dumbfounded.

The principal, greatly disturbed, accompanied them to the

superintendent of police. Afterwards father and daughter stayed the night at the hotel.

The young man was discovered next day in the company of a kept woman in the town. His grandfather and mother carried him off with them to Les Peuples without a word being exchanged throughout the journey. Jeanne buried her face in her handkerchief and wept. Paul gazed out at the surroundings with an air of indifference.

It came to light after a week that he had run up debts to a total of fifteen thousand francs during the last three months. His creditors had as yet made no move, knowing that he would soon come of age.

There were no demands for an explanation. It was hoped that he might be won over with kindness. He was given special delicacies, pampered, indulged. It was spring; notwithstanding Jeanne's fears, a boat was hired for him at Yport so that he could go out for a sail whenever he pleased.

No horse was put at his disposal, for fear that he might ride back to Le Havre.

He was without occupation, irritable, at times even rough-tongued. The baron was concerned about his interrupted studies. The prospect of another parting filled Jeanne with dread, yet she wondered what was to be done with him.

One evening he did not come home. It was found that he had gone out with two seamen in a boat. His mother was so distraught that she went down through the darkness to Yport with her head uncovered.

There were a few men waiting on the beach for the boat to come in.

A small light showed out at sea; it came nearer, swaying to and fro. Paul was not on board. He had had the boatmen take him to Le Havre.

The police searched for him without success; he was not to be found. The girl who had hidden him once before had also disappeared without trace, her furniture sold and her quarter's rent paid. Two letters from this creature were found in Paul's room at Les Peuples, from which she appeared to be wildly in love with him. She wrote of a journey to England, for which, she said, the necessary money had been found.

The three people in the château dwelt in sombre silence, in the hell of mental torment. Jeanne's grey hair had turned white. Naively she wondered why fate should deal so harshly with her.

A letter came for her from Father Tolbiac: 'Madame, the hand of God is heavy upon you. You have denied Him your child; He in His turn has taken him from you, to throw him into the arms of a prostitute. Are your eyes not opened by this lesson from Heaven? The Lord's mercy is infinite. It may be that He will pardon you if you turn to Him again and kneel before Him. I am His humble servant, I will open the door of His dwelling when you knock.'

She held this letter on her knee for a long time. What this priest said might be true. Religious doubts began to gnaw at her conscience. Could God be vindictive and jealous, as humans are? yet if He did not manifest Himself as a jealous god, no one would fear Him, no one would worship Him any longer. No doubt he appeared to us humans as having feelings like our own in order that we should know Him better. Moved by that ignoble fear that drives the vacillating and the distressed into the churches, she went in secret to the presbytery one evening at nightfall to kneel at the gaunt priest's feet and beg for absolution.

He promised her half a pardon, since it was impossible that God should pour down His mercies upon a house which sheltered a man like the baron: 'Soon,' he announced, 'you will feel the effects of the Divine Forbearance.'

Indeed, two days later she received a letter from her son; in her pain and distress she took it to be the beginning of the solace the priest had promised her.

MY DEAR MAMA

Do not be afraid. I am in London, and in good health, but sadly in need of money. We have not a penny left, and there are days when we have nothing to eat. My companion, whom

I love with my whole heart, has spent everything she had in order to remain with me: five thousand francs; and you will understand that I am in honour bound to pay that debt before any other. It would be a great kindness, therefore, if you could advance me fifteen thousand francs on my inheritance from Papa, as I shall soon be of age; you would be helping me out of a serious difficulty.

Goodbye, my dear Mama, I embrace you most fondly, also grandfather and Aunt Lison. I hope to see you again soon.

Your son,

VISCOUNT PAUL DE LAMARE

He had written! Then he had not forgotten her. She thought nothing of his asking for money. If he had none left, some would be sent to him. What did money matter? He had written!

She ran in tears to show this letter to the baron. Aunt Lison was summoned; and they read each word on the piece of paper that had come from him. Each phrase was discussed.

Jeanne's spirits rose from utter despair to the wildest hope, and she defended Paul: 'He will come home, surely he is coming home, since he has written to us.'

More calmly, the baron pointed out: 'Just the same, he has left us to go to that creature. He must love her more than us, as he did not hesitate to do that.'

A sudden agonizing pain pierced Jeanne to the heart; and instantly hatred welled up in her for the mistress who had stolen her son from her: the primitive, implacable hatred of a jealous mother. Until that moment she had had no concern for anything but Paul. She had barely given a thought to the hussy who had led him astray. But the baron's words had brought her rival suddenly to life, made plain how fatal was her power; and she felt that a desperate struggle was beginning between that woman and herself, and moreover that she would rather lose her son than share him with the other.

All her happiness was spoiled.

They despatched the fifteen thousand francs requested, and no word reached them for five months.

At the end of that time a man of business presented himself to settle the details of Julien's inheritance. Jeanne and the baron rendered the accounts without argument, even giving up the life interest which would have gone to the mother. Paul, who had returned to Paris, received a hundred and twenty thousand francs. After this he wrote four letters in six months, briefly giving news of himself and ending with cold expressions of affection: 'I am working,' he wrote; 'I have taken a position in the Stock Exchange. I hope to come to Les Peuples one day to embrace you, my dear parents.'

He did not mention his mistress; and his silence told them more than if he had written four pages about her. In these cold letters Jeanne could sense the woman lurking unappeasable, the eternal enemy of the mother, the woman of easy virtue.

The three people Paul had deserted talked of what could be done to save him; and they could think of nothing. A journey to Paris? What use would that be?

'This passion of his must be left to burn itself out,' said the baron. 'He will come back to us of his own accord.'

They led a pitiable existence.

Jeanne and Lison went to Mass together without the baron's knowledge.

A long time passed without news, until one morning a desperate letter arrived which filled them with alarm.

MY DEAR MAMA

I am ruined, there is nothing for me to do but blow my brains out if you do not come to my help. A speculation has just failed, one that offered every chance of success; and I am eighty-five thousand francs in debt. If I do not repay it I shall be disgraced, ruined, I shall never be able to do anything again. I am lost. I repeat, I will blow out my brains, for I cannot survive the disgrace. I would probably have done so before now if it had not been for the support of a woman of whom I never speak to you, but who is Providence itself to me.

I embrace you with all my heart, dear Mama; perhaps for ever.

Farewell

PAUL

Enclosed with this letter were bundles of documents setting out in detail the facts which had led to the disaster.

The baron replied by return post, saying that he would look into it. He went to Le Havre to make investigations; and mortgaged some land to obtain the money to send to Paul.

The young man wrote three letters in return expressing warm gratitude and fervent affection and announcing that he was coming to see his dear parents without delay.

He did not come.

A whole year passed.

Jeanne and the baron were on the point of leaving for Paris to seek him out and make one final attempt to bring him back to them, when a note arrived with the news that he was again in London, starting up a steamboat company under the name of 'Paul Delamare and Co'. He wrote: 'It is certain to do well, and it may make my fortune. There are no risks. The advantages are plain. When I next see you I shall have a good position in the world. Nowadays it is only in business that one can get out of a tight corner.'

Three months later the steamboat company went into liquidation and the director was prosecuted for irregularities in the accounts. Jeanne had an attack of hysterics lasting several hours; then she retired to bed.

Once more the baron went to Le Havre to interview lawyers and agents, attorneys and bailiffs, from whom he ascertained that the firm of Delamare was in deficit to the extent of two hundred and thirty-five thousand francs, and again mortgaged some of his property. The manor-house of Les Peuples and the two farms were mortgaged for a large sum.

One evening, when he was settling the last of the formalities at an agent's office, he fell to the floor in an apoplectic fit.

A messenger was sent to ride to Les Peuples with the news. By the time Jeanne arrived he was dead.

As she brought him home to Les Peuples she was too numb with shock to feel more than a dull grief at her loss.

In spite of the two women's urgent pleading, Father Tolbiac refused to admit the body into the church. The burial took place at nightfall without ceremony of any kind.

Paul heard of the baron's death from one of his company's liquidators. He was still in England, in hiding. He wrote to send his apologies, explaining that he had not known of the unhappy event until it was too late for him to come home. 'Besides, now that you have come to the rescue, my dear Mama, I am returning to France and shall soon be coming to pay you a visit.'

Jeanne was in such a state of collapse that she seemed to take in nothing that went on round her.

Towards the end of the winter Aunt Lison, who was now sixty-eight, had an attack of bronchitis which turned to pneumonia; she murmured, as she quietly breathed her last: 'My poor little Jeanne, I shall ask the good God to take pity on you.'

Jeanne followed her to the cemetery and looked on as the earth fell on the coffin; then, just as she was sinking to the ground in a longing to die herself, to suffer no longer, think no longer, a sturdy peasant woman took her up in her arms and bore her off as though she were a child.

Jeanne had spent five days at Aunt Lison's bedside, and after she returned to the château she let herself be put to bed unresisting by this unknown village woman who treated her gently but with authority; she fell into an exhausted sleep, worn out with fatigue and grief.

She awoke in the middle of the night. A night-light was burning on the mantelpiece. A woman was sleeping in a chair. Who was she? Jeanne did not recognize her, and leaned out from her bed in an effort to distinguish her features in the wavering gleam of the wick floating on oil in a kitchen glass.

She had the impression that she had seen that face before. But when? And where? The woman was peacefully asleep, her head tipped over on her shoulder, her cap fallen to the floor. She might have been forty or forty-five. She was robust, with a high colour, well-built and strong. Her large hands dangled at the sides of the chair. Her hair was greying. Jeanne gazed at her with her mind in confusion as she awoke from the troubled sleep that comes after great misfortunes.

Surely she had seen that face! Was it long ago? Was it recently? She had no idea, and the question obsessed and worried her. She rose quietly from her bed to look more closely at the sleeper, and tiptoed nearer to her. It was the woman who had lifted her up at the cemetery, carried her away and put her to bed. Obscurely, the memory returned to her.

But had she not met her in another place, at another time in her life? Or did she only think she recognized her from a vague recollection of the day before? And then, how did the woman come to be there, in her room?

The sleeping woman opened her eyes, saw Jeanne and immediately rose to her feet. They stood face to face, so close that their breasts touched. The stranger muttered: 'Well! Now you're on your feet! That won't do any good this time of night. Back to bed!'

'Who are you?' Jeanne asked her.

The other put her arms round Jeanne and lifted her up again, seeming as strong as a man as she carried her back to her bed. She gently laid her down on the sheets, bending over until she was almost lying on top of her; then she began to weep and covered Jeanne's face, hair and eyes with feverish kisses, bathing her face with tears and babbling: 'My dear mistress, Mam'zelle Jeanne, my dear mistress, don't you know me any more?'

Jeanne exclaimed: 'Rosalie, my girl.' She threw her arms round her, hugged and kissed her; and they both sobbed and held each other close, mingling their tears and unable to let each other go.

Rosalie was the first to compose herself: 'Now, now, we've got to be sensible,' she said, 'and not catch cold.' She gathered up the blankets, remade the bed and replaced the pillow under the head of her former mistress, who was still gasping and trembling as old memories came back to her mind.

At last Jeanne asked her: 'Why have you come back, my poor child?'

Rosalie answered: 'Well, you never thought I'd leave you all alone like that, did you?'

Jeanne persisted: 'Light a candle and let me look at you.' When the light had been set on the bedside table, they regarded each other for a long time without speaking. Then Jeanne stretched out her hand to her former maid and whispered: 'I should never have recognized you, my girl, you are very much changed, you know, although not as much as I am.'

Rosalie looked at the white-haired woman, gaunt and faded, who at the time she left her had been young and fresh and beautiful, and replied: 'It's true you've changed, Madame Jeanne, and more than's natural. But there, it's twenty-four years ago since we saw each other last.'

They were silent, reflecting. At last Jeanne said in a murmur: 'At least you have been happy?'

Afraid of awakening some too painful memory, Rosalie answered hesitantly: 'Well . . . yes . . . yes . . . Madame, I can't complain, really, I've been happier than you . . . that I have. There was only the one thing wrong, and that was me having to go away from here . . .' Then she fell abruptly silent, feeling that she had touched unwittingly on that delicate subject. But Jeanne took her up, saying gently: 'What did you expect, my girl, one can't always do as one would like. You are a widow too, are you not?' Then pain brought a tremor to her voice as she went on: 'Have you any other . . . other children?'

'No, Madame.'

'And your . . . your son . . . what has become of him? Is he doing well?'

'Yes, Madame, he's a good boy, works his fingers to the bone. It's six months now he's been married, and he's taking over my farm, that's how I'm back with you.'

Jeanne was deeply moved and her voice trembled: 'Then you will not leave me again?'

Rosalie's reply was abrupt: 'That's right, Madame, I've settled everything.'

After this they did not speak for a time.

In spite of herself Jeanne fell to comparing their two lives, yet without bitterness, resigned as she had become to the cruel injustice of fate. She said: 'And your husband, how did he treat you?'

'Oh! He was a good man Madame, and no mistake, did very well for himself. He died of a bad chest.'

Then Jeanne was filled with an urge to know, and she sat upright in bed: 'Come now, child, tell me everything, all about your life. That will do me good just now.'

Rosalie drew up a chair close to the bed and began talking about herself, her house and her neighbours in the minute detail dear to country folk, describing her farmyard, laughing now and then over things long past which reminded her of happy times in the old days, and gradually raising her voice, the voice of a farmer's wife accustomed to authority. Finally she declared: 'Oh! I've got my own bit of land now. I'm all right, there's nothing for me to worry about.' Then she felt ill at ease again and went on more quietly: 'It's you I owe it to, just the same: so you know I won't be asking for wages. No, that I won't! And then, if you don't want me here, I'll be leaving you.'

Jeanne replied: 'But you cannot mean you'll work for me for nothing!'

'Ah! that's just what I will do, Madame. Money! You'd give me money? Why, I've got just about as much as you. D'you know how much you've got left after all that scribbling about mortgagings and the like, and the interest never paid that's going up every quarter? Do you know? You don't, do you? Well, I can tell you this, you haven't got so much as ten thousand livres coming in. Not ten thousand, you understand? But I'm going to put all that right for you, straight away.'

Her voice had risen again as she became carried away with indignation at the thought of the interests neglected, the threatened ruin. As a dim smile of affection flickered over her mistress's features she protested, shocked: 'You ought never to laugh about that, Madame, not about money, because where there's no money you won't find any but low, ignorant people.'

Jeanne took her hands and held them in her own; then she said slowly, still haunted by one obsessive idea: 'Oh! I have had nothing but misfortune. Everything has turned against me. Disaster has pursued me all my life.'

Rosalie shook her head. 'You shouldn't talk like that, Madame, you shouldn't go saying such things. You had a bad husband, that's all. Nobody ought to be married like that, anyway, not without knowing a bit about their intended.'

They continued their exchange of confidences, like old friends.

They were still talking when the sun rose.

12

WITHIN A WEEK ROSALIE HAD ASSUMED FULL charge of everyone and everything in the château. Jeanne submitted passively to her rule. She went out leaning on her maid's arm, with feeble dragging steps, as dear Mama used to do, while Rosalie walked slowly beside her, preaching at her or comforting her with brisk, affectionate chatter, treating her like a sick child.

They always talked about old times, Jeanne with a lump in her throat and Rosalie in the placid tones of the stolid peasantry. The former maid-servant reverted more than once to the subject of interest in abeyance; then she insisted that her mistress should hand over the papers that Jeanne, in her ignorance of business matters, had been ashamed on her son's account to show her maid.

Rosalie then made a daily journey to Fécamp for a week, to have matters explained to her by an attorney of her acquaintance.

One evening after she had attended her mistress to bed she sat herself down beside her and announced in her abrupt way: 'Now you're in bed, Madame, we're going to have a talk.'

She proceeded to explain the situation.

After everything had been settled there would remain an income of seven or eight thousand francs. No more.

Jeanne replied to this: 'Never mind, my girl. I know I am not long for this world; I shall always have enough.'

Her answer angered Rosalie: 'And so you may, Madame, just for yourself; but what about Monsieur Paul, aren't you going to leave anything for him?'

Jeanne shuddered. 'Pray do not speak of him again. It gives me too much pain to think of him.'

'Well, that's just what I do mean to talk about, because you're not being fair to him, don't you see, Madame Jeanne. He does act silly at times; but he won't do always; and then, he'll be getting married; there'll be children. He's going to want money to bring them up. Now you listen to me: you're going to sell Les Peuples! . . .'

Jeanne sprang up in bed: 'Sell Les Peuples! What are you thinking of? I would never dream of such a thing!'

Rosalie was unmoved: 'I tell you, Madame, you will sell it, because you're going to have to.'

She explained the calculations and plans she had made, and the way she had worked things out.

After Les Peuples and the two adjoining farms had been sold to somebody she had found who wished to have them, they would keep four farms at St Léonard which, after the mortgages had been redeemed, would bring in eight thousand three hundred francs. Thirteen hundred would be set aside each year for the repair and upkeep of the property; that would leave seven thousand francs, of which five thousand would go to current expenditure; and the balance of two thousand would form a reserve fund.

Rosalie added: 'The rest's all gone down the drain, and that's that. From now on, it's me that'll hold the purse strings, you see; as for Monsieur Paul, he'll get nothing, nothing at all; he'd take the last penny out of your pocket.'

Jeanne was by now in tears, and murmured:

'But suppose he has not enough to eat?'

'He can come and eat with us, if he's that hungry. There'll always be a bed for him, and a morsel of food. Do you think he'd've done all them stupid things if you'd given him nothing from the start?'

'But he had debts, he would have been disgraced.'

'And when you've got nothing left, is that going to stop him having a lot more? You've paid up, and that's done with; but you're not going to pay one penny more; I can tell you that. Good night now, Madame.'

She went out of the room.

Jeanne was too distressed and agitated to sleep at the thought of selling Les Peuples, going away and leaving the home with which her whole life was bound up.

As soon as Rosalie entered her room the next day she said to her: 'My dear child, I shall never be able to bring myself to leave this house.'

This made Rosalie angry: 'Just the same, Madame, that's what you've got to do. The lawyer's coming soon with the person that's got his eye on the château. If you set yourself against it, in four years' time you won't have anything left, not a radish.'

Jeanne, prostrate with distress, only repeated: 'I cannot do it; I shall never be able to.'

An hour later the postman brought a letter from Paul asking for another ten thousand francs. What was she to do? In distraction she consulted Rosalie, who raised both arms in the air: 'What did I tell you, Madame? Ah! you'd've been in a fine pickle, the two of you, if I hadn't come along.' Jeanne bowed to her maid's will and wrote to the young man in reply:

MY DEAR SON

I can do nothing more for you. You have ruined me; I even find myself forced to sell Les Peuples. But do not forget there will always be a home for you if you care to come and take refuge with your old mother, whom you have pained so much.

JEANNE

When the attorney arrived bringing Monsieur Jeoffrin, a retired sugar-refiner, with him she received them herself and invited them to go over every part of the property.

She signed the deed of sale a month later and purchased a modest little house at the same time, near Goderville on the road to Montivilliers, in the hamlet of Batteville.

Then she walked alone in dear Mama's avenue until dark, in anguish of heart and distress of mind, addressing herself to the horizon and the trees, the worm-eaten seat under the plane-tree, all those features of the landscape so familiar that they seemed to have entered into her mental vision, into her soul – the copse, the mound overlooking the heath where she had often sat and from which she had seen Count de Fourville running towards the sea on that terrible day of Julien's death, an old headless elm against which she had often leaned – to everything in that familiar scene she bade farewell with sorrowful tears.

Rosalie came out at last to take her arm and bring her back to the house.

A tall peasant youth of twenty-five was waiting at the door. He greeted her in a friendly tone as though he had known her a long time. 'Good evening, Madame Jeanne, how are you? Mother told me to come and see to your move. I'll want to know what you're going to take away, seeing as I'll have to do it a bit at a time, not to interfere with the farm work.'

This was her maid's son, Julien's son, Paul's brother.

Her heart seemed to stop beating; and yet she would have liked to embrace the lad.

She looked at him, to see if he resembled her husband or her son. He was a sturdy fellow with a ruddy complexion, fair hair and blue eyes like his mother's. And yet there was a likeness to Julien. What was it? How did it show itself? She could not be certain, but there was something of his father in his looks as a whole.

The young peasant repeated: 'If you could show me right away, I'd be obliged.'

She had not yet decided, however, what to take with her, since the new house was very small; and she asked him to return in a week's time.

She became absorbed in the removal, which brought some distraction into her dull existence where there was no hope or promise.

She went from room to room seeking out the pieces of furniture which held memories for her, like those well-loved possessions which are almost part of ourselves, things we have known since childhood, to which a memory of joy or sorrow clings; they are dates in our private history, those objects which were once the mute companions of our brightest and our darkest hours, and have grown old and worn along with us until the fabric is split in places and the lining torn, with shaky joints and faded colours.

She picked them out one by one, often hesitating, as painstaking as though each decision were of capital importance, changing her mind every minute, weighing the merits of two armchairs or an old writing-desk as compared with those of an antique work-table.

She pulled drawers open, trying to remember things; and when she had announced firmly: 'Yes, I will take this,' the piece was carried down to the dining-room.

She decided to keep all the furniture of her own room, her bed, her tapestries, her clock, everything.

The drawing-room chairs that she chose were those with pictures which had been her favourites as a child: the fox and the stork, the fox and the crow, the grasshopper and the ant, and the melancholy heron.

One day, exploring every corner of the home she was to leave, she went up into the loft.

She was startled at what she saw; there was a medley of objects of every kind, some broken, some merely dirty, others left up there no one knew why, perhaps because they were no longer wanted or had been replaced. She came upon a number of knick-knacks which had disappeared unremarked, small things she had handled, old things, the trivia of her surroundings for fifteen years which she had seen every day without paying attention to them and now rediscovered there in the loft, together with others even older which she perfectly remembered seeing in their places when she first arrived – suddenly each of these assumed the importance of a forgotten presence, a friend re-encountered. They made an impression on her like that of people one has met frequently over a long period without ever coming to know them, who one evening for no particular reason suddenly begin to prattle interminably, baring their very souls in unsuspected revelations.

Her heart beat faster as she wandered from one object to the next, saying to herself: 'Why, that is the china cup I cracked one evening a few days before I was married. – Ah! there is Mama's little lamp, and the stick dear Papa broke trying to open the gate when the wood was swollen after the rain.'

There were many things there besides that she did not recognize and that held no memories for her, possessions of her grandparents or great-grandparents, covered with dust and looking like exiles in a period not their own, sad at being thus abandoned where there was no one acquainted with their history or what had happened to them and no one who knew the people who had chosen and bought them, owned and cared for them, handled them with a familiar touch and looked at them with pleasure.

The dust long gathered left marks on Jeanne's fingers as she turned these objects over; and she stood there among that old bric-a-brac in the wan light from a small skylight in the roof.

She examined with close attention, in case they might recall something to her, such things as three-legged chairs, a copper warming-pan and a battered foot-warmer that she thought she recognized in a heap of disused household utensils.

At last she made a collection of everything she wished to take with her and went downstairs to send Rosalie to fetch it. Her maid at first indignantly refused to carry down 'those dirty old things'. However, although Jeanne seemed no longer to have any will of her own, she insisted on this; and Rosalie had to obey her.

One morning the young farmer Denis Lecoq, Julien's son, brought his cart to the manor-house to begin the removal. Rosalie went with him to attend to the unloading and see that the furniture was put in the proper places.

Left to herself, Jeanne began wandering through all the rooms in the château in a state of great distress, her eyes streaming with tears, embracing in transports of nostalgia everything she could not take away, the big white birds on the drawing-room tapestries, old candlesticks, anything that met her eyes; then she left the house to 'say farewell' to the sea.

It was the end of September; a grey lowering sky hung heavy over the earth, and the waves were a dull ochre as far as the eye could see. Jeanne stood for a long time on the cliff, while painful thoughts passed through her mind. When it grew dark she turned to go back, after a day in which she had suffered as much as she ever had in times of great sorrow.

Rosalie had returned and was waiting for her, pleased with the new house and declaring that it was very much more cheerful than this box of a building which did not even stand on a highway.

Jeanne wept all that evening.

From the moment the farmers heard that the manor-house was sold they had shown her no more than the exact measure of respect that was due to her, calling her 'the madwoman' among themselves without quite knowing why, but doubtless because with their primitive instincts they sensed her morbid and increasing sentimentality, her high-flown imaginings and all the disorder of her pitiful storm-tossed spirit.

On the day before their departure she chanced to visit the stables. She was startled at hearing a groan. It was Massacre, to whom she had not given a thought for months. Blind and paralysed, he had reached a greater age than most of his kind and lived on a bed of straw, looked after by Ludivine, who did not neglect him. Jeanne took him up in her arms, kissed him and carried him into the house. He had grown as big as a barrel and could scarcely drag himself along on his stiff, splayed legs; he barked like one of those toy wooden dogs that children play with.

The last day dawned. Jeanne had slept in Julien's old room, since her own had been dismantled.

She rose from bed weak and panting, as after a long journey. The cart was waiting at the entrance, loaded with trunks and the rest of her possessions. A second two-wheeled conveyance, a gig for the mistress and maid, stood ready behind it.

Old Simon and Ludivine were to stay on alone at the manor-house until the new owner arrived; then they would retire to live with relations, Jeanne having provided for them to receive a small pension. They had, besides, savings of their own. By now the two servants were very old, useless and garrulous. Marius had taken a wife and long ago left the manor.

At eight o'clock it began to rain, a fine cold drizzle borne on a light breeze off the sea. Covers had to be put over the cart. The leaves were already falling from the trees.

Cups of coffee steamed on the table in the kitchen. Jeanne took a chair, sipped her coffee and then rose and said: 'Let us start!'

She put on her hat and shawl, and said in a choked voice as Rosalie was fitting galoshes on her feet: 'Do you remember how hard it rained when we started out from Rouen to come here . . .'

She shuddered violently, put both hands to her breast and fell back unconscious.

For more than an hour she lay as still as the dead; then she opened her eyes and went into convulsions, amid floods of tears.

When the attack subsided she felt too weak to get to her feet. Rosalie however feared that there might be further attacks if they delayed their departure, and went to fetch her son. They lifted her up, carried her out and set her down in the gig on the oilcloth-covered seat; the old servant climbed in and took her place beside Jeanne, wrapped up her legs and put a big cloak round her shoulders, then opened an umbrella and held it over her mistress's head, calling out: 'Quick now, Denis, let's be off.'

The young man mounted beside his mother, with only half a seat to sit on, and put his horse into a brisk, jerky trot that jolted the two women up and down.

When they turned the corner in the village there was somebody pacing up and down in the roadway: it was Father Tolbiac, who appeared to be waiting to see them leave.

He stopped to let the gig pass. He was holding up his cassock with one hand to keep it out of the puddles, and his lean black-stockinged shanks could be seen ending in enormous muddy shoes.

Jeanne lowered her eyes to avoid meeting his; and Rosalie, who knew the whole story, was furious. She muttered: 'The beast, the beast!' then, gripping her son's hand: 'Give him a touch of the whip.'

However, when the young man drew level with the priest and they were moving at a smart pace he let one of the wheels of his boneshaker drop sharply into a rut, and a stream of mud shot up and covered the cleric from head to foot.

Rosalie turned round beaming and shook her fist at him, while the priest dried himself with a large handkerchief.

They had not gone much further before Jeanne exclaimed: 'Massacre – we have left him behind!'

They pulled up, and Denis jumped down and ran back to fetch the dog, while Rosalie held the reins.

The young man reappeared at last with the bald, shapeless

creature heavy in his arms and put him down between the two women's skirts.

13

TWO HOURS LATER THE CART PULLED UP IN front of a small brick house beside the highway, set in an orchard of quenouille-trained pear trees.*

There was a pergola in each corner of the garden covered with honeysuckle and clematis, and the centre was laid out in small vegetable plots with narrow paths between them and a border of fruit trees.

The whole property was enclosed by a high quickset hedge and separated by a field from the neighbouring farm. A hundred paces away along the road was a blacksmith's forge. Apart from these, the nearest habitation was a kilometre away.

It was possible to glimpse a view of the countryside through four double rows of tall trees round an apple orchard, a landscape which extended over the plain of Caux with its scattered farmsteads.

Jeanne wished to retire and rest as soon as they arrived, but Rosalie feared that she would start to brood again and would not allow it.

A carpenter from Goderville was waiting to help them to settle in; and they immediately set about the task of arranging the furniture which had already been brought, while they waited for the last cartload which could not be long in coming.

The labour was considerable, involving much lengthy reflection and discussion.

An hour later the cart drew up at the gate and had to be unloaded in the rain.

By the evening the house was in total disorder with everything piled up at random; and Jeanne fell into an exhausted sleep as soon as her head touched the pillow.

* Trees pruned to a long, narrow pyramid. (*Quenouille:* distaff.)

There was so much to be done in the days that followed that she had no time for sentiment. She even took an interest in the arrangement of her possessions in her new home, for the thought of her son coming to see her there was constantly in her mind. The tapestries from her old room were hung in the dining-room, which served also as drawing-room; and she gave particular care to the furnishing of one of the two rooms on the first floor, which she privately called 'Poulet's room'.

She kept the other for herself, while Rosalie's was on the floor above, next to the loft.

It was a pleasant little house after so much care had been spent on it; and Jeanne felt at home there from the first, although something – she did not quite know what – was lacking.

One morning the attorney's clerk from Fécamp called to bring her a sum of three thousand six hundred francs, payment for the furniture she had left at Les Peuples to be valued by an auctioneer. She thrilled with pleasure as she took the money; and as soon as the man had left she put on her hat, intending to go with all speed to Goderville to hand over this windfall to Paul.

She was hurrying along the road when she met Rosalie returning from market. The maid was suspicious, although she did not guess at once what had happened: when she found out – for Jeanne could no longer keep anything from her – she put down her basket on the ground and gave free rein to her wrath.

Hands on hips, she screamed at Jeanne; then she took her mistress on her right arm, her basket on her left, and with anger undiminished marched back to the house.

As soon as they were indoors the maid demanded that Jeanne should hand over the money to her. Jeanne did so, only keeping back the odd six hundred francs; but Rosalie's suspicions were aroused and she was on her guard, and was not taken in for long; Jeanne was obliged to give up that small sum as well.

Rosalie agreed, however, that it should be sent to the young man.

He returned thanks for it a few days later. 'You have done me a great service, my dear Mama, for we were in a sorry state.'

Jeanne nevertheless did not settle down well at Batteville; she constantly had the sensation that there was a change in her breathing, and she felt even more solitary, more forsaken and lost than before. She would go out to take the air, walk as far as the hamlet of Verneuil and return by way of Trois-Mares, then no sooner was she indoors than she would feel a sudden urgent desire to leave the house again, as though she had failed to go exactly where she intended, where she wished to walk.

Every day it was the same, yet still she could not understand why she felt that strange compulsion. Then one evening she unconsciously used an expression which revealed the secret of her restlessness. She said as she sat down to dinner: 'Oh! how I wish that I could see the sea!'

It was the sea that she was missing so much, the wide ocean which had been her neighbour for twenty-five years, with its salt air, its storms, its scolding voice and stinging breezes, the waters she used to see every morning from her window at Les Peuples and whose air she had breathed day and night, the sea whose near presence she had unknowingly felt and come to love like a living being.

Massacre also lived in a state of extreme disarray. On the evening of his arrival he had settled down in the bottom of the kitchen dresser, from which no one was able to dislodge him. He stayed there all day, hardly moving, only turning round occasionally with a low growl.

As soon as darkness fell he got upon his legs and dragged himself to the garden door, bumping against the walls. After he had been outside for the few minutes he needed he came in again, sat down on his haunches in front of the stove which was still hot, and as soon as both his owners had retired to bed he began to howl.

He howled all night on a plaintive, mournful note, occasionally breaking off for an hour only to begin again on one even more heart-rending. They chained him up in a barrel in front of the house. He howled beneath the windows. Then, as he was old and feeble and could not live much longer, he was brought back into the kitchen.

Jeanne found it impossible to sleep when she heard the old dog moaning and scrabbling, trying to find his way about this new house, knowing very well that he was not in his own home any longer.

Nothing could quiet him. He drowsed in the daytime half asleep, as though his blurred sight and the sense of his infirmity kept him from trying to move about at a time when other creatures were alive and astir, but as soon as it was dark he would wander restlessly abroad, only then perhaps daring to live and move when the night made all beings blind.

One morning he was found dead. It came as a great relief.

The winter wore on; and Jeanne fell prey to an incurable hopelessness. It was not the agony of grief that seems to wring the soul, but a dull, oppressive melancholy.

There was nothing to rouse or distract her, no one to pay her any attention. The highway stretching to right and left of her door was almost always deserted. Occasionally a trap went trotting past, driven by a red-faced man whose smock was blown out by the wind of his motion into a sort of blue balloon; sometimes there was a slow-moving cart; two figures might be seen like specks on the horizon, tiny figures at first which grew slowly larger and then, when they had passed the house, shrank again to the size of insects at the extreme end of the white line that unrolled itself into the distance, rising and falling with the shallow undulations of the ground.

When the grass began to grow again a little girl in short skirts passed the gate every morning, driving two lean cows which cropped the grass at the roadside along the edge of the ditches. She returned each evening at dusk at the same drowsy pace, taking one step in ten minutes as she followed her charges.

Jeanne dreamed every night that she was still at Les Peuples.

She was there again as she used to be with Papa and dear Mama, sometimes even with Aunt Lison. She was doing again things that were now long past and forgotten; she imagined she was supporting Madame Adélaïde when she took the air in her avenue. Each time she awoke she burst into tears.

She thought constantly of Paul, wondering: 'What is he doing? How is he now? Does he sometimes think of me?' As she went slowly along the sunken lane between the farms, she turned over in her mind all the thoughts that tormented her; but above everything she suffered from an unquenchable jealousy of the unknown woman who had robbed her of her son. That hatred was all that restrained her and kept her from taking action, from going to find him and enter the house where he lived. She seemed to see his mistress standing in the doorway and asking: 'What are you doing here, Madame?' Her pride as a mother rebelled at the possibility of such an encounter; and the arrogance of a virtuous woman, one who is without stain or weakness, went to swell her indignation at all the baseness men can stoop to when they are enslaved by the obscenities of carnal love, which coarsens their whole nature. She saw all humankind as tainted when she thought of the impure secrets of the senses, the degrading caresses and manifold mysteries of couples joined in copulation.

Another spring and summer passed.

When autumn came round again with its long hours of rain, lowering skies and sombre clouds, she felt so weary of her present existence that she decided to make one last attempt to win back her Poulet.

Surely by this time the young man's passion would have spent itself.

She wrote him a pitiful letter.

MY DEAR BOY
I am writing to implore you to come back to me. You must realize that I am old and ill, quite alone with my one maid all the year. I am living now in a small house on the high road. It is very sad for me. But if you were here, everything would be

different. I have no one but you in the world, and I have not seen you for seven years! You will never know how unhappy I have been, how my heart has found refuge in thinking of you. You were what I lived for and dreamed of, my only hope, my only love, and I miss you, and you have abandoned me!

Come back to me, my little Poulet, come back and hold me in your arms once more, your old mother who appeals to you in despair.

JEANNE

He answered a few days later.

MY DEAR MAMA

There is nothing I should like better than to come and see you, but I haven't a penny. Send me some money, and I will come. I did, in any case, intend to come and look you up to discuss a plan that would make it possible to do as you ask.

In all that I have gone through, my dear companion has never spared herself; her devotion to me has been beyond bounds. I cannot go on any longer without giving proper recognition to her loyalty and love. Besides these qualities she has very good manners, something you will appreciate. And she is well educated, fond of reading. In short, you cannot imagine what she has been to me all this time. I should be inhuman if I did not give her proof of my gratitude. So I am asking your permission to marry her. Then you would forgive me for my escapades and we would all live together in your new house.

If you knew her, you would grant your consent instantly. She is the best of women, I assure you, and very well bred. You would like her, I am sure. As for myself, I cannot live without her.

I await your reply with impatience, my dear Mama, and we embrace you with all our hearts.

Your son,

VISCOUNT PAUL DE LAMARE

Jeanne was thunderstruck. She sat motionless with the letter in her lap, while it dawned on her what a cunning scheme that woman had employed, keeping a continual hold on her son and never once allowing him to come near her, biding her time, the time when the old mother would be driven to despair and unable to resist any longer the yearning to take her child in her arms, when she would weaken and agree to anything.

She suffered acutely at the thought of Paul's obstinate preference for that creature. She said to herself over and over again: 'He does not love me. He does not love me.'

Rosalie came into the room. Jeanne burst out: 'He means to marry her now.'

The maid was startled. 'Oh! Madame, you can't allow that. Monsieur Paul's not going to take up with that streetwalker.'

Crushed though she was, Jeanne was not defeated. 'No, my girl, never. Since he will not come, I will go to him myself, and we shall see which one of us has the best of it.'

She wrote to Paul then and there to announce her coming, so that she should meet him somewhere other than at the lodging where that hussy lived.

While she was waiting for an answer she made preparations for her journey. Rosalie began packing an old trunk with her mistress's linen and personal belongings. As she was folding a shabby, countrified old gown she exclaimed: 'You haven't so much as a rag to put on your back. I can't let you go like that. You'd be a disgrace to us all; the Paris ladies would think you were a servant.'

Jeanne let her have her way. The two women went together to Goderville to choose some material, a green check, which was put in the hands of the town dressmaker. Then they went back to ask information of the attorney, Maître Roussel, who stayed a fortnight in the capital every year. It was twenty-eight years since Jeanne had been in Paris.

He gave them plentiful advice on avoiding the traffic in the streets and taking precautions against theft, advising them to sew their money into the lining of their clothes and keep in their pockets no more than would suffice for their immediate needs; he discoursed to them lengthily on medium-priced restaurants and mentioned two or three suitable for women;

and recommended the Hotel Normandie where he stayed himself. They should give his name as an introduction.

The railways of which everyone was talking had been in operation for six years between Paris and Le Havre. But Jeanne, obsessed with her sorrows, had not yet seen the steam-driven carriages which were revolutionizing the whole country.

In the meantime, no answer came from Paul.

She waited one week, then two, walking along the road every morning to meet the postman and trembling as she accosted him: 'You have nothing for me, Monsieur Malandain?' The man always answered, in a voice hoarse from being out in all weathers: 'Nought for you today, mistress.'

It was surely that woman who kept Paul from writing!

At last Jeanne decided to leave without further delay. She wished to take Rosalie with her, but the maid refused, since it would have added to the expense of the journey.

She would not allow her mistress to take more than three hundred francs: 'If you need more than that you write to me and I'll go and see the lawyer, he'll let you have it. If I give you any more it'll only go into Monsieur Paul's pocket.'

One December morning Denis Lecoq came to take them to the station and they both stepped into his gig, since Rosalie was escorting her mistress to the train.

They first inquired the price of the ticket, and then when the trunk had been registered and everything was settled they waited beside the railway line, trying to make out how the contraption worked and so intent on this mystery that they thought no more of the sad occasion for the journey.

At last a whistle sounded in the distance and they turned their heads, to behold a black machine that was growing steadily larger. It came in and passed them with a terrible clamour, pulling behind it a long chain of small houses on wheels; a railway employee opened the door of one of these, and Jeanne in tears kissed Rosalie and climbed inside.

Rosalie called out with emotion:

'Bye-bye, Madame; a safe journey, see you again soon!'

'Goodbye, my girl.'

There was another blast on the whistle and the whole string of carriages began to move, slowly at first, then faster and then with alarming speed.

Two of the corners in Jeanne's compartment were occupied, each by a gentleman sleeping.

She watched the countryside go past with its trees, farms and villages, nervous at the speed, feeling that she was caught up in a new life and being carried off into a world that was no longer her own, no longer the world of her peaceful youth and monotonous existence.

It was growing dark when the train arrived in Paris.

A porter took Jeanne's trunk; and she followed him, scared, jostled, unpractised in making her way through the swarming crowd, almost running after the man in fear of losing sight of him.

When she was in the hotel she hastened to announce:

'I have been recommended to come here by Monsieur Roussel.'

The landlady, a large, solemn woman seated behind a desk, asked her:

'Who's he, Monsieur Roussel?'

Jeanne told her, somewhat surprised: 'Why, he is the attorney from Goderville, who stays with you every year.'

The big woman assented:

'Likely enough. I don't know him. You want a room?'

'Yes, Madame.'

A boy took her luggage and went before her up the stairs.

Her heart sank. She took a chair at a small table and ordered soup and a chicken wing to be sent up to her. She had eaten nothing since dawn.

She made a sad little meal by candle-light, thinking of many things, remembering how she had passed through this same city on the return from her wedding trip, how the first signs of Julien's disposition had shown themselves during that stay in Paris. She had been young and confident then, and full of spirit. Now she felt old, ill at ease, even timorous, weak and easily put out. After she had finished her meal she sat at the window and looked out at the crowded street. She would have liked to venture out, but did not dare. She felt sure that she would soon be lost. She retired to bed; and blew out her candle.

The noise, the sense of being in a strange city and the unsettling effect of the journey kept her wakeful. Hours passed. Although the medley of sounds outside gradually grew quieter she still could not sleep, with the great city round her never completely at rest. She was accustomed to the deep, calm sleep of the country which plunged everything into torpor, men, beasts and plants, and she now felt a mysterious stirring all about her. Voices, almost imperceptible, came to her ears as though they had stolen into the walls of the hotel. Sometimes a floor creaked, a door was shut, a bell rang.

Suddenly at two in the morning, just as she was beginning to feel drowsy, a woman screamed in a room nearby. Jeanne sat up quickly in bed; then she thought she heard a man laugh.

The approach of dawn brought back the thought of Paul; and she dressed as soon as it was light.

He lived in the Cité, in the rue du Sauvage. Remembering that Rosalie had urged her to economize, she decided to go there on foot. It was a fine day; there was a bite in the air; people were hurrying along the pavements. She walked as fast as she could to the end of a street where she had been directed to turn right, then left; then she would come to a square where she was to ask again. She could not find the square and asked her way at a baker's, who gave her different directions. She started off again, lost her way, wandered about and inquired again, until she was completely lost.

By this time she was in a panic; she had stopped choosing which way to turn, and was walking almost at random. She had just decided to call a cab, when she caught sight of the Seine. She continued then on foot along the riverside.

She had been walking nearly an hour when she came to the

rue du Sauvage, which proved to be an unlit alley. She stopped in front of the door, too agitated to take another step.

He was there, Poulet, in that house.

Her hands and knees were shaking; at last she entered the house, found her way along a passage to the concierge's room, proffered a coin and asked the man: 'Will you go up and tell Monsieur Paul de Lamare that an old lady is here to see him, a friend of his mother?'

The concierge answered:

'He's not living here now, Madame.'

A violent shudder ran through her whole body. Her voice quavered:

'Ah! where . . . where is he staying now?'

'That I don't know.'

It was like a blow; she felt dizzy as though she might fall, and it was some few minutes before she could speak. At last with a great effort she recovered herself and said in a whisper:

'When did he leave?'

The man was full of information. 'That was a fortnight since. They went out one evening, just like that, and they never came back. Owed money all over the place. So they wouldn't leave an address, would they, stands to reason.'

Jeanne had an impression of flashing lights, great jets of flame blazing up before her eyes as though a gun were being fired. A single thought remained in her mind, however, sustaining her and keeping her upright on her feet, outwardly calm and self-possessed. She would find out where Poulet was and go to see him.

'Then he did not say anything to you before he left?'

'Oh! not a word, they ran away so they wouldn't have to pay, that's how it was.'

'Surely he sent someone for his letters?'

'More often than I'd have given them. And then, they didn't get no more than ten in a twelvemonth. Still, I did take one up to them a day or two before they ran off.'

That would have been her letter. She said hastily: 'Listen, I am his mother, and I have come to see him. Here are ten francs for you. If you have any news of him, if you should hear anything, come to see me at the Hotel Normandie, rue du Havre, and I will pay you well.'

He replied: 'You can count on me, Madame.'

She hurried away.

She started again on foot, without caring where she was going. She walked quickly as though she had important business; she kept close to the wall and was hustled by people carrying bundles; she crossed roads without looking at the traffic, and coachmen swore at her; she stumbled on pavement kerbs without seeing them; she ran on straight ahead, like a lost soul.

Presently she found herself in a garden, so fatigued that she sank down on a bench. She must have stayed there a long time, weeping without knowing it, while passers-by turned round to stare at her. Then she was aware of being very cold; and she rose to go on; she was so weak and exhausted that her legs would hardly carry her.

She would have liked to go into a restaurant for some soup; but she dared not set foot in one of those establishments, for she knew that her distress must show in her features, and this filled her with a sort of shame, or diffidence. She stopped for a moment to look in through a doorway, but fled in discouragement when she saw people at tables eating, saying to herself: 'I will go into the next one.' But she went no further inside the next.

At last she bought a croissant at a baker's and munched it as she went along. She was very thirsty, but did not know where to find something to drink and went without.

Passing through an archway, she came into another garden enclosed by arcades. She recognized this as the Palais-Royal.

She felt warmer after walking in the sun, and rested again on a seat for an hour or two.

A crush of people entered the quadrangle, an elegant crowd who bowed and smiled to each other as they conversed, one of those gatherings of the fortunate among whom the women are beautiful and the men rich, whose sole interests are dress and pleasure.

Jeanne rose to make her escape, nervous at finding herself in the midst of that brilliant throng; but suddenly it occurred to her that she might come upon Paul in these surroundings; and she began walking about the garden with her quick, nervous step from one end to the other, peering at the faces passing to and fro.

People turned to stare at her; others laughed and pointed her out to each other. She ran away when she saw this, thinking that doubtless they were laughing at her appearance and the green check dress that Rosalie had chosen and had made up by the dressmaker in Goderville.

She dared not even ask her way of passers-by. At last, however, she did venture to do this and ended by reaching her hotel.

She did not stir again all the rest of that day, but sank into a chair at the foot of her bed, where she remained. She dined as she had the day before, on soup and a little meat. She went through each stage of her toilet mechanically, from habit, as she prepared for bed.

Next day she went to the police headquarters to demand that a search be made for her child. They could promise her nothing; but told her that the matter would be investigated.

She wandered about the streets in the hope of meeting him. She felt more alone, more lost and forlorn among the bustling crowds than in the midst of empty fields.

When she returned that evening to her hotel she was told that a man had asked to see her in the name of Monsieur Paul, and that he would come back the next day. A warm flush spread through her, and she did not close her eyes that night. Could it be he? Yes, it was surely Paul, although she did not recognize him from the description she had been given.

At nine in the morning there was a knock on her door, and she called: 'Come in!' ready to rush forward with open arms. A stranger presented himself. As he apologised for disturbing her and explained why he was there – to claim payment of a sum that Paul owed him – she began to weep but did not want him to see, and brushed away her tears with a finger-tip as they trickled into the corners of her eyes.

He had heard of her visit to the rue du Sauvage from the concierge, and since he could not find the young man he addressed himself to the mother. He held out a piece of paper, which she took without thinking. She made out a figure: ninety francs; she drew out her purse and paid it.

She did not leave her room that day.

The next day other creditors made their appearance. She gave them most of what she had left, keeping back only twenty francs; she wrote to Rosalie to tell her how she was situated.

Waiting for an answer from her maid she passed her time in aimlessly wandering the streets, not knowing what to do or where to go to kill the sad, interminable hours with no loving companion at her side, no one who knew of her misfortunes. She walked at random, beset now by a desire to leave the city and go home to her little house beside the lonely highway.

A few days earlier she had been too low-spirited and sad to stay there; now however it was clear to her that, on the contrary, she would be able to live nowhere else but in that house where her few forlorn habits had taken root.

At last one evening a letter came from her maid containing two hundred francs. Rosalie had written:

Madame Jeanne, come back very soon, I am not going to send you any more money. About Monsieur Paul, I will go and look for him myself when we have some news of him.

I send my respects.

Your servant,

ROSALIE

On a bitterly cold, snowy morning Jeanne left Paris to return to Batteville.

14

AFTER JEANNE'S RETURN TO BATTEVILLE SHE never left the house, never bestirred herself in any way. She rose at the same hour every morning, looked out of her window at the weather and then came downstairs to sit beside the fire in the drawing-room.

There she would remain all day without moving, her eyes fixed on the flames, letting her sad thoughts roam uncontrolled as her misfortunes passed in melancholy procession through her mind. Darkness would steal in and gradually fill the little room, and still she had not moved except to put more wood on the fire. Rosalie, bringing in the lamp, would exclaim: 'Now, Madame Jeanne, you must rouse up or you won't have no appetite again come dinner-time.'

She often became obsessed with an idea or disturbed by the merest trifle, for the most trivial things took on an exaggerated importance in her sick mind.

She lived above all in the past, the distant past, haunted by the early days of her life and her wedding journey to Corsica. Long forgotten landscapes in that island took shape before her eyes in the embers on the hearth; and every detail came to her recollection, every minute particular, every one of the figures she had seen there; the face of the guide Jean Ravoli appeared repeatedly; and at times she imagined that she heard his voice.

Then her thoughts turned to the delightful years of Paul's boyhood, when he had made her plant out salad vegetables and she knelt on the rich soil with Aunt Lison, the two of them rivalling each other in the pains they took to please the little boy, at odds over who would be more skilled in rooting the young plants and who would raise most seedlings.

Very softly her lips formed the words: 'Poulet, my little Poulet,' as though she were talking to him; and as she came to rest on that word in her musing she essayed, sometimes for hours, to trace the letters of it in the air with a pointing finger. She moved it slowly as she sat by the fire, imagining that she could see the letters and then, when she thought she had been mistaken, she began the P again with a hand that trembled with fatigue, straining to draw the whole of the name; as soon as this was accomplished she started over again.

The time came when she was unable to go on, confusing everything, shaping different words, driving herself into a frenzy.

All the fantasies of solitary people came to plague her. It would vex her to find the least thing out of place.

Rosalie used often to force her to go out of doors, and take her for a walk along the road; but after twenty minutes Jeanne would say: 'I cannot go any further, child,' and sit down by the roadside.

Before long she came to detest movement of any kind, and stayed in bed as long as possible.

A childhood habit had clung to her, that of rising from bed as soon as she had drunk her coffee. She was excessively fond of this drink, and would have suffered more at being deprived of it than of anything else. There was something sensual in her expectation as she waited impatiently for Rosalie to bring it in the morning; and when the full cup was set down on her bedside table she sat up in bed and emptied it rapidly, almost greedily. Then she threw back the sheets and began to dress.

Gradually however she fell into the way of daydreaming for a few moments after she had replaced the empty bowl in its saucer; then she stretched out again, and those idle minutes grew longer from day to day, until Rosalie lost patience and came back to dress her mistress almost by force.

She appeared no longer to have any will of her own, and whenever her maid required her advice or opinion, or asked her a question, she answered: 'Do as you like, my girl.'

She believed herself to be dogged so closely by a personal, persistently malevolent fate that she became as fatalistic as an Oriental; and after repeatedly seeing her dreams come to nothing and her hopes fall to pieces she had become reluctant to embark on anything, and would hesitate for whole days before doing the smallest thing, convinced that she would always go the wrong way about it and it would end in failure.

She was always saying: 'I have never had good fortune in

all my life.' Then Rosalie would protest: 'What would you say then if you had to earn your bread, get up at six o'clock every morning and go out and do a day's work! There's plenty that do, just the same, and when they're too old to work they starve.'

Jeanne would answer: 'You must remember that I am quite alone, for my son has abandoned me.' Rosalie would fly into a rage: 'Just think of that! Well! And what about the boys doing their military service! and the ones who go off to America and never come back!'

She had a dim notion of America as a country where people went to make a fortune and never returned.

She went on: 'The time always comes when they have to leave each other, young ones and old, because they're not made to get on together.' She ended on a savage note: 'Now then, what would you say if he was dead?'

After that, Jeanne had nothing more to say.

A little strength returned to her with the first days of spring when the air grew milder, but she employed it only to plunge even more deeply into sombre brooding.

One morning she went up into the loft to look something out, and chanced to open a box of old calendars; it is the habit of country folk sometimes to keep such things, and these had escaped destruction.

She felt as though she had rediscovered the actual years of her own past, and she was overcome by a strange, obscure emotion at the sight of the heap of cardboard squares.

She gathered them up and took them downstairs. They were of all sizes, big and small. She began arranging them on the table in chronological order. Presently she came to the first one, the calendar she had brought with her to Les Peuples.

She pored over it for a long time, gazing at the dates she had struck off on the morning she left Rouen, the day after she had come home from the convent. She wept. She wept sad, slow tears, the piteous tears of the old, at the sight of her unhappy life spread out on the table before her.

Next, an idea came into her mind which soon became a fearful, incessant, desperate obsession. She wished to go through everything she had done, rediscover it almost, day by day.

She pinned up the yellowed pieces of cardboard on the walls and tapestries, and spent hours in looking at one or another of them while she asked herself: 'What happened in that month?'

She had underlined the memorable dates in her history and sometimes succeeded in recovering a whole month, reconstructing, grouping and linking together one by one all the details that preceded and followed an important event.

By dint of persistent attention, efforts of memory and concentrated willpower she succeeded in reconstructing almost the whole of her first two years at Les Peuples, as memories of her distant past returned to her with singular ease, bringing a sense of relief.

The later years, however, appeared to her shrouded in mist, mingling and overlapping; and she would sometimes pass long minutes with her head bent over a calendar and her mind reaching out over the past, unable even to be sure it was in that particular calendar that such and such a memory was to be found.

She moved from one to the next round the room, which was papered with these pictures of bygone days as it might have been with engravings of the Stations of the Cross. She would halt suddenly, set down her chair in front of one and never move until dark while she gazed at it, deep in her researches.

Presently when the sap began to rise everywhere in the heat of the sun, when the young crops thrust up spears of green in the fields, trees put on their foliage and rosy bubbles of apple blossom in the farmyards scented all the plain, she became uncontrollably restless.

She could not stay still; she went from one room to another, out of doors and into the house again twenty times a day, and sometimes wandered far along the tracks between the farms, carried away by a sort of fever of nostalgia.

She was moved by the sight of a daisy deep in a tuft of grass, a shaft of sunlight stealing through the leaves, a puddle in a lane that reflected the blue of the sky – things like these affected and disturbed her as they brought back sensations of long ago, an echo of what she had felt as a young girl when she dreamed the hours away in the country.

She had thrilled with the same tremors and delighted in the same disturbing, heady sweetness in those warm days of spring when she awaited her future. Now, when that future was closed, she rediscovered it all. At heart she rejoiced in it still; but at the same time she suffered, as though the perennial joy of the awakening world as it penetrated her withered flesh, chilled blood and troubled mind could bring to them now no more than an attenuated and painful delight.

It seemed to her, besides, that there was a change in everything about her. The sun was a little less warm than it had been when she was young, the sky a dimmer blue, the grass a less vivid green; flowers were paler and their scent was weaker, less heady.

There were days, however, when she had such a sense of well-being that she abandoned herself again to dreams, hopes and expectations; for however harsh or savage fate may be, can one ever give up hope when the weather is fine?

She walked on and on, straight before her for hours on end, driven by the restless spirit aroused in her. At times she came to a sudden halt and sank down by the wayside to abandon herself to sorrowful thoughts. Why had she not been loved as others were loved? Why had she not known even the ordinary pleasures of an untroubled life?

At times, again, she would forget for a moment that she was old and had nothing to look forward to but a few lonely, melancholy years, that all her race was run; at such moments she fell happily into the way of making plans, as she had when she was sixteen; she picked out fragments and put them together in a charming mosaic of the future. Then she became aware of the harsh reality; she rose to her feet stiff all over, as though a heavy weight had fallen and broken her back; and she followed the path back to her house with slower steps,

muttering to herself: 'Foolish old woman! Foolish old woman!'

Rosalie now was always saying to her: 'Why don't you stay still, Madame? What's the matter with you, always on the move like this?'

Jeanne answered sadly: 'I cannot help it, I am like Massacre in his old age.'

One morning the maid came to her room earlier than usual, and said as she set down the bowl of coffee on the bedside table: 'Come along now, drink up quickly. Denis is waiting at the door. We're going to Les Peuples, I've got something there to see to.'

Jeanne was so much affected when she heard this that she thought she was going to faint; she was shaking as she dressed, and weak with apprehension at the thought of seeing her beloved home again.

A radiant sky spread over the earth; the horse was fresh and occasionally broke into a gallop. When they drove into the parish of Etouvent, Jeanne's heart beat so hard that she could scarcely breathe; and when she saw the brick pillars at the gateway she repeated 'Oh! Oh! Oh!' several times in spite of herself, as though her heart turned over at the prospect before her.

They left the gig at the Couillards' farm; since the new owners of the château were away, the farmers suggested to Jeanne that she should go over the house while Rosalie and her son attended to their affairs; and they gave her the keys.

She went alone, and when she came within sight of the old manor-house beside the sea she stood still for a moment to view it. Outwardly nothing had changed. The sun was smiling that day on the walls of the weatherbeaten building, grey and streaked with age. The shutters were all closed.

A twig from a dead branch fell on her dress, and she looked up: it had come from the plane-tree. She went up to the great tree with its smooth, pale bark and stroked it as she would an animal. Her foot struck a piece of rotten wood lying in the grass; it was the remains of the seat where she had rested so often with one or other of her family beside her, the seat which had been placed there on the day Julien first came to the château.

The double door of the main entrance was difficult to open and at first she could not turn the heavy, rusty key. The lock yielded at last with a groaning of the spring; the door itself was stiff, but swung open at a push.

Jeanne went straight up to her old room, almost running up the stairs. It had a new, light wallpaper and she did not recognize it; but when she opened a window she was touched to the heart at the sight of that well-loved scene, the little wood, the elms, the heath and the sea dotted with brown sails so far away that they looked motionless.

Then she wandered all over the big empty building. She observed long-familiar marks on the walls. She stopped when she saw a small hole in the plaster where the baron had amused himself by making a pass with his cane as he went by, in recollection of his fencing days.

In dear Mama's room she found a slender gold-headed pin that she had left there long ago (as she now remembered) and searched for for years afterwards, stuck behind a door in a dark corner near the bed. No one had ever found it. Here was a precious relic; she picked it up and kissed it.

She went into every room and looked about, recognizing almost invisible traces in rooms which had not been redecorated, discovering again the curious figures that imagination often sees in the pattern of a fabric, in marble, in ceilings shaded with the dust of time.

Her steps made no sound as she walked alone through the big, silent house, as though she were in a cemetery. All her life was there.

She went down to the drawing-room. It was dark behind the closed shutters, and at first she could distinguish nothing; then as her eyes became accustomed to the gloom she gradually recognized the big tapestries with pictures of birds. Two armchairs had been left beside the hearth, as though they had only lately been abandoned; and the very odour of the room, an odour peculiar to it as it might be to a person, indistinct and yet entirely recognizable, the faint uncertain smell of an old apartment – this penetrated Jeanne's senses and enveloped her in a wave of heady recollection. She stood gasping, breathing that atmosphere of the past, with her eyes fixed on the two chairs. Then in a moment's hallucination, born of her great obsession, she thought she saw her father and mother as she had so often seen them, warming their feet at the fire.

She sprang back in terror and caught her back on the edge of the door, which supported her and saved her from falling, while she still gazed at the armchairs.

The vision had gone.

She stood motionless with shock; when she recovered she wanted to run away, afraid that she was mad. She happened then to glance at the frame of the door on which she was leaning; and her eyes fell on Poulet's ladder.

The shallow markings scaled the paintwork at unequal intervals; and figures scored with a penknife showed her son's age, the month of the year and his growth in height. Here was the baron's larger writing, there was her own smaller hand, and there again Aunt Lison's slightly shaky one. It seemed to her that the little boy of other days was standing there before her, fair-haired, with his small forehead glued to the wall as his height was measured.

In her memory the baron exclaimed: 'Jeanne, he has grown a centimetre in six weeks.'

She put her lips to the place in a passion of love.

Her name was being called. It was Rosalie's voice: 'Madame Jeanne, Madame Jeanne, they're waiting for you to come to lunch.' She went out with her head in the clouds. She no longer understood what was said to her. She ate whatever was put before her, heard people talking without taking in what they said, doubtless replied to the farmers' wives when they inquired about her health, allowed them to kiss her and in return kissed the faces presented to her, and at last stepped into the gig.

It was anguish to her to see the high roof of the château

disappear out of sight among the trees. She felt in her heart that she had just said farewell to her home for ever.

Denis Lecoq drove them back to Batteville.

Just as she was about to enter her new home she saw something white under the door: it was a letter that the postman had slipped in while she was away. She saw immediately that it was from Paul, and opened it with painful apprehension. It read:

MY DEAR MAMA

I have not written to you before because I did not want you to make an unnecessary journey to Paris, when I meant to go to see you myself before long. I have just suffered a heavy blow, and am in a most difficult situation. My wife is dying, after giving birth to a little girl three days ago; and I have not a penny. I do not know what to do with the child, which the concierge here is feeding on the bottle as best she can, but I am afraid we may lose her. Could you not take care of her? I am at my wits' end, and have no money to put her out to nurse. Answer by return.

Your loving son,

PAUL

Jeanne dropped into a chair; she had scarcely strength enough to call Rosalie. When the maid came they read the letter together and then sat for a long time without speaking.

Rosalie said at last: 'I'll go and fetch the little thing myself, Madame. We can't leave her like that.'

Jeanne answered: 'Do, my girl – go.'

They were silent again, then the maid went on: 'You put on your hat, Madame, and we'll go into Goderville to see the lawyer. If that woman's going to die, Monsieur Paul's going to have to marry her, for the little one's sake later on.'

Jeanne said nothing in reply, but put on her hat. Joy, deep and unconfessed, welled up in her heart – a treacherous joy that she would conceal at any cost, one of those fearful delights for which we blush even while we revel in them in the inmost recesses of the soul: her son's mistress was dying.

The attorney gave detailed directions to the maid which she made him repeat several times; when she was certain of making no mistake, she told him: 'Don't you be afraid, I'll see to it now.'

She left for Paris the same night.

For the next two days Jeanne's mind was in such turmoil that she was incapable of thought. On the third morning she received a note from Rosalie stating merely that she would return by the evening train. Nothing more.

At three o'clock she asked a neighbour to drive her to the station at Beuzeville to meet her maid.

She stood on the platform, gazing at the rails that ran out in a straight line and came nearer, ever nearer together as they fled into the distance. From time to time she glanced at the clock. – Ten minutes more – five minutes – two – now was the time. There was nothing to be seen on the track. Presently she could make out a white speck, a puff of smoke, then beneath it a black dot which grew and grew as it came swiftly nearer. The great machine at last slackened its speed, snorting as it rolled past Jeanne, while she avidly scanned the doors of the carriages. Several of these swung open; people descended, peasants in smock frocks, farmers' wives with baskets, small tradesmen wearing felt hats. At last she saw Rosalie, carrying something in her arms that looked like a bundle of linen.

Jeanne tried to go to meet her, but her legs had turned to jelly and she was afraid she might fall. As soon as her maid saw her she came up, calm and stolid as usual, and said: 'Good day, Madame; here I am again, though I've had my troubles.'

Jeanne quavered: 'Well?'

Rosalie replied: 'Well, she died last night. They did get married, and here's the baby.' She held out the infant, invisible in its wrappings.

Mechanically Jeanne took the bundle from her, and they went out of the station and climbed into the trap.

Rosalie went on: 'Monsieur Paul, he's coming as soon as they've had the burial. Same time tomorrow, I expect.'

Jeanne murmured, 'Paul . . .' and said nothing more.

The sun slipped down to the horizon, shedding its radiance over the green of the plains, the specks of yellow rape in flower and blood-red poppies. An infinite stillness lay over the peaceful earth in which the sap was beginning to rise. The trap went along at full tilt as the peasant clicked his tongue to urge on his horse.

Jeanne looked straight in front of her, up into the air where swallows soared like rockets in their arching flight across the sky. She felt a gentle warmth through her clothing, penetrating her legs and body; it came from the small being asleep on her lap.

She was deeply moved. With a quick movement she uncovered the face of the baby she had not yet seen: the daughter of her son. As the frail little thing opened its blue eyes to the bright light and moved its lips, Jeanne lifted it up in a passionate embrace and covered it with kisses.

Rosalie, in great content, scolded her: 'Now, now, Madame Jeanne, that's enough; you'll make her cry.'

She added, no doubt in answer to thoughts of her own: 'You see, life isn't ever as good as you think, and it isn't ever as bad either.'